THE FINAL INDIGNITY

He might have been taking a nap or sleeping off a night of revels. He might even have been "playing possum," as we used to say when I was a kid. Unfortunately for both of us, he wasn't doing any of those things.

He looked very peaceful: he was lying on his back, hands neatly folded over his lean stomach; there was something grotesque about that seeming serenity, because a few inches from his hands, and protruding from his dark sport shirt, were six inches or so of knife handle . . .

CRIME of PASSION

KAY HOOPER

AVON BOOKS NEW YORK

CRIME OF PASSION is an original publication of Avon Books. This work has never before appeared in book form. This work is a novel. Any similarity to actual persons or events is purely coincidental.

AVON BOOKS
A division of
The Hearst Corporation
105 Madison Avenue
New York, New York 10016

Copyright © 1991 by Kay Hooper
Published by arrangement with the author
Library of Congress Catalog Card Number: 90-93391
ISBN: 0-380-76197-1

First Avon Books Printing: February 1991

AVON TRADEMARK REG. U.S. PAT. OFF. AND IN OTHER COUNTRIES, MARCA REGISTRADA, HECHO EN U.S.A.

Printed in the U.S.A.

RA 10 9 8 7 6 5 4 3 2 1

ONE

HE MIGHT have been taking a nap. Or sleeping off a night of revels. He might even have been "playing possum," as we used to say when I was a kid. Unfortunately for both of us, I knew he wasn't doing any of those things.

He was dead.

My first thought was the natural one of self-preservation. In other words, I wanted to get the hell out of there. My second thought was along the lines of curiosity. In other words, I couldn't help wondering what this man had done to get himself dead. I should have paid more attention to the first thought.

And the smell was getting to me. There are certain involuntary bodily functions which death . . . well, if you know what I'm talking about, it's probably because you have to know, or because you've had the misfortune to stumble across a dead person. If you *don't* know, you don't want to. Put it this way: it's no cliché that death is the final indignity.

As I've already indicated, he looked very peaceful. He was lying on his back, hands neatly folded over his lean stomach; and there was something grotesque about that seeming serenity, because a few inches above his hands, protruding from his dark sport shirt, was six inches or so of knife handle. It didn't look as though the wound had bled very much, but that was hardly surprising since he must have died instantly.

1

I always wonder about that phrase. "Died instantly," the coroner says with a judicious nod, and everybody looks satisfied, the nightmare horror of a human being living even a few seconds in mortal pain laid to rest. They never say, "He lived ten minutes and suffered dreadfully." Not in the newspapers, the television reports, the books—except for a certain kind of book, of course.

I'm digressing. I do that a lot, so you'd better get used to it. I also tend to get emotionally involved with people and situations, which is probably why I tried to summon up a clinical inner voice now.

The victim (she noted with assumed professional detachment) was in his forties, handsome if you liked the broody type, and looked in pretty good shape physically. Which indicated (she decided) that either he hadn't gotten a chance to fight for his life, or else hadn't felt the need to. He was fully dressed in casual clothing, and not a strand of his medium-brown hair was out of place. He was lying on a peach-colored couch with a burgundy pillow under his head, his ankles crossed, and black shoes hanging a bit off the edge of the cushion, as if he didn't want to get the furniture dirty.

It was nice furniture. In fact, it was a nice house; nice meaning a place Donald Trump might have claimed as a summer cottage. At least thirty rooms.

This living room was about thirty by forty feet, with lots of windows (all closed), and the only door, slightly behind me now, leading to the foyer. There was a floor-to-ceiling bookshelf between two of the windows, filled with the kind of expensive leather-bound volumes that are strictly for show. Big green plants crouched here and there, behind and beside chairs and in corners. There were a few artlessly scattered "reading" chairs with small tables and lamps beside them.

The peach-colored couch occupied by the deceased was one of three in the room, grouped in an open-ended square. There were more casual burgundy and coral pillows, and the coffee table held a delicate vase of fresh flowers in shades to match the room; a small crystal decanter on the opposite corner of the table almost overflowed with a colorful collection of jelly beans.

I don't know why I examined the room so carefully. Maybe just the eternal human questions of how and why; the need to make sense of chaos. There was a dead man in a lovely, peaceful room, and he hadn't died naturally. It was obscene.

So I stood there. And I looked.

At first glance, the dead man seemed the only item (well, it's better than "thing") out of place. When I looked harder, forcing myself to take stock as calmly as possible, there were a couple of other items that struck me as wrong somehow.

I hadn't come more than three steps into the room, and looking back over my shoulder I could see that my shoes had left indentations in the deep-pile carpet. But there weren't, as far as I could see, any tracks near the couches. In fact, the carpet looked freshly vacuumed, the nap raised and pristine. I couldn't believe the maid had come in and cheerfully vacuumed with a corpse on the couch.

Not, at least, without telling somebody about it.

There was a big rock fireplace to my right between two of the windows and at the open end of the couches, and I had the vague feeling there should have been a rug there, but there was only a neatly swept hearth, fireplace tools of gleaming brass, and a wicker basket full of wood.

To my left and just inside the door was a narrow table holding the phone; I made a note, but didn't move. The next bit of furnishing, going clockwise around the room, was a rather luxurious wet bar, T-shaped; the crossbar of the T was set out from the wall, obviously hiding a sink and other necessities behind its raised frontage, and the stem of the T stuck outward into the room, boasting four barstools whose cushions matched the color scheme of the room.

Next was a corner containing a chair flanked by two tables, the grouping set out from a window. Then the bookshelf and another window with a similar reading arrangement. Then a corner, another window, the fireplace, another window, and a chair in the corner directly to my right. Squarely in front of me were the couches, end tables, coffee table—and the corpse.

From my position three steps into the room, I was gazing over the back of one couch at the one on the other side of the coffee table where the corpse lay.

The drapes were made of thick, heavy material, tied back on either side of each window with those silky-looking tasseled cords. One of the things that bothered me about the room was the fact that one of those cords was missing, so that the window to the left of the fireplace had a lopsided appearance.

So. A missing drapery cord. No footprints on what looked like a freshly vacuumed carpet. The vague insistence of my mind that there should have been a rug before the fireplace. A very peaceful-looking man with a butcher knife sticking in his chest. And yours truly on the spot.

Great.

If you're wondering what I was doing in this somewhat luxurious living room a little before midnight with a corpse, the answer is that I had come in response to an invitation; a message on my answering machine. It isn't often I do that without at least confirming the message by phone, but I have to admit that this particular voice got to me.

Have you ever eaten chocolate candy on a day when you *really* wanted it? When your mouth was watering for it, and you knew you just had to have it no matter what? And then the taste of it, thick and dark on your tongue, rich and sweet and faintly grainy so there was just enough to get your teeth into . . .

No, I'm not digressing again. The voice on my answering machine had affected me just like that. I had even felt my mouth water.

Mind you, I'm not given to that kind of reaction to voices in general and masculine ones in particular. I'm rather happily single, barring the occasional flights of madness which compel me to do strange things like . . . well, never mind. You don't know me well enough to hear *that* story. But then, you don't know me at all, do you? Sorry.

My name is Lane Montana (Yes, I know, terrible!) and I'm thirty-one. Single, never married. About average in looks; women don't feel threatened by me, and men don't run into lampposts trying to get a second look at me. I don't grieve over it. I'm five four, a hundred and ten pounds, with short black hair that hasn't made up its mind whether it wants to curl, and green eyes. I tan easily whether I want to or not, never gain weight—fortunately (remember the chocolate?)—and tend to get fierce about injustice. I live in a loft, drive an unassuming economy-type station wagon, and am owned by a temperamental Siamese cat named Choo.

I am not a private investigator; I want that understood up front. I don't do divorce cases, or security work, or investigate stuff like murder. What I *do* is find things. People sometimes, but more usually just *things*. You'd be surprised how many people lose things: their wallets, a cherished antique ring, packages in the mail, or objects otherwise in transit. I stay pretty busy.

My official business is called Montana Lost, which gets me some pretty weird calls, let me tell you. I thought about calling it Montana Lost and Found, but that sounds like a little cubbyhole in the rear of a department store where they keep the hats and gloves and assorted junk found after the doors are locked at night.

Anyway. I work out of my loft, and my answering machine is my secretary when I leave—which brings us to this dead man. I had to assume this *was* his house, and that he *was* the man who had called me; working from those assumptions, his name was Jeffrey Townsend.

Which meant that I was very likely in deep trouble.

You have to understand who Jeffrey Townsend is—was. You might have called him a big fish in a little pond, except that this particular pond was hardly a little one. Specifically, we both happened to live in Atlanta, Georgia, which is by no stretch of the imagination a little *anything*. And, in Atlanta, Jeffrey Townsend was a pretty big fish. His family had owned properties and businesses here since before Sherman marched through, and the war had been little more than a minor setback for them.

I might have been expected to recognize Townsend right off the bat considering just how big a fish he was, but I have to admit I don't pay much attention to the society pages, and he and I are hardly in the same league businesswise. I knew the name, though, like any other person in the city who watched television and read the newspapers. And knowing what little I did about him, the self-preservation bell in my head was clanging loudly.

I was alone in a gracious old mansion on the outskirts of the city, not a servant in sight, not another soul stirring, and the master of the house lay quite definitely dead in front of me, and not from natural causes.

A glance at my watch told me I'd already been standing here like a knot on a log for a good ten minutes, and I could almost hear the police asking suspiciously why I had waited so long to call them. If I called them at all, that is, which is what I was currently debating. The front door had been standing open, but except for three lit lamps in this room, the entire house was dark.

As far as I could remember, Townsend had a wife, a son in college, and a daughter of about eighteen. Some or all of them could have been upstairs asleep. Murdered like Townsend, for all I knew. There could well be half a dozen live-in servants also abed, breathing or not. Probably not. I could be the only living thing in a house full of corpses. The murderer could still be here. I could—

I decided to stop scaring myself.

I tossed a mental coin, then sighed and moved toward the phone on the table to my left. *I* didn't have a reason to kill him, after all; I'd never even met the man. The message on my answering machine, which I had thankfully not erased, was proof of my reason for being here. I dialed 911, and when the operator came on the line, I heard my voice speak with a coolness I was far from feeling.

"I want to report a murder."

ACCORDING TO TELEVISION SHOWS AND NOVELS, private investigators always seem to have a good friend in the police department. You know the type. He's generally a captain or lieutenant, always roaring, "I'll have your license!" whenever his good buddy, the heroic P.I., butts into a case, but then, of course, helping said P.I. even at the risk of losing his job. There's usually a lot of rule bending and an occasional "All right, damn it, you've got twenty-four hours to break the case!"

Well, as I've already explained, I'm not a private investigator. The only cops I know (and slightly, at that) are in the Juvenile Division, where I've gone once or twice to get information about runaways. What I'm trying to say is that none of these guys knew me from Adam.

A patrol car arrived to check out the report, and one of the uniformed cops stood with one hand near his gun eyeing me suspiciously while his partner went to call it in. Then we pretty much stared at each other until the homicide detectives arrived.

I was sitting in a high-backed chair near the door, as far away from the body as I'd been able to get without leaving the room. Somehow, I didn't think the patrolmen would like the idea of my going outside, which was what I very much wanted to do. The older of the two, a hard-faced guy somewhere in his forties, had asked me the basic questions and taken notes in a little black notebook. There wasn't much I could tell him, but I answered truthfully.

No, I'd never met Mr. Townsend and didn't know why he'd left a message asking me to come here tonight; I'd assumed he wanted me to find something or someone for him. No, I hadn't rung the bell; the front door had been open. No, I hadn't seen or heard anyone else. No, I hadn't touched anything; when I called the police, I had used my handkerchief to cover the receiver and a pen I carried to punch the number.

The officer had asked to see my license right off, and I handed it over, even though I was reluctant. You have to understand, I'm a bit hard to classify as a business. I'm *not* a private investigator; I'm a finder of lost things. But city hall couldn't figure out what kind of license to issue, so they decided on a basic business license and then told me that if I wanted to be a business, I'd have to be classified as a private investigator. That was what I *did*, they insisted.

I even had to be an apprentice for two years and then take the damned test.

So, anyway, I'm officially licensed as a private investigator. But I'm not one. Remember that.

We got through the basics pretty fast, and our long silence was finally broken by the arrival of a number of cars and other vehicles outside the mansion.

From that point on, things got very lively. The room that had felt so large and cold filled rapidly with people, and hot lights, and the occasional jarring sound of laughter. I told myself these people were accustomed to death— it *was*, after all, their job—but I still felt unsettled by the fact that anyone could laugh in this room.

After a few keen glances, I was totally ignored, except by the younger patrolman who was presumably standing guard so I wouldn't escape. My hands were cold, and I was aware that by rubbing them together I made myself look nervous. *Was* I nervous? No, of course not. Am I a liar? You betcha.

You try meeting the big boys of your local police department for the first time while standing (almost literally) over the murdered body of a pillar of your community. Just try it.

Having been declared temporarily invisible, I took the opportunity to study the people doing their jobs with casual expertise. As you might expect, they were a varied lot: all shapes and sizes, ranging in age from about twenty-five to around forty; two women, one of them clearly a lab technician. I could pick the technical specialists out by watching them do technical things; they took photos of the body and the room, dusted various surfaces for finger-prints, and collected samples of everything from carpet fibers to ashes in the fireplace.

The medical examiner (or police surgeon, or whatever), a long, thin man with the gloomiest face I'd ever seen on anything human, made his specialty obvious by poking at the body, apparently checking for temperature and (as I vaguely remembered from television, damn it) degree of rigor, among other things. Things I really didn't want to think about. I heard somebody call him Carl, and some-body else called him Dr. Douglas, so I deduced that he was Dr. Carl Douglas.

Bright, that's me.

The homicide detectives seemed fairly obvious among the rest, and I occupied myself by sorting the names I heard and matching them with faces and personalities. The woman was, I gathered, Sarah Jensen. She was a bit un-expected to me, which just goes to show that we're all prejudiced. For one thing, she was beautiful: tall, slender, and fragile looking, the way old porcelain is. She was pale and auburn haired. Her delicate features blended in a per-fect picture of serenity. Her voice was deep and throaty. Late twenties or early thirties, I decided.

The second detective was named Rudy Flint. He wasn't in charge, but he must have been pretty high up, because he directed most of the activities going on in the house. He was a bit unexpected as well. Big. Very big. He was somewhere between thirty-five and forty-five; I couldn't call it any closer than that. He looked like nothing so much as an ex-football player, complete with thick neck, massive shoulders, and huge hands. He was black, and his voice was a continuous roll of thunder from the bottom of a deep well. He was the kind of guy you would want on your side, no matter what the fight was about.

The third detective was Darrel Hughes, a slender, fast-moving man of about thirty-five. He talked quickly, almost nervously, in an interesting tenor. He was also black, and his hair formed a widow's peak atop his high forehead. He clearly had a habit of cracking his knuckles, smoked constantly, and carried an ashtray around with him. He had a quick smile that would probably inspire just about any woman to do just about anything he asked. (A completely impartial observation.)

The fourth detective was apparently named Link Carpenter. He would have looked more at home on a farm somewhere, and I don't mean anything offensive by that. It's just that he looked like the prototypical hayseed, complete with tousled red hair, freckles, and a shambling gait. He had a voice so soft I had to strain to hear it, a shy, elusive smile, and he seemed not to know what to do with his hands when they were empty. More than once I saw him look at one or the other in vague bewilderment, as if he wondered what on earth they were doing attached to his wrists.

And then there was the other one. The final detective.

The medical examiner, like the other technicians, reported his findings in a low voice to this man, the only person in the room who didn't seem to be doing anything at all.

I'd heard him addressed only as "Lieutenant" and assumed he was in charge here, since I hadn't heard a higher rank. When I got a good look at him, I felt as unsettled as if someone had opened the wrong door and let the tiger out. I didn't know why. Then.

Elegant was the word that came to mind. He was about six feet tall, built leanly but with muscles to spare, judging by the way he moved. At a guess, mid-thirties; forty would have been pushing it. There was a bit of silver at his temples, and the rest of his thick hair was russet brown. He had batwing brows flying above eyes that were deeply set, sleepily hooded, and curiously both hard and luminous; I couldn't guess the color. His nose had been thin and straight according to nature's plan, but had encountered a fist or some other hard object at least once along the way and was now kinked faintly in the middle of its aristocratic bridge.

He had a jaw. Determined, very determined, maybe even obstinate. Lips that were neither too thin nor too full, and beautifully shaped. The high cheekbones of an Indian.

He was dressed with a meticulousness that was almost foppish, from the spotless, creaseless fawn raincoat to the knife-edge pleat of his dark trousers. His shirt was snowy white, his dark tie knotted precisely. His hair was cut in the thick, layered look that had finally—in my opinion—given men's hair some kind of style to boast of, and barely brushed his snowy collar in back. No sideburns to speak of, but a neat mustache. He didn't look like a cop. A lawyer, yes; a businessman, certainly.

Not a cop.

I watched him gesture slightly, gracefully, while talking to the medical examiner, and my attention was drawn to his hands. I felt something catch in the back of my throat. I would have expected slender hands, perhaps even strong hands, but hands as elegant and precise as the rest of the man. Instead . . .

How can I describe them? Powerful? God, yes. They were large hands, wide across the palm, long fingered. And they were ugly. The knuckles were rawboned knots, the wrists thick and heavy, with hair sprinkled across the backs almost to the fingers. They were the brutally strong hands of a man who had worked all his life to wrench beauty out of stone or crops out of the reluctant earth.

He kept them mostly in the pockets of his raincoat, and I thought he was probably at least conscious of their incongruity, if not downright sensitive about them. It was an effort to look away from those hands, a greater effort to look away from that man, and I didn't like what I was feeling.

"Miss—Ms. Montana?"

I looked up to find the very large Rudy Flint standing in front of my chair holding the photostat of my license in his big paw. "Miss is fine," I said dryly, letting him know that I didn't go around shouting about being liberated. What was the point, after all? *I* knew I was liberated—as much as anyone can be, that is—and if he didn't automatically assume I was, there was no hope for him anyway.

He nodded, looking down at me with spaniel-brown eyes that were probably deceptively mild. "Sorry to keep you so long, Miss Montana, but when the lab people have cleared out, the lieutenant'll want to talk to you."

"There isn't much I can tell him." I kept my gaze on Flint and away from that elegant figure in the periphery of my vision; he didn't appear to be listening, but I somehow knew he was. "Just what I've already told the two patrolmen. I didn't know Jeffrey Townsend except by reputation, and I have no idea why he called me here tonight."

Flint pursed his lips unconsciously. "Yes, ma'am. Still. If there's someone you'd like to call—being kept here so late, I mean . . ."

"No."

He nodded, then wandered away after a faintly apologetic smile. I trusted that smile about as much as I would have if a paranoid Doberman had worn it.

Please understand, I wasn't getting paranoid myself. At least, not unreasonably paranoid, if that isn't a contradiction in terms. It was just that I'd had time to think a bit more, and I had the uneasy feeling that there was more to my being here than what I thought I knew.

Consider: I'd gotten home at eleven to find the message on my machine, and it had been logged in (isn't technology wonderful?) at ten P.M. So, sometime between ten P.M. tonight and when I walked into the house at eleven-thirty, Jeffrey Townsend had been murdered, apparently while taking a nap. Now, I'd heard the detectives talking, and I knew that the family was absent. The kid, they'd said, was away at college; that was the son. The daughter was apparently away on some kind of trip with friends, although how they'd found that out so quickly . . .

Mrs. Amy Townsend was also away, in New York, apparently, visiting a friend.

There were no live-in servants; the cook/housekeeper and butler were a married couple with their own house near the estate, and I'd heard Darrel Hughes report to the lieutenant that they had been peacefully asleep at home. A cleaning service came daily, but they were always out of the house by six.

The door had not been forced, nor had any of the windows. The alarm system had been deactivated from inside with no damage done; the front gate had been open. A datebook on Townsend's desk, which I hadn't seen (in his study down the hall), apparently had my name on it for eleven P.M. tonight, with no other visitor mentioned.

My hands felt colder than before.

It didn't help to *know* I'd had nothing to do with the murder. Maybe it was a common reaction to the situation, but I found myself minutely examining my life these past few days and trying to find a connection somewhere. I came up empty. As far as I could tell, I didn't even know anyone who knew Townsend personally.

I locked my fingers together over my stomach and slumped in the chair, feeling understandably defensive as I watched the technicians packing up their gear. The knife had been removed from Townsend, a procedure I had thankfully not witnessed, and he was zipped into a black bodybag. I wished I hadn't seen that. Within a few minutes, I was alone in the living room with the detectives. With three of them, that is. Rudy Flint, Sarah Jensen, and the lieutenant. The patrolman had left.

It was very quiet.

The lieutenant stood facing me, hands in his pockets, while the others found seats on a couch—not the one Townsend had occupied.

"Miss Montana."

I met those luminous eyes, deciding absently that they were gray. "Yes?"

"I'm Lieutenant Fortier."

I almost said "of course you are," but contented myself with a nod. Fortier? Sounded French, which wasn't all that uncommon in the South. He had an interesting voice, somewhere between bass and tenor, and faintly husky. The tone was impersonal, his lean face expressionless and his eyes unreadable. He'd be a good poker player.

Unfortunately, I am not.

"According to your statement, you arrived home at eleven and found a message from Jeffrey Townsend asking you to come here tonight. What time did he expect you?"

"Eleven." I knew damned well that he knew the answer to that question. "Obviously, I was late."

"You then drove here," he said, making no comment on my answer, "finding the gate open when you arrived at eleven-thirty. Is the time exact?"

"Yes. The porch light was on and I looked at my watch as I came up the walk, because I knew I was late. It was eleven-thirty when I reached the door."

"Which was standing open?"

"About a foot. I could see the lights from this room spilling out into the entrance hall, but the rest of the house was dark."

"You didn't suspect anything when you found the door ajar?"

"Of course I did." I tried not to bristle. Bad habit of mine, bristling. "I called out Mr. Townsend's name. When there was no answer, I pushed open the door and went inside the house. I came into this room, naturally. He was lying there, just the way he was when the patrolmen arrived. I didn't go near him. I didn't touch him. I didn't have to."

"And what was your reaction to what you found?"

I stared at him for a moment, sensing a trap and baffled by it. "My reaction, Lieutenant?"

He nodded, and his voice remained impersonal. "Your

reaction, Miss Montana. The dispatcher logged your call in at eleven forty-five. According to you, it required a minute at most for you to cross the foyer and enter this room. There are a number of minutes unaccounted for. What were you doing?''

Well, it wasn't as if I hadn't expected the question. I took a deep breath. ''I wasn't doing anything, Lieutenant. I just stood there inside the doorway and looked around the room. Nothing made sense, and I suppose I was trying to think—''

''What do you mean, 'nothing made sense'?''

I gestured toward the currently unoccupied couch. ''Him. Lying there so . . . peacefully. With a knife sticking in him. Everything looked so normal, except for him.'' I decided not to mention my vague doubts for the moment. ''The house was silent. I knew there were other family members, but I wasn't about to go upstairs and find out if they were here.''

The lieutenant nodded slightly. ''All right. You said you supposed you were trying to think. About what, specifically?''

''Well, why he'd been killed. How somebody could have just walked up and stabbed him while he was taking a nap. Why he'd asked me to come here. And I guess I wondered if it would have happened if I'd been here when he had expected me to be.''

Fortier nodded again, then asked mildly, ''Where were you tonight, Miss Montana?''

I'd known he would ask that, but I didn't want to answer. Still, I hardly had a choice. ''From seven until nine, I was at a movie. Alone.''

''And during the next two hours?''

''Driving.''

''Driving where, Miss Montana?''

I sighed. ''Just around the Perimeter, Lieutenant. I do that sometimes. It helps me to relax.''

''Alone?''

''Yes.'' Damn it.

"So between the time you say Townsend called and left a message for you and the time you arrived here at eleven-thirty, there were no witnesses to your movements."

I suddenly remembered something. "Not quite. My landlady talked to me before I went into the loft. That must have been about ten minutes to eleven." I had a hollow feeling that hadn't helped me very much, and asked hesitantly, "Do you know when—"

"He was killed?" It was Flint who responded. He was sitting on the couch, turning the photostat of my license in his big paws and staring at it. "You're a P.I., you should know better than that. The M.E. can't be exact—"

"I'm not a P.I." I felt that needed to be explained. "Well, technically, maybe. But not really. I just find things for people. Or people for people." I had the feeling I was babbling nervously and shut it down, finishing evenly, "I'm not a private investigator. And I've never seen a murdered body except on television."

"You're handling it very well," Fortier commented coolly.

I looked at him, feeling hostile. I always feel that way when someone hints that I haven't behaved the way I should have. "I'm not the hysterical type, Lieutenant. It was certainly a shock to find him like that, but I didn't know the man and I didn't fall apart." I could have added that I tended to get torn and bloody inside where no one could see, but that was hardly his business.

He studied me for a moment in silence, those luminous gray eyes hooded and unreadable. "You stated that you didn't erase the message Townsend left on your machine."

"That's right. I usually don't, I just record over them later."

"We'll need that tape, Miss Montana."

"Fine."

He glanced at the other two detectives. "I'll follow Miss Montana back to her loft. You two get started; we'll have a circus as soon as the press gets onto this."

"They'll be on it by morning," Sarah Jensen murmured. "If not sooner."

Fortier looked at me. "Shall we go, Miss Montana?"

As if I had a choice.

I COULD SOUND BUSINESSLIKE and methodical here by telling you that I thought long and hard on the drive back to my loft about Jeffrey Townsend's murder and why I was involved in it (I don't believe in coincidence, at least not this kind). I could sound like a professional private investigator, which is what the police thought I was, if I told you that I was reviewing every tiny fact I knew about the case. Unfortunately, I would have been lying.

What I was thinking was that if Lieutenant Fortier called me Miss Montana in that bland voice of his one more time, I'd probably throw the nearest heavy object at him.

Yeah, I know. Hardly professional, huh? I couldn't put my finger on why, exactly, but the man bothered me. Maybe it was just because I felt like a suspect. Or maybe not.

Anyway, he followed me to the loft, driving a light-colored sedan which, I saw when we arrived, was a Mercedes. Obviously, judging by his clothes and car, the man liked to live well. I wondered if he had a source of income other than the police force. I wondered if he was one of the inevitable few on every police force in the world who was on the take. I wondered if he thought of me as a suspect.

I wondered if he had a wife. Or a lover.

We parked in the lot in front of my building, and I led the way inside. The building was an old warehouse converted to lofts, three of them besides my own. The stairwell was central and well lit, and he followed me up to my second-floor loft in silence. I unlocked the sliding door and pulled it open, flipping on the lights as I stepped inside.

"Choo?"

"I beg your pardon?" Fortier said as he followed me inside the loft.

I turned back and went rather stiffly around him to close the door, feeling very self-conscious. "My cat. Choo. I was calling him."

Fortier nodded, still expressionless. "I see."

He stood looking around the loft, and I wondered what he thought. To the right of the door as we came in was a small space containing my desk, filing cabinets, and a couple of chairs for visitors; it was partitioned by my bookcase, which was so stuffed that every shelf sagged noticeably. Barring a few outdated almanacs and a couple of battered paperback dictionaries, I have no reference books, just fiction. My taste runs to mystery, from the classics to modern stuff, and to adventure and intrigue.

Well, all the books *look* professional, as long as you don't start scanning the titles. Unfortunately, I thought the lieutenant scanned a few.

Beyond the bookcase was an entertainment center at right angles against the brick wall, holding my stereo, television, VCR, and collection of tapes and records. Directly ahead of us was the living area—couch, coffee table and end tables, one chair. Beyond that was my bedroom, partitioned from the rest of the loft by an oriental screen. And to our left was the kitchen area.

Everything looked fairly neat. It's not that I'm a good housekeeper, it's just that I'm not necessarily sloppy in day-to-day living. I mean, it *looked* okay, but it wouldn't stand a white-glove test. I clean maniacally every spring and fall, and on the rare occasions when I'm extremely upset about something, but other than that . . .

I hadn't given much thought to decorating since I'd moved in two years ago, just adding bits and pieces as I went along, a few houseplants that thrive no matter what I do to them. The brick walls were painted white, just as when I moved in, the high windows uncurtained, the furniture overstuffed and comfortable but hardly stylish. The rugs dotting the wood floor and throw pillows on the couch and chairs provided splashes of color, but the color scheme was somewhat bland.

I had a few paintings hanging about; I know next to nothing about art, but being related to an artist who hates bare walls I had, over the years, acquired quite a few really good oils, watercolors, and pen-and-ink sketches.

Fortier's hooded gaze swept the place (missing very little, no doubt), coming to rest at last on a freestanding glass-and-oak curio cabinet near my desk. He stepped closer and regarded it silently, studying the array of glass, ceramic, pewter, brass, bronze, copper, and porcelain figures on the three shelves. He didn't comment.

And he didn't even start in surprise when a twenty-pound, chocolate-point Siamese tomcat (neutered) leaped out of nowhere onto my desk to face him with a lashing tail and glared at him with hideously crossed china-blue eyes, which can be a very disconcerting experience.

"Hello," Fortier said to the cat.

I blinked. When you're a cat person, you can recognize it in someone else, usually instantly. I don't mean one of those silly people who talk baby talk to their furry friends and buy them little outfits and treat them like children; I mean a genuine cat person who honestly respects the feline personality, admires their self-sufficiency and independence, and isn't unsettled by their sly intelligence.

You can always tell. Maybe it's the tone of voice.

Choo clearly recognized the mysterious trait as soon as I did. He stopped lashing his tail, sat down on the corner of the desk, tilted his head, and contemplated this interesting man with the eerily wise (albeit crossed) eyes of the ancient feline race. After a moment, he said, "Wauur."

Fortier nodded slightly, as if he understood he had been accepted. Of course he understood. He was a cat person.

Damn it.

He looked at me, his eyes still unreadable. "The tape?"

I went over to the desk, aware that both man and cat were watching me. I indicated the machine, which sat on the corner opposite Choo. "Do you want to hear the message?"

"Yes."

I rewound the tape all the way, then started it. An unimportant message played itself out, and I talked over the recorded voice to explain to Fortier that the machine recorded the time of every incoming call, then displayed the time as the message was replayed. Something was nagging at me as I talked, but I didn't pay much attention. Then.

He stepped closer to look down at the LED indicator. "Do you get many messages like that?" he asked.

We were listening, unfortunately, to one of those weird calls I mentioned before. An obscene one. The male caller, clearly undisturbed (even gleeful) that his voice was being recorded, was explaining with some relish all the things we would do together once he "found" me. His vocabulary left nothing to the imagination. It still surprised me that obscene callers seem to *enjoy* knowing that their messages are being recorded; according to the experts, obscene callers get their kicks from your reaction—but machines don't react. It's enough to make you question your faith in experts.

I cleared my throat. "Some, yes. They don't bother me."

The lieutenant said nothing else, merely listening with me as the caller finally wearied of his game and hung up. I had just noticed the flashing time of the LED indicator myself and felt a chill feather suddenly down my spine. Now I knew what had been nagging at me. That call had been logged in at midnight, and it had been first on the tape. But that meant . . .

After the obscene call there was only the faint hiss of blank tape.

Nothing.

No call from Jeffrey Townsend.

The message had been erased.

TWO

IT WAS IMPOSSIBLE. I stood staring down at that damned machine, my mind whirling, vaguely aware that my heart was pounding, my hands cold and damp. Townsend's message should have been first on the tape; no matter what other calls had come in, the machine should have begun recording immediately after Townsend's message, where I had earlier stopped the tape. I felt my skin crawl and watched blankly as one of Fortier's big, ugly hands cut across my line of vision and punched the stop button on the machine.

"No message," he said.

I looked at him. He was standing right beside me, too close, and yet somehow I didn't feel threatened the way you normally do whenever a stranger invades your personal space. I couldn't breathe, though. His eyes were almost silver. No wonder they were luminous.

"It was there," I said, hearing a strained note in my voice that I didn't like. "First on the tape. I played it through twice before I left."

"Maybe you erased it."

I couldn't tell if he believed me or not. "No. I told you, I hardly ever do that. And I didn't do it tonight. Not even accidentally; I've had this machine for over a year, and I know how to work the damned thing. That message was on the tape when I left."

After a moment, he moved away from me, and I could

breathe again. I followed him a few steps around the partition so that I could watch him. He didn't seem to have any specific destination in mind; he just wandered around the loft, hands in his pockets, face expressionless. I would have given my bank account to know what he was thinking.

"So," he said, still wandering, "you're saying that someone got in here during the last couple of hours and erased one single message from your answering-machine tape. One rather important message that just happens to be proof of your reason for being on the Townsend estate tonight."

It sounded ridiculous, put like that. I decided I hated him. I decided I hated him even more when Choo abandoned his seat on the desk without so much as a glance at me and began pacing at his heels like a fawning lapdog. As evenly as I could manage, I said, "That's what I'm saying." Reluctantly, I damned myself further. "And they had less than an hour to do it. I left here at eleven; that call we just heard was logged in at midnight."

"There were no signs of tampering on your door," he said.

"No," I agreed.

"Is there a fire escape?"

"No. I have a collapsible ladder to hook to the window in case of fire."

"Any other way in?"

I gritted my teeth. "No."

"Who has a key to the loft?" he asked.

I had to stop and think about that a minute. Had I changed the lock after . . . ? Yes. I had. "My landlady, of course. My brother. No one else."

He continued his perambulation, halting briefly near the foot of my bed to contemplate my hope chest. (For the record, I want to state that the chest had been made for me by an uncle when I was sixteen, and that it now contained a few extra blankets rather than virginal hopes.) Choo sat down at the lieutenant's heel and contemplated as well. After a moment, they moved on, perfectly in step, both expressionless.

"Is anything else missing?"

It only took a glance to show me the answer was no. I don't have jewelry, at least not to speak of, and my stereo, VCR, and television were in place. All my paintings and sketches were still hanging inside their neat frames. A tug at the locked drawers of my filing cabinet found them still "securely" locked, which apparently didn't mean a damned thing. Anyway, it would take hours to go through the files, which I was in no mood to do.

"I don't think so." I went and sat on the couch. I picked up a colorful throw pillow and hugged it. I was feeling insecure.

"Did either your landlady or your brother know Townsend?" he asked.

"No. At least, I'm pretty sure my brother doesn't—I mean didn't—know him. My landlady never mentioned it."

"Is there anyone with a grudge against you, a strong enough grudge that they would feel the need to frame you for a murder? Or, at the very least, make you a strong suspect?"

"I can't think of anyone."

"And you have absolutely no idea why Townsend would call you out to his estate late at night with no warning, no prior contact, and no explanation?"

"None. I just assumed he wanted me to find something or someone for him."

"Since you received the message late," Fortier continued, still wandering around, "why didn't you call Townsend? Why did you immediately drive across town late at night without confirming his call?"

I wished he hadn't asked that. I wasn't about to explain a compulsive response to a chocolate voice. "Maybe," I tried, "I was impressed by who he was. My clients run the gamut, but there isn't a Townsend in the lot."

He shook his head slightly, but I couldn't tell if it was

because of my comment or some negative thought of his own.

"Tell me about your business," he said abruptly.

"Well . . . I find things."

He sent me a glance I couldn't define to save my life. "Care to elaborate?" he suggested mildly.

I resisted the urge to chew on a thumbnail. I was trying to break the habit because I thought it was childish. "I find lost things." I shrugged helplessly. "Look, Lieutenant, that's what I do. A client calls me because they've lost something. Maybe they're pretty sure it's in their own house or yard, or they lost it moving here or away from here. A package. Great-aunt Matilda's antique ring, or Grandmother's string of pearls. Or maybe it's a little more serious, and fourteen-year-old Susie ran away from home. Maybe Mrs. Smith's husband took a walk one night to get cigarettes and never came back. Or maybe Rover slipped his leash and vanished, and the kids are crying themselves to sleep."

He stopped wandering and stood a couple of feet away, looking at me. "Suppose I called you about a missing ring. How would you go about finding it?" he asked.

I still couldn't read his face, damn it. "I'd check your house or apartment first, if you weren't sure where you'd lost the ring. If it was there, I'd find it within an hour." I stopped suddenly, having said more than I'd meant to.

"How can you be sure of that? I might have a big house."

I never liked explaining my peculiar talent, mostly because it sounded like . . . well, you'll see. "Some people are good at fixing machinery, some people have green thumbs, I'm good at finding things. Once I have a clear idea what the object looks like, I just get a strong feeling where it is. A sense of direction, usually."

Lieutenant Fortier didn't say anything for a moment, just continued to look at me. I met that hooded gaze with all the steadiness I could muster, but the truth was I was feeling quite shaken by the events of tonight. And I won-

dered if that was his game, asking me these fairly innoc-
uous questions until I got defensive and/or off my guard.
Then he'd go for the throat.

"Tell me," he said, "what was the greatest distance
between you and an object or person you were able to
locate?"

The answer to that really *did* sound like witchcraft, but
I'd be damned if I'd try to avoid it. (See? I was already
getting defensive.) "I was here, and the object was in San
Francisco. One of her enterprising nieces or nephews had
hidden Aunt Stacy's emerald ring in their mother's suit-
case. When Aunt Stacy described the ring, I suddenly
thought of the Golden Gate Bridge. It developed that her
sister had visited from San Francisco with the children and
had only recently gone home. They found the ring tucked
inside one of the sister's shoes. Next question?"

"You're psychic?" he asked.

I glowered at him. "No. At least, I flunked all the tests
at Duke University years ago when my brother insisted I
find out for sure. I'm not psychic. I just find things."

He nodded slightly. The man was maddeningly unreadable, and it was a good thing I was feeling too insecure
to let go of the pillow I was hugging. I would have thrown
it at him.

Turning away abruptly, he went over to my desk and
pulled the phone book out from under the phone. He
checked the yellow pages, then replaced the book and returned to that mysteriously exact spot a couple of feet away
from me.

"Has there been anyone recently—say in the last few
months—whom you were unable to help?"

"A disappointed client, you mean?" I thought about it.
"No. About a year ago, I had some trouble with a client's
runaway ex-husband, though. I found him twice, and both
times he was hauled up in court and forced to pay back
child support."

The lieutenant's luminous eyes never wavered from my
face. "Did he make threats against you?"

"Against me, the judge, his wife, the judicial system. He was pretty ineffective, though. The closest he ever came to carrying out his threats was when he slashed my tires. I caught him at it."

"Where is he now?"

"Florida. He sends his support checks promptly, according to his delighted ex-wife. She keeps in touch with me."

"Not a promising lead," Fortier noted.

"Hardly," I agreed, and then had a sudden thought. "Are you saying you really believe someone came in here and erased the message?"

"Shouldn't I?"

I gave him a baffled look. "Am I a suspect in the murder?"

"Did you kill Townsend?"

"No."

"Perhaps you were having a torrid affair with him, and when he refused to divorce his wife, you stabbed him in a fit of rage while he lay peacefully and unsuspectingly asleep?"

I blinked. No expression on his face except polite attention, but I had an odd feeling something abruptly . . . softened in him. Ridiculous, of course. "No. I mean, *hell*, no!"

"You weren't blackmailing him?"

"No!"

"He didn't owe you money?"

"If he had," I pointed out reasonably, "he would have paid me. Money doesn't—*didn't*—seem to be one of his problems. And, no, he didn't owe me money." I was having more trouble than the lieutenant was with keeping Jeffrey Townsend in the correct tense.

"Are you one of his heirs?"

"Of course not."

"Was there any reason you would have killed him for revenge?"

"Revenge?"

"My question."

"Not that I know of. And knowledge is something of a prerequisite for revenge, don't you think?"

"I would think."

We stared at each other.

"Offhand," Lieutenant Fortier said, "I can't think of a single reason why you would have stabbed Jeffrey Townsend in the chest. I could be wrong, of course."

I thought about it while he waited in silence. This was getting interesting. "Well, I can't think of a reason either. But I also can't think of a reason why anyone would have come in here and erased one message from my answering machine. I mean, what's the point?"

"That message gave you a legitimate reason for being at the Townsend estate tonight."

"And without it, you'd think my story was fishy?"

"Stands to reason."

"But you don't?"

"You aren't stupid," Fortier said, surprising me. "If you had known the message wasn't on the tape, you would have simply claimed to have erased it yourself. It's a logical action, after all. You can't prove a negative; just because the message wasn't there, I couldn't have proven it never had been. And I gave you the opportunity more than once to make use of that explanation. But you maintained the message had been there when you left here."

"I could have been lying all along," I offered thoughtfully. "To give myself a reason for being at the estate."

The lieutenant nodded. "Certainly. And you might possibly have even studied Townsend's handwriting meticulously enough to have forged the entry about your appointment tonight in his datebook."

"Are you sure it's his handwriting?"

"Verification tomorrow. But it's probably his."

I believed him. Continuing to play devil's advocate out of some perverse instinct—or maybe just because I was enjoying the conversation—I said, "Well, I could have asked for the appointment myself. Called Townsend. That would explain his entry in the datebook."

"It would," he agreed. "And I'll have the phone company verify all the outgoing calls from the Townsend estate in the last twenty-four hours—as well as outgoing calls from your number. But you didn't call him."

"How can you be sure?"

"We've agreed you didn't have a motive," he reminded me. "Unless I uncover something in your lurid past, that is."

I felt disgruntled. "Damn it, are you going to be digging around in my lurid past?"

"S.O.P.," he murmured. "Sorry."

"You said I wasn't a suspect."

"No, but you're involved, so you're on the list. Someone, presumably the killer, apparently went to a great deal of trouble to slip into your home and erase—are you sure it was Townsend's voice?"

I wished he hadn't mentioned the killer coming in here. I also wished he hadn't asked me that question, because suddenly I wasn't sure. "I . . . guess not. I've never heard Townsend's voice, or at least never listened to it. You know, on television."

"Would you recognize the voice on the message if you heard it again?"

"Yes, I think so." I knew so.

For the first time, Lieutenant Fortier displayed a genuine expression: dry amusement. "Wonderful. We'll round up every man in Atlanta and let you listen to them one at a time."

I ignored the joke, mainly because I suddenly realized what all this meant. Absently, I said, "At least we can rule out Townsend; there's bound to be a recording of his voice. Wait a minute, though. Are we considering the possibility that someone who knew both me and Townsend deliberately set things up so I'd look bad? Maybe even guilty?"

"It's possible. Likely, in fact. It's also possible that the killer knew Townsend, knew *of* you through someone else—possibly a former client of yours—and decided you'd make a dandy suspect. It's possible that your involvement is only a red herring, intended to lead us to waste as much time as possible. It's even possible that you know the killer well enough that he didn't dare allow that message to remain on tape for fear you'd recognize his voice if you got another chance to listen to it.''

I was liking this less and less. "He got in here," I said uneasily, "whoever he is. Did he leave fingerprints on the knife?''

"No.''

"Then I suppose it's foolish to expect he'd leave some here?''

"Probably. However he got in here, it was carefully. He doesn't seem the type to make basic mistakes.''

If I gulped, at least it was silently. "Um . . . do you think I could be in danger?''

He looked at me for a moment, then said, "That, unfortunately, is possible. Until we know exactly what role you were cast for, we just can't be sure. I've posted a couple of men at this building, front and back; they'll stand watch for the rest of tonight. Tomorrow, we should have at least a few answers. Or a different set of questions. You don't have a gun permit," he added abruptly.

I answered the tacit question. "I never needed a gun, so I never got one.''

"Wauur,'' Choo said.

The lieutenant looked down at him. "Pity you can't talk, Choo,'' he said absently.

Choo blinked up at him seraphically, tail curled neatly around his forepaws.

Fortier sighed, wearily, I thought. He consulted his watch, and I found myself staring at that incongruous hand. Hastily, I looked away. Whether I accepted his professed belief in my innocence, I stood a chance of having at least one of the local constabulary on my side; there was no need to alienate the man by staring at his strangely ugly hands.

"I'm sorry I've kept you so late," he said formally, with none of the mellowing I'd sensed in him earlier.

Damn it, he'd seen me staring like an idiot! I cleared my throat. "That's all right. I'm a night owl anyway."

"I'll need a complete statement from you tomorrow," he said, still formal. "Your license will be returned to you then. We're hoping to keep your involvement quiet for the time being so, with luck, you won't be bothered by reporters. If you could come to my office sometime after lunch, I'd appreciate it."

"Of course." I rose and followed him to the door. Before he opened it, I bent down and picked up Choo, partly because he regarded opened doors as blatant invitations and partly because I was feeling insecure again and needed something to hug. "I'll—I'll see you tomorrow afternoon, then, Lieutenant."

"Yes." He stood looking at me for a moment, then shook his head slightly and left without another word.

It occurred to me only then that Lieutenant Fortier had posted his men outside *before* he'd known about the erased message. The question was, what did that mean? I locked the door behind him and set Choo on the floor. "Traitor," I accused. "You followed him around like a puppy."

"Wauur!" Choo said in an indignant tone. He hated being compared to anything canine.

"Learn to talk English, why don't you? Then you could tell us who came in here and erased the message."

"Wauur," Choo said.

AND, you know something? Lieutenant Fortier hadn't called me Miss Montana in that bland tone of voice once. In fact, he hadn't called me anything at all.

I DIDN'T SLEEP WELL. I hardly expected to. It was nearly dawn before I really closed my eyes, and consequently it was late when I dragged myself out of bed in response to the hungry yowls and persistent weight of the Siamese who had chosen, with some feline logic beyond fathoming, to share my life. I fed Choo and put coffee on, then stumbled to the shower and stood under steaming water long enough to clear away the cobwebs.

By the time I'd dressed in jeans and a pullover sweater, shaken my wet hair a couple of times so it would dry in its usual (and occasionally fashionable) tousled style, and injected myself with the first shot of coffee for the day, I felt reasonably human. I turned on the television to catch whatever news was forthcoming, rummaged in the cabinets for cereal, and ate it standing at the work island while I looked blearily at an indecipherable game show on the TV.

I don't know if I've mentioned it, but I don't cook. It isn't that I can't follow a recipe in a cookbook, it's just that when I do, the results are never edible. Dinner guests have been known to take a single bite and blanch in horror. No emergency-room treatment has been required to date, but probably only because none of my guests has been able to ingest enough to do serious damage.

Needless to say, I never have dinner guests unless they bring the food and cook it themselves, or unless it's their first time and they haven't been warned. Even Choo, amazingly nondiscriminating for a cat, examines everything I put in his dish warily before tasting it; he was a victim of some of my culinary efforts, and he's a smart cat. And my brother is fond (to extreme) of saying that the obesity problem in this country could be solved if only the government shut down McDonald's and let me cook for everybody.

Well, it doesn't really bother me. It used to. But then, my generation had—and has—to deal with quite a few role conflicts, so that's hardly surprising. Like many of the girls I went to high school with, it occurred to me in something like a spiritual revelation somewhere during the pompous graduation ceremony (somebody ought to outlaw them—they warp the psyche by making one think that one is far more important in the general scheme of things than is at all necessary, or even rational) that I didn't *have* to find myself a man and move to suburbia. (I gave my boyfriend his class ring back the very next day. I think he later joined the navy, but it wasn't because of me, I'm sure.) It occurred to me that I didn't have to know how to sew on buttons or make biscuits. I could have a *career,* by golly, and live alone without much risk of being called a spinster. I could learn to change a tire and take care of my own finances. I could, by golly, be independent.

It wasn't until considerably later that I finally understood that sewing on buttons had nothing to do with being female and everything to do with being clothed. I might have made the same discovery about food but it's cheaper to eat out. Really.

And all of this explains, if you think about it, why I don't cook. It also explains why I still get touchy whenever somebody hints that I'm not acting like I'm supposed to. I mean, I *know* I'm independent, and I like being alone, and it's really no sin to be hopeless in the kitchen, but . . . well, I do live in the South, after all. Hoopskirts and simpering manners may well be behind us, but that damned notion of genteel southern womanhood has warped as many psyches as graduation ceremonies have.

Do you suppose our wretched preoccupation with what we're *supposed* to be is stamped in our genes, all knotted up and ready to spring on us with a gleeful giggle at odd moments?

What I'm trying to say (at length, I know, but I did warn you about my digressions), is that my inability to cook could be as simple as a lack of natural talent, or it could be a vestigial bit of role confusion. At least, I hope it's vestigial. At thirty-one, I am only beginning to realize who I am, unfettered by all those weighty chains composed of excessive youth, ridiculous and unearned guilt, racial memories (I'm convinced that's what they are), and the role models of previous and future generations.

I'm Lane Montana, that's who I am. I can't cook for

toffee, but I can sure as hell change a tire. I find lost things. I am owned by a cat. I can sew on buttons. I do my own income tax, accompanied by swearing of extraordinary magnitude. I get obsessive about remaining independent, and I am not at all willing to leave my fate in someone else's hands. I have a singular weakness when it comes to accumulating objects, a passion for collecting something I refuse to discuss because it sounds so damned frivolous.

I'm not frivolous. My brother, who maintains that he's been fascinated by me for years because he knows if he can only figure me out he'll have the eternal male problem of understanding women licked, says there's nothing at all frivolous about me. Several combustible traits, but no inanities.

My brother, by the way, is named Jason—just so you'll recognize him when you meet him later.

I don't know why I'm telling you this.

My name is Lane Montana, and I find things. In a couple of hours, I'm going to the police station to make a formal statement to an elegant lieutenant with hooded, luminous eyes and ugly hands, because last night I found a dead man.

A murdered man.

I WON'T SAY I was disappointed to find, upon arriving at the police station, that Lieutenant Fortier wouldn't be taking my statement after all. I won't say it. I was directed to his office, but found Sergeant Rudy Flint waiting for me. Alone. He had a tape recorder, which I viewed with misgivings: recording devices hadn't been kind to me lately.

In his bear-rumble voice, he invited me to sit down in front of the lieutenant's immaculate desk, whereupon I became fascinated to learn from a brass nameplate that the missing lieutenant was named Trey Fortier. Trey. Unusual, and I liked it.

"Miss Montana?" Sergeant Flint ventured from his position behind the desk.

I blinked at him. "Oh. Yes, Sergeant?"

"Your license." He was holding it out.

I took it. "Thanks."

In a businesslike tone, he said, "We usually have a stenographer, but not today." He didn't offer to explain why. "I'll tape your statement and then have it typed for your signature. All right?"

I wanted to ask what would happen if it wasn't all right. "Fine, Sergeant," I murmured.

"Just describe the events of last night, ending with your calling us." He turned on the machine, efficiently recited the date and circumstances, then looked at me expectantly.

I cleared my throat and began with the message on my answering machine . . .

Sergeant Flint brought me coffee while the statement was being typed up, for which I blessed him. He seemed disposed to stay in the office and talk, which faintly surprised me but was interesting because he obviously had something specific on his mind despite the trivial conversation.

"How long have you been in business, Miss Montana?" he asked chattily.

"Four years. My friends call me Lane, Sergeant— unless it would be improper for you to do so?"

He grinned. "Improper. That's an old-fashioned word."

Hoopskirts and simpering manners, damn it. I didn't blush only because I've trained myself not to. "I'm a great one for etiquette."

He nodded, serious again despite a twinkle in his mild brown eyes. "Four years, huh? Do you find mostly people or objects?"

"More objects than people."

"And you make a living at it?"

Since I had taken the lieutenant at his word when he mentioned digging into my lurid past, I knew damned well that whatever Rudy Flint didn't know about me already, he soon would. Therefore, I replied honestly. "It would probably be a marginal living, but I inherited a few investments that keep me solvent."

"Lucky you. Working on anything at the moment?"

"No."

We looked at each other. Behind the rugged and, I thought, deceptively bovine expression, Rudy Flint was thinking. He seemed to be trying to make up his mind about something. I had a feeling it was me.

"Tell me," he said suddenly, having apparently acquired his lieutenant's trick of that abrupt lead-in, "how you'd go about finding a murderer."

I blinked at him. "I wouldn't."

"Why not?"

"Because I'm a coward," I said, and stared him defiantly in the eye.

It was his turn to blink, and then his eyes narrowed. "No," he said softly, "I don't think you are. But it might be better if you were, Lane. It might be a lot better."

I didn't have to respond to that, because an officer brought in my statement and I could concentrate on reading it through. Not that I did. Read it, I mean. When I signed my name, I might well have signed a confession for all I knew.

"Is that all, Sergeant?" I asked him lightly.

He nodded, expressionless. "For now. The lieutenant said to ask if you'd try to catch one of the news reports on Townsend today and let us know if the voice on the machine was his; they're airing some of his civic speeches."

"Right." I got up and headed for the door, then turned back and stared at his massive form as he rose from the desk. "Tell me, Sergeant." Damn it, I was doing it too! "Am I going to be followed until this case is over?"

"I thought you weren't a private investigator."

I smiled, with all my teeth showing. "I had to apprentice for two years, so I learned the basics. I took the test.

And even a novice can spot a tail if she's looking for one.''

"I'll check with the lieutenant," Flint said woodenly.

I half saluted him and sauntered out. Sauntered. Stylish, huh? Actually, I was jumpy as hell. I didn't like the idea of being followed, even though that murderer was still out there and seemingly knew me a lot better than I knew him. Or her. Truth to tell, I would have been happy to accept the escort except that I wanted to do a little investigating.

Yeah, I know, dumb. I'm not a private investigator, or a cop, and I don't even have a gun. But I didn't like the way things were shaping up. I'd read somewhere that the law didn't have to prove a motive for murder, and given that, I had two strikes against me—means and opportunity. That knife had looked like the kitchen variety, available anywhere and probably filched from the Townsends' kitchen; and I had a depressing feeling that if I had been able to bring myself to touch Townsend last night, I would have found him still warm.

Granted, there were a number of points in my favor. No motive, of course. The fact that my landlady could place me at home just before eleven; I'd have to have a hell of a nerve as a murderess to drive to the estate, kill Townsend at eleven-thirty (I couldn't possibly have gotten there sooner), then call the cops fifteen minutes later. The police would have to admit that sounded a mite peculiar. I mean, I certainly hadn't had time to vacuum. Even if Townsend had been killed between ten and eleven, it wouldn't have left me much time to return to the loft—and why on earth would I have gone *back* there after killing him sometime after ten?

I suppose I could have gone back to keep the appointment on the off chance that he'd written it down somewhere, but why bother? I could always have said that I got the message too late and had decided to call him in the morning. It would have taken more than nerve to keep an appointment with a man I'd earlier killed. It would've taken balls.

Still, until somebody else turned up, I was most likely a suspect no matter what the lieutenant said.

I told myself, as I worked my way through the crowded police department and outside, that this wasn't a television show. I could hardly count on stumbling onto some clue the professionals had blindly overlooked, nor would the cavalry come charging over the hill if I went and got myself in some stupid confrontation with the murderer—even if I figured out who he was.

He. Why did I keep assuming it was a man? Hadn't I read somewhere that knives were a woman's weapon? Or was that poison? Damn it.

It all came down to why. *Why* was Jeffrey Townsend killed? Because he had called me? Or was I intended to be either a red herring or a genuine suspect? Had the murderer neatly boxed me in with a faked message and then taken considerable risk to erase that message?

When I drove away from the station, I had the doubtful comfort of knowing my escort dutifully followed. I could lose them, of course; it's child's play to lose a tail in heavy traffic as long as you're a reasonably adept driver and know the streets—which I was and did. It'd look damned suspicious, though.

Well, hell. I already looked suspicious, even to me and despite the lieutenant's professed belief in my innocence. And I didn't really believe the murderer would be chasing after me, because that would rather defeat his apparent purpose. That's what I told myself. Several times, in fact. Then I gritted my teeth, turned my station wagon onto Peachtree, and proceeded to lose my tail.

MY BROTHER HAD, like me, a loft. In his case, however, the loft was the entire top floor of a warehouse, and the main floor was a garage in which certain questionable activities took place. In street language, the place was a chop shop. Shiny, expensive (stolen) cars were driven in, taken apart or drastically altered, and resold later up north— either wholly or in pieces.

And, no, my brother wasn't involved, except in the same sense as me: because we both knew damned well what was going on. And it wasn't because I approved of what he was doing that I went in on the ground floor to warn Drew; I went to warn him because he'd saved my life three years ago.

"You did *what?*" Drew asked politely.

"I found a body. Anyway, the police are going to be checking me out, and that means Jason too, so I thought you should know about it."

Drew stared at me. Somebody was operating a welder behind him, sparks flying everywhere, and with the fiery halo he looked like Zeus during a storm. I've never quite figured Drew out, but I like him. He's tall, with snow-white hair down to his shoulders and a full white beard; he's muscled and handsome and, whatever his age, he's obviously in his prime. I've never known his last name; Jason pays his rent to a holding company and we've never really been sure if Drew rents too, or if he owns the building.

"You found a body," Drew said. "You found a body." He seemed to be trying the words on for size, altering his tone consideringly from matter-of-fact to mildly surprised. "You . . . found . . . a . . . body. Whose body?" It was obviously an afterthought.

"Jeffrey Townsend's. Look, Drew, I lost my police escort, but it's only a matter of time before they come to check out Jason. So maybe you'd better stop chopping."

Drew looked mildly offended. "I have the pink slip on every car in the place."

"Oh. Well, you don't, usually."

"No. I *do* usually. I just don't sometimes. Thanks for the warning, though, Lane."

I waved and headed back outside, thankfully escaping the noise of Drew's establishment. I climbed the iron stairs to Jason's loft and made use of the tarnished brass lion's-head door knocker, knocking twice before pushing open the heavy fire door that was never locked.

It was quiet up here. Excellent soundproofing.

To understand my brother, you have to really study his place. There's an awful lot to see, mostly paintings in various stages of completion. They're stacked against the walls, propped on easels, hanging here and there, framed and unframed. There are sketches in charcoal and water-color, pen-and-ink drawings. Coffee cans filled with brushes decorate a huge paint-spattered worktable at the entrance end of the loft, surrounded by tubes of paint, jars of turpentine, and piles of rags.

There are, by the way, no paintings or sketches of either me or our mother, and no self-portraits of Jason. He's refused to paint Mother despite her yearly requests (to her absolute fury); stubbornly maintains that a self-portrait is the rankest sort of vanity, and told me years ago that he'd paint me when I fell in love and not before. I haven't asked why.

Anyway.

This end of the two-hundred-by-fifty-foot loft is parti-tioned from the living area by three Japanese screens. There are odd pieces of furniture for props, vases and dried flowers, bolts of material leaning here and there. One of those demure little "changing" screens in one cor-ner where Jason's models disrobe if nakedness is called for (although why anyone would need to strip in privacy before modeling in the nude is something of a mystery to me, but Jason says they do that), or change into something other than street clothes if that's necessary.

Once you walk past the Japanese screens, you come into the living area, which is definitely in stark contrast to the rest of the place. From bare wooden floors you step onto pale, plush carpet, an off-white pit grouping forms a con-versational area around a wood stove set into a brick hearth; an entertainment center boasts a huge-screen pro-jection television, an ungodly number of neatly labeled videotapes, audio tapes, and records, and a complex stereo system complete with five-foot speakers.

There's a wet bar that's better stocked than the corner

tavern and is cozily complete with taps and a framed picture of the Budweiser Clydesdales, a massive desk made of dark oak, and framed paintings (not painted by Jason) hang on the white brick walls.

A Sheetrock wall provides the partition between living room/kitchenette and bedroom, and tucked away in his bedroom area my brother has a bathroom that would bring envious tears to your eyes, complete with a Jacuzzi the size of a small swimming pool that's set in place and surrounded with decidedly erotic decorative mosaic tiles.

Jason calls himself a Sybarite, which is about as far wide of the mark as you can get, but he is a very tactile creature; textures influence his moods the way colors affect most people. He likes softness. His bed, for instance, is a water bed with a free-float mattress, which is like sleeping on a cloud that's never completely still.

Anyway, Jason is a prolific and immensely talented artist given to painting murals for schools and businesses (the former without pay) and teaching kids who couldn't ordinarily afford lessons in how to paint. He has buckets of charm, the kind of looks that make women check their makeup in the nearest available mirror, and is frighteningly intelligent.

I was on my way across the living room toward the kitchen, where the welcome scent of coffee beckoned, when my brother stormed in his usual energetic fashion from his bedroom with a towel wrapped around his waist, his face half-lathered (we're both late risers), and a razor in his hand.

He got all the leftover inches in the family, being over six feet and somewhat gangly for a man of nearly thirty. He also got, like me, the family trademark of black hair and green eyes, although his eyes are flecked with gold. Damn it.

To the uninitiated, his eyes would have looked wild; to me, they looked bright with interest. We're unusually close as siblings go, possibly because we were mostly raised by one parent who occasionally forgot that's what she was, but more likely because we're suited temperamentally and not at all competitive. But we were hardly psychic with one another, so his first words to me were a bit startling.

"All I want to know," he said as if his retreat to shower and shave had interrupted a conversation, "is how in the name of hell you managed to find Jeffrey Townsend's murdered body?"

THREE

THE LOGICAL response, of course, was, "How did you know?"

Jason followed me into the brick-and-tile kitchen, leaning back against the counter near the sink and tilting his head back to finish shaving under his chin while I fixed a cup of coffee. "Sharon called."

"Who's Sharon?"

He turned on the hot water and rinsed his razor, continuing with his shaving, and mumbling at me because he was contorting his face. "Sharon York. You remember—I went out with her a few times two years ago."

I did remember. Sharon was a typist for the police department, and it figured that she'd still remember my brother two years later. Women remember Jason, no matter how long ago it was. "Oh. Well, what'd she say?"

"She typed your statement," Jason said, using a kitchen towel to wipe the remainder of the lather off his face. "Thought I might be interested. Plasma?"

I poured him a cup and handed it over, then responded to his lifted brows. "Well, it isn't much, after all. I just found him. Somebody left a message on my answering machine for me to meet him, so I went out there. And he was dead."

"Somebody? Not Townsend?"

"It's beginning to look that way. When we got back to my loft, the message had been erased."

42

"We?"

"They found me standing over a murdered body, Jase; of course somebody went back to the loft with me to get the tape. Only it turns out there wasn't a message, but the lieutenant believes me. I think."

Jason sipped his coffee for a moment, bright eyes fixed on my face. "Uh-*huh*. Well, somebody must have believed you, since you're still footloose and fancy free today."

"I lost an unwelcome escort," I confessed.

"They put a tail on you?"

"Yeah. Either because they really do suspect me, or else they think the murderer might have me on his 'Must-Get' list."

Jason took that with his usual aplomb. "Christ, Lanie, you need a keeper."

My brother is the only person who could (and does) call me Lanie and live to tell. "Hey, if you think walking in on a dead body is any picnic, let me reassure you! He had a big kitchen knife sticking out of his chest, Jase. And somebody—*somebody*—must have planned for me to find him like that. I've got one hell of a rabid enemy out there, and I don't know who it is!"

"You must know," Jason said. "You just don't know that you know. But if you think about it—"

"I dreamed about it," I told him. "I've asked myself a hundred times, gone through every major event of the past four years trying to come up with—"

"What about minor events?" He carried his coffee toward the bedroom and I followed, sitting on the footrail of his water bed while he disappeared into the bathroom.

"If it was something minor," I called to my brother, "then why the hell involve me in a murder? That's a little drastic, isn't it?"

"Maybe it wasn't minor to him," Jason called back. "Goddamn it, where did I put my—oh, there it is. The man's a killer, Lanie, he doesn't have to be logical. Maybe you smiled at him one day and ignored him the next, so he decided on a spot of murder to gain your interest.''

I shivered. "That isn't funny. Besides, I'm hardly the type of siren men murder for, brother mine."

"You underestimate yourself," he said in a muffled voice, wandering back into the bedroom with a sweater half-on and the zipper of his jeans at half-mast. He yanked the sweater down and absently smoothed his hair with both hands, then fished a belt from an open drawer of his dresser and began threading it through the loops of his jeans.

"Not to that extent I don't, pal," I told him. "Besides, all he had to do was ask."

"Maybe he was afraid to." Jason went back into the bathroom long enough to get his coffee, returning to the bedroom fully dressed but for his bare feet. "Maybe—"

"You're barking up the wrong tree," I told him with what patience I could muster. "Jase, this guy *got into my loft* to erase that message. And if he broke in, he did a damned subtle job of it."

Jason's faint amusement disappeared, and he looked at me steadily. "Didn't think of that, did I? Sorry, Lanie."

I got up and went into the living room, collapsing on the couch. "Hell of a note, isn't it? You and Mary are the only ones with a key to my place. And you know how she is—she sleeps with the keys on a chain around her neck, she's so afraid of somebody breaking into the building. You haven't misplaced yours recently, have you?"

Jason sat down at a right angle to me, lifting his key ring from the glass-topped end table. "Right here. But I suppose somebody could have made a wax impression in a stray moment. Isn't that how it's done?"

"Beats me. I'd better see about getting the lock changed as soon as possible." I brooded for a moment. "I keep coming back to *why*. Why was Townsend murdered, and why was I involved in it? There has to be a reason."

"To give the police a suspect?" Jason suggested.

"Ummm. That's what the lieutenant said. But, why *me*, Jase? You don't carefully arrange to pin a murder on someone else—I mean a specific someone else—without at least a vague reason. Do you?''

''I shouldn't think so. Are you sure you haven't put someone's nose rather badly out of joint recently, Lanie?''

I opened my mouth to retort, but the distant, hollow sound of Jason's door knocker forestalled me. ''I'll bet that's the police. They aren't going to be happy with me.''

Jason grinned as he got to his feet. ''Shall I draw their fire?''

''Don't,'' I begged, alarmed. ''Jason Montana, don't you dare! This is serious.''

He wiped the grin off his face, but I knew that bright look in his eyes and sighed inwardly as he went to answer the door. You have to understand, my brother can be a flake at times. He gets possessed by a demon of mischief, and the only rational thing to do is just wait until it passes.

I wondered, suddenly and with intense curiosity, what the lieutenant would make of him.

They came into the living room a couple of minutes later: Jason, Lieutenant Trey Fortier, and Sergeant Rudy Flint. The sergeant looked, as before, huge, faintly rumpled, deceptively mild, and unexpressive. The lieutenant was as elegant as before, his fawn raincoat worn over a dark suit and spotless white shirt. I wanted to yank the knot of his tie askew just for the hell of it.

''Coffee, gentlemen?'' Jason asked politely as he gestured for them to sit and resumed his own place on the couch.

Flint sat down at one end on Jason's side of the grouping, shaking his head at the offer; Lieutenant Fortier sat down on my side, about two feet away. ''No, thank you, Mr. Montana,'' he said calmly.

I felt boxed in.

''I feel I should mention,'' Jason said solemnly, ''that I hate being called 'Mister.' I'll answer to anything else, you understand. Just the first or last name, or 'you ugly bastard,' or whatever. As long as you don't put a 'Mister' in front of it.''

Jason was going to be difficult. I half closed my eyes and glanced sideways at the lieutenant, and when his luminous gaze flickered to meet mine I felt like giggling. I looked away hastily and saw that Rudy Flint was glancing from Jason to me with a kind of faint surprise.

I'd seen that reaction before. Lots of siblings resemble each other, of course, and both Jase and I have black hair and greenish eyes. We're unmistakably brother and sister despite the considerable difference in height and build, but there's more to it than that. In fact, pictures of us together always startle even me just a bit.

Jason says it's the shape of our bones, and I imagine he'd know. At any rate, people who see us together always seem fascinated, and we've gotten used to explaining that, no, we aren't twins.

"Fine, Jason," the lieutenant said, still calm. "I expect your sister has discussed the situation with you?"

"Well, we'd just gotten started, Lieu—d'you mind if I call you something else? Lanie's been referring to you as THE LIEUTENANT—all caps—and it's scared the hell out of me. A phobia about authority figures, I guess."

"My name," the lieutenant said, "is Trey."

Jason nodded affably. "Fine, Trey."

I looked into my coffee and concentrated on remembering that I had trained myself not to blush. I was going to kill Jason. Slowly. I'd start by pouring hot coffee on him, and then . . .

"You were saying?" the lieutenant prompted my brother.

"Oh, right. Well, we'd just gotten started talking about it, really. Lanie was wondering why somebody would kill Townsend, and wondering why she was involved."

"Do you have any ideas on that?"

"Not a one. I don't suppose it could have been the odd homicidal maniac?"

"Not likely," the lieutenant told him gently.

Jason frowned. "Then I'm stumped. I knew Townsend by reputation, of course, I even did a mural for one of his office buildings, but never met the man. Met his daughter, though.''

"When?''

"While I was doing the mural. It was at his office downtown . . . oh, a few months ago. At the beginning of the summer. She must have been home from boarding school or something—she was wearing one of those god-awful uniforms. Anyway, I was doing the mural there, in the building's lobby, and she followed me around during the afternoons for a few days. Didn't talk much, acted like a scared rabbit. Let's see, her name was—''

"Samantha,'' the lieutenant said.

"Right. Samantha. I called her Sam, and she held brushes for me.''

"I remember her,'' I said suddenly. "I'd forgotten all about it. You were craving barbecue, so I brought some by a few days for lunch. It wasn't a school uniform, though, Jase, just a skirt and blazer and kneesocks.''

Jason frowned. "It should have been a uniform. No girl should dress like that willingly.''

"Maybe she was trying to look grown-up—even if it did have the opposite effect. She was in her father's office building after all. And she had a crush on you.''

"She was a baby, Lanie!''

"Eighteen is not a baby. She had a crush.''

The lieutenant, silent throughout our exchange, then said to me, "So you met her as well?''

"Well, informally. Jase casually introduced us. She didn't care for me, I think. I doubt she'll grow up to be a woman's kind of woman.''

"As opposed to a man's kind of woman?'' Jason asked interestedly.

"Oh, you know,'' I said vaguely. "Some women just don't care too much for their own sex. They don't have female friends. To them, the world is divided into me, men, and the rest of them. Sam'll probably be like that.''

"Why do you think so?'' the lieutenant asked.

I thought about it. "Hard to say, exactly. Intuition,

maybe, if you believe in that stuff. Her mouth smiled at me, but her eyes didn't.''

"They didn't smile at me either," Jason objected.

"No, they adored you."

"Bullshit," my brother said.

I waved off the subject. "Well, anyway, we both met Samantha. But not the wife or son, and certainly not Townsend himself."

"That's about it," Jason said, looking at the lieutenant. "Lanie and I know roughly the same pool of people around here, overlapping as it were, except for some of our individual clients. I've done portraits for a few of Townsend's set, but not recently."

"Where were you last night, Jason?" the lieutenant asked.

Grinning, Jason said, "According to all the novels I've read, my answer will render me instantly suspect. It seems I have an airtight alibi, unlikely as it sounds. From seven o'clock last night until almost one A.M. I attended a dinner party at a client's home."

"Could you have slipped out?" the lieutenant asked politely.

"Well," Jason said with a sigh. "I really wanted to, but since the daughter of the house was attached to my arm as if by Krazy Glue the entire evening, I couldn't manage it. There was, I remember fondly, one brief trip to the john, but she waited outside the door and the window was too small for me to escape through."

"Jason," I muttered.

"True, I swear. I'll be glad to furnish the name and address of the client, Trey." He rattled it off, while Flint solemnly wrote it down in his notebook.

I'd like to explain here that Jason isn't at all vain. Yes, I know his blithe "alibi" sounded that way, but he really isn't. Hard as it is to believe, he's actually a bit shy around admiring women and covers it up by being flippant. And women generally *do* tend to go overboard on the side of flattery with my brother, which makes him uncomfortable.

They seem to have the idea that artists need their egos stroked regularly, which is a false idea where Jason is concerned.

Though I've never mentioned it to him, I've always had a hunch that when my brother falls in love it'll be with some woman who prefers fair men to dark ones, house painters to artists, and brute muscle to feline grace. Jason is as stubborn as I am, and neither one of us has ever in our life taken the easy path to anything.

Just so you know.

The lieutenant brought out a small tape recorder and looked at me. "There are three separate voices recorded here. Will you tell me, please, if any are familiar?"

"Sure." I watched him push the play button and listened intently to the first voice. It wasn't familiar. Nor was the second. But the third had me sitting up. "That's it!"

The lieutenant asked, "Which voice?"

"The third one. It's the voice on the message."

"You're certain?" He was looking at me intently.

"Positive. I could swear to it in court." Something about his gaze unnerved me suddenly. "Um, whose voice. . . ?"

He slipped the recorder back into his pocket, still watching me. After a long and silent moment, he replied softly, "Jeffrey Townsend's."

I hope you never feel what I felt then. On the surface of things, the lieutenant's revelation should have simplified matters. Townsend had called me, and I had gone; therefore, I had a good reason to have been at the estate. Great. Wonderful.

But if *Townsend* had indeed called me out to his place last night, how had the murderer known about the message? Had Townsend told him? ("I'm going to call this Lane Montana and hire her to find———." Whatever.) Had Townsend been killed because he was going to hire me? And had the murderer, having killed Townsend (who had stupidly and with a total lack of manners gone to sleep in his presence), then rushed to my loft sometime between eleven and midnight (knowing right where I lived, of course), let himself in without leaving a sign of a break-in, erased the damning message from my machine (which he knew about because Townsend had also said to him, "I left a message on Lane Montana's answering machine"), let himself back out, and then gone blithely on his way, confident that I either hadn't gotten the message or else wouldn't be interested in finding out what the hell was going on?

Was my involvement purely accidental and unwanted—from the murderer's point of view, at least? Or was it the other way, was my involvement deliberate, a carefully planned frame?

And if that was so . . . then *why me?*

"So what now?" Jason asked, finally sobered.

The lieutenant shook his head slightly. "We start checking out everything. Everyone involved. Places, times, alibis. And we try to discover why Townsend would have called your sister. If we know that, we may be able to work out who went to the trouble of erasing the message, and why. Then we'll have the killer."

I thought he was being amazingly forthcoming for a cop, and Flint seemed to agree with me; I caught the glance he sent the lieutenant, and it was a bit startled. But he didn't say anything as they rose to leave.

The lieutenant, however, did. He looked at me, hands in his pockets, expressionless. Politely, he said, "If you attempt to lose your escort one more time, I'll lock you up."

I could feel my hackles rising. "You said I wasn't a suspect."

"I said you were still on the list. Lose the escort again, and I'll lock you up."

I faced him squarely, clutching my coffee cup and annoyed because I had to look up so far. "I'd be out in an hour."

"Then," he said very softly, "I'll lock you up every

hour on the hour. For spitting on the sidewalk. For jay-walking. For any goddamned thing that comes to mind. Lose your tail again, Montana, and I'll throw away the key. Understand?''

From the corner of my eye, I thought I saw Flint's mouth drop open. I heard my brother choke a couple of times. But I couldn't look away from those luminous eyes. ''The last time I checked,'' I said evenly, ''I was free, over twenty-one, and living in a democratic society. I will be damned, *Lieutenant*, if I knuckle under to a tyrant with a badge.''

For the first time, he smiled. If sharks could smile, that's what they'd look like. ''Well, why don't I just mention to the press that you found the body? Would you like that, Montana? All that speculation in the newspapers? Guilty by the press until proven innocent by the courts? Strangers camped out on your doorstep and calling at all hours with rude questions? How does that sound?''

''Like shit,'' I muttered, hating him.

''Then behave.''

I grinned at him with all my teeth. ''Don't you mean 'heel'?''

''Whatever works.''

I stood there watching him walk away, and I didn't say a damned word. Don't think I was giving in, though. I was just too busy gnashing my teeth to be verbal.

''Whew,'' Jason murmured when he returned from see-ing them to the door. ''Your lieutenant reminds me of a lion tamer I saw once, except he didn't need a whip and chair. Hell, he didn't need anything at all.''

Through my (still-bared) teeth, I said, ''He isn't *my* lieutenant, damn it. He's a tinhorn dictator with a vastly inflated idea of his own importance. He's a little Hitler—''

''Not so little.''

''—and somebody needs to take him down a peg or two.''

''Lanie,'' Jason said in a thoughtful tone, ''we both know I'm the last man in the world to preach caution.

And, under ordinary circumstances, I'd be tickled to get myself a ringside seat while you went head to head with Lieutenant Trey Fortier of the Atlanta Metropolitan Police Department, Homicide Division. However. A man has been shuffled off this mortal coil by person or persons unknown with the aid of a kitchen knife. After which, said person or persons unknown slipped into your loft and erased the victim's voice from your trusty machine.

"Now, it seems to me that our dark lieutenant has your best interests at heart, however he chooses to state his case. It might behoove the both of us to take the man seriously."

I stared at him.

"Besides," he said, descending to normality, "I'd feel a lot better if you let the cops tag along while you investigate."

I looked down at my cold coffee, then swore and headed for the kitchen. "What makes you think I'm going to investigate anything? I'm not a P.I. I wouldn't have the faintest idea where to start investigating."

Jason followed me with his own cup. "I think you know exactly where to start. What's more, I think Fortier knows you have something in mind. You'll notice he didn't order you to barricade yourself in the castle, pull up the drawbridge, and flood the moat, which would have been easier on his men. No, he just told you not to lose the tail. And he also, in case you missed the point, riled you enough so you'd go charging off in pursuit of truth, justice, and the American way. He played you like a champ, sweetie."

I burned my tongue with an unwary sip of coffee and stared at him in dawning horror. "My God, he did, didn't he? But why on earth would he think I could find out anything the police couldn't?"

"You find things," Jason reminded succinctly. "When you start looking, you find. He just started you looking."

"That devious bastard!"

"I like him too," Jason confided gravely.

* * *

THE UNMARKED CAR was waiting outside and fell in behind me as I left, making no attempt to be discreet. Maybe those guys (there were two of them) were smarting after having been reprimanded for losing me earlier; I thought—having felt the effect myself—that Lieutenant Trey Fortier could probably tear strips off an oak tree at thirty paces with that impersonal voice of his. At any rate, my escort very definitely wanted me to know that they were sticking like glue this time.

It was, of course, ridiculous. I wasn't a detective, damn it. But I wasn't really surprised to find myself at the public library. When I finally emerged hours later, starving, weary, and with a pounding headache, I had an armful of xeroxed magazine and newspaper articles, documents, and other junk. I didn't try to lose my escort, but drove sedately back to my loft with only one brief stop at McDonald's.

"Waaurr!"

"Well, I'm hungry too," I said irritably, dishing out the latest gourmet flavor from Friskies. While Choo was delicately devouring his feast, I sat down at the breakfast bar with mine and looked over the copies I'd made while I munched a chef's salad and inhaled french fries.

Townsend had been decidedly newsworthy. The whole family had been, in fact, and I had as much of their history here as was public knowledge. I skimmed over most of the early stuff, provided by in-depth articles from some of our better city and state magazines. Some of it was fascinating. I was tickled to note that Amabel Townsend née Culpepper, after marrying into the family just after the Civil War, had managed to lose her husband on a trek out west, returning tearfully "great with child," which, duly brought into the world, turned out to have raven-black hair and high cheekbones and was popularly believed to be a result of the Indian raid that had cost Charles Townsend his life. Amabel held to it tooth and nail that the interestingly dark baby was Charles's son, and he got the Townsend name.

Oh, for a peek into her journal . . .

Three of the early Townsends, all of them women, had been discreetly committed to asylums; two male Townsends had been lost at sea and several killed in the Civil War, Korean War, and both World Wars. There had been a somewhat ruthless feud between the Townsends and Culpeppers, which had also claimed a few on both sides, but which had been more or less settled when Amabel married Charles.

The occasional "bad" marriage popped up in print, complete with details of divorce and/or gossipy speculation of infidelity. There were court battles among the family, more of them with all the family on the same side against somebody else, and a few cases of dubious as well as patently valid paternity suits.

The family had gradually died out, helped along by wars and the like, until Jeffrey came along post–World War II, just in time to be a member of the baby boom. The apple of his parents' eyes, he'd been born with the proverbial silver spoon in his mouth and lost no time leaving teeth marks on it.

It's amazing what you can piece together with a stack of public records. Jeffrey hadn't been a good boy. There was nothing screamingly obvious, just hints and mentions here and there, suitably couched to avoid libel accusations. (I'm great at reading between the lines.) Jeffrey had attended four different private schools before he reached his teens, and though his grades were reportedly outstanding, his teachers didn't want to answer questions about him from occasional curious reporters.

There was also a faint hint of scandal from his college days, although I couldn't really get a handle on it. Something about a girl, I thought, which figured. He had "changed" colleges at that point, and it was, perhaps, coincidental that his poor mama had "visited" a popular rest home for the very rich about the same time.

Jeffrey Townsend, Jr., (I hadn't known he was a junior) had served in Vietnam. In a sign of those confusing times, the gossip columns and magazines had gotten a bit bolder when discussing his military service, one announcing baldly that he'd been up for disciplinary action, again involving a girl, although the details were murky. One column slyly reported a "substantial" withdrawal of funds from Jeffrey senior's bank account, tacitly suggesting a payoff of some kind.

Then Jeffrey junior came home, settled down with the young bride of his family's choice after a truly spectacular wedding, and promptly got her pregnant. The first child was lost due to a miscarriage after Amy Townsend took a bad fall. The papers clucked in sympathy. A second pregnancy was triumphantly announced rather quickly.

Jeffrey Townsend III was born with suitable pomp and ceremony.

Two more miscarriages occurred during the next two years, until Samantha Townsend's reportedly difficult birth. (God, was her doctor crazy? Or had either Amy or Jeffrey—or both—ignored the standard advice to wait and heal after a miscarriage before trying again?) Then Amy very wisely either stopped trying, or else quietly got her tubes tied so that Jeffrey's trying wouldn't produce any results.

Jeffrey settled down to build on his family's fortune after both Mama (details on her were a bit murky) and Jeffrey senior (heart attack) obligingly shuffled off and left him the kitty. He was awfully good at it too.

One particular name kept popping up in articles about his suspectedly unscrupulous business dealings, and I gradually realized that the man was a sort of silent partner of Jeffrey's and had been for at least ten years. Aside from his dealings with Jeffrey, he looked clean, yet another pillar of the community, but by now I was suspicious of everyone . . . A bit thoughtfully, I added Luther Dumont's name to my list of people and events I wanted to learn more about.

And I went back to my reading.

It seemed that the Townsends figured that any publicity

was worth having, because not one of them had tried very hard to suppress anything. Or, at least, if they had, they'd done a damned thorough job of it. And Jeffrey junior seemed even more oblivious than his ancestors.

That fall of Amy's, for instance, resulting in the first miscarriage. I thought I could probably finagle the medical records somehow; I had the feeling that hadn't been quite the accident it was reported to be. Mind you, I could have been wrong . . . but I didn't think so.

Yes, I was beginning to get a feeling about the Townsends. A lot of feelings, as a matter of fact, and most of them negative and disturbing ones. I was very tired, so I stripped down and climbed into bed naked (my normal mode of sleeping) with the final, most recent accounts.

I banked pillows behind me and spread the papers out atop Choo, who was in my lap. And, somewhere between Jeffrey III's graduation from high school and Amy's redecorating of the Townsend mansion, I fell asleep.

"THE SECURITY SYSTEM." I came awake with a jolt, sitting bolt upright and nearly bumping heads with Choo, who was sitting on my legs.

"Errpp," Choo said.

I stared at him, feeling my eyes cross like his and coping with a vague memory about something to do with a security system. Or maybe it had been a dream. "You always make that sound when I wake up," I said to Choo, still more than half asleep. "I don't know what it means."

"Yah!" Choo said, and stalked—no mean feat on a surface that gave with every step—across the bed. He hit the floor with a thump and headed for the kitchen, looking back at me and saying, "Yah!" again.

I knew what that meant. Flinging back the covers and sending what was left of the research on my bed flying, I padded naked into the kitchen and obediently opened a can of Friskies. I started the coffee and stumbled into the bathroom, praying, as always, that a hot shower would prepare me to face the day.

I remembered the security system after the first cup of coffee and sat at the breakfast bar sipping a second cup while I thought about it. Jeffrey's security system, of course. It had been off last night, the gate standing open. Well, okay, he'd apparently expected a visitor: me. Odd, though, that he hadn't locked up tight and buzzed me through at the gate. There was an intercom out there.

What did I know about the system? Not much, but at a guess it was pretty complex and extensive. I knew from what the police had said that the system had been deactivated, apparently from inside and with no harm done. So someone had known just how to turn the thing off. Had Townsend done it himself, and if so, why?

I needed to know more about that system. And even though the lieutenant had egged me on to stick my nose in this, I could imagine what his superiors would have to say if word got out that he was handing out information to someone who herself was a subject of the investigation. Assuming he would.

Whatever Trey Fortier thought of my ability to "find" the murderer, I doubted he'd reported officially that he'd nudged me in that direction. In fact, I knew damned well that *officially* I was a suspect.

I brooded for a few minutes, chewing on a thumbnail until I caught myself at it and stopped. What I needed, I decided finally, was someone able to find out who had installed the security system, and able to tell me what the thing consisted of in case the lieutenant wasn't forthcoming.

I thought immediately of Drew.

Calling him was out; my phone could be tapped for all I knew, and I preferred to be paranoid about it. But going to see Drew would be just as bad, likely focusing the police's attention where Drew wouldn't appreciate it.

The phone rang before I could make up my mind. It was the lieutenant, and what he had to say was brief and to the point. He wanted to see me, because of a development in the case. When he told me what the development was, all I could do was mumble that I was on my way.

As it turned out, the butcher knife in his chest hadn't ended Jeffrey Townsend's life; he'd been dead when it went in. The muscle relaxers he'd ingested had done a dandy job of stopping his heart, instead.

THE LIEUTENANT'S OFFICE wasn't a surprise to me, since I'd been there before. But I looked closer this time. It wasn't much more than a cubbyhole, separated from the large squad room by partitions that were glass from the waist up. There were blinds for privacy and a door, which the lieutenant shut when I came in.

Two visitor's chairs (one occupied by me) sat before the big wooden desk that was scrupulously neat, his chair was the regulation desk type that is never comfortable enough, a huge map of the city hung on the wall behind the desk, there were a couple of filing cabinets, and his phone had at least half a dozen lines. What can I say? It was an office.

And an interesting one, to me. No certificates or commendations neatly framed on the walls, although I thought he could have produced a few if he'd wanted. No decorative personal touches that I could see, such as artwork or photographs, on his desk, or even a coffee mug with a funny saying on it. And though he was clearly fastidious about his appearance, he didn't pander to vanity here: his fawn-colored coat was hung, not on a hanger, but on a scarred, old wooden coat tree in one corner.

I suddenly wanted to run out and buy him a plant or a big stuffed bear to sit on top of one of the filing cabinets. Conquering the urge, I spoke as he was settling into his chair. "A question."

He nodded, watching me and giving nothing away, as usual.

"Am I here as a suspect?"

He sat back in his chair, and I wasn't surprised that it didn't creak. He'd probably trained it not to. He was immaculately dressed, as usual. I looked at the neat, dark tie and imagined bright red polka dots.

"No," he said finally.

I'd gotten over my hostility about the unwelcome tail, but still wasn't satisfied with the answer. "I want to be absolutely clear on this," I told him. "If I'm not a suspect, I won't expect to hear any more veiled threats, Lieutenant." I sounded brave. I hoped.

He might have smiled, but it was hard to tell. "You didn't kill Jeffrey Townsend. Is that clear enough?"

I thought about it. "So I'm off the list?"

"You're off my list."

I appreciated the distinction, and winced. "But not someone else's? Like maybe your superiors'?"

He seemed to weigh the question, studying me in silence until he reached whatever conclusions he'd been after. "My superiors like a neat case," he said at last. "They're also under a certain amount of pressure from various groups and individual citizens."

"Who move in the same circles Townsend did," I finished for him grimly. "And who would no doubt prefer a murderer ready to hang, with no need for poking and prying into those elite circles."

The lieutenant nodded slightly. "An understandable attitude, from their viewpoint," he pointed out dryly. "Townsend had an iron in every fire going, and a great many 'friends' in high places. A cliché, but so often true. Those same friends are yelling for a quick arrest and conviction."

"And they'd much rather it be me than one of their own?"

"Words to that effect. A murder investigation often rattles tightly sealed closets, and most people prefer their skeletons decently in the dark."

"Damn," I muttered. I stared at him for a moment, then asked, "So why're you being so forthcoming with the official number-one suspect?"

This time, he definitely smiled. "Suspicious Montana. You feel the jaws of a trap?"

"I can hear them creaking."

Calmly, he said, "No physical evidence ties you to the murder. You had an appointment to be there, confirmed by Townsend's note, you left no fingerprints, except on the front door, which was perfectly natural. You had no prior connection to the dead man and, so, no discernable motive.

"Your landlady states that you were at your loft just before eleven; you couldn't possibly have driven to Townsend's estate in under half an hour; I believe he was killed before eleven, which makes your return—supposing you killed him—a bit hard to understand. You called the police upon finding the corpse and answered all questions put to you without hesitating and without, so far as we can determine, hiding anything. Not even my nervous superiors would go to the D.A. with your name as a suspect as things stand now."

"But?" I prompted.

He shrugged. "But, Townsend's wife, son, and daughter each have an alibi I couldn't break with a pickax. And now that the man's dead, he's all but become a saint. We haven't found a trace of a motive. We have a court order to search Townsend's offices, both at his business and home, but aren't likely to find anything new. And according to the elderly lady who lives across the street from Townsend's front gate, the only car to enter the estate that night was yours. She remembers that distinctly, by the way, because she thought at the time that a station wagon wasn't the usual type of car to visit Townsend."

"Did she say what time she saw the car?"

"She couldn't pin it down. Sometime after nine o'clock and before midnight. She'd been dozing in her chair and got up to let her cat in."

"Great." I could see it clearly enough. The lieutenant was being pressured to find the killer quickly, while at the same time those "nervous" superiors of his were urging him to make a case against me. Cynical, I know. Wouldn't you be, in my position? Damn right.

"Is this an official meeting?" I asked suddenly. "I mean, are you officially questioning me again?"

"Certainly. And my report will state that you stuck to your story."

I decided to abandon oblique questions and come straight to the point. "But—unofficially—you believe I can help you find out what really happened that night."

He nodded.

"Why? I mean, why do you believe I can do that?"

After a moment, he said slowly, "I knew of you before you found Townsend dead. A friend of mine is a former client of yours."

"Who?"

"Frank Beaufort."

I remembered him instantly. "About a year ago. His daughter was a runaway." I wondered if the lieutenant knew the whole story, but decided not to ask. Beaufort had later tipped the police about the place where I had found his fourteen-year-old daughter, but may have done so anonymously. I had managed to talk him out of going down there with a shotgun and a few pounds of plastic explosive. Even though he'd wanted revenge, he wouldn't have wanted his daughter in court testifying against the men who had abused her sexually; and she *hadn't* testified. So he probably hadn't told his friend the lieutenant all the details.

"Yes. And you tracked her down. Frank talked about it to me. He was . . . quite impressed with both your instincts and your tenacity."

I felt a little bewildered. "But it was something entirely different. A runaway versus a murderer?"

"Not so different," the lieutenant said definitely. "In both cases it's a question of instinct. You find things. You know how to look, what to look for. And, in this situation, you do have a vested interest in the outcome of the case."

I decided to ignore that last for the moment; it sounded

like one of those veiled threats he wasn't supposed to be making anymore, and I was busy feeling unsettled by a few realizations. "It is different, and we both know it. I'm a total amateur at this kind of thing, and I don't have any official status. I can't—"

"You can go places I can't," he interrupted, "ask questions I'd be hung for asking. And you have a legitimate reason, because you *are* involved. You found him. He apparently wanted to hire you, but you don't know why. And the police are suspicious."

"So, in effect, I'd be your spy," I said slowly, not liking it. "Inside, as it were. Just another suspect, worried and logically trying to find out what the hell's going on."

"Yes."

I didn't like it at all. What had seemed almost like an interesting puzzle until now suddenly took on a different appearance. I'd have to get involved with the people in this case, watching and listening and probing. And if I was successful, I'd be the Judas, leading one of them to slaughter . . .

"Make it clear you have a police escort," he said abruptly, frowning a little. "Let it be known to everyone involved that you're always followed. *Everyone.*"

"For my own safety, you mean?" I asked evenly.

His eyes held mine steadily. "It's a dangerous game, Montana, and you could become a target if you get too close."

"I don't seem to have much choice."

"No. Neither do I."

I could believe that. He didn't seem the type to use people needlessly—though it was obvious he could use them when he had to. And I couldn't even feel exploited. Not really. I was too aware that I *did*, in fact, have a vested interest in finding the murderer.

FOUR

"ALL RIGHT," I said finally. "I'll do my best. But I hope to hell you aren't pinning all your hopes on me."

He didn't answer that, just nodded briskly. "Fine. Now. It wouldn't do for you to take notes. How good is your memory?"

"It hasn't failed me yet," I muttered.

The lieutenant wasn't amused. Before he could respond, there was a knock at the door and Rudy Flint came in, bearing cups of coffee.

"Thought you could use this," he said, handing one cup to me and the other to his lieutenant.

"Thanks, Rudy."

I nodded my thanks as well and caught the shadow of a wink from the bear of a man before he retreated from the office.

"Does he know what you're up to?" I asked.

"Yes. He's the only one. If you need to get in touch with me and can't, talk to Rudy."

"Right," I murmured. I had caught myself staring at the hand holding his cup, feeling the same catch in my throat at the sight of that ugly, powerful hand. And I realized that if he was indeed sensitive about that incongruity, as I thought he was, my avoiding any glance would just make matters worse. So I told myself to stop being silly about the whole thing.

He had ugly hands. Big deal. They were . . . curiously moving. Maybe one day I'd tell him that. Maybe.

Setting his coffee to one side, the lieutenant opened the single file on his blotter. "The first point, as I told you on the phone, is that Townsend didn't die of a knife wound. He was given enough muscle relaxers to stop his heart, then stabbed sometime later."

"How much later?"

"Hard to say. The M.E. estimates anything up to an hour after he was dead."

"And what time was that?"

"Sometime between six P.M. and midnight."

"It had to be after ten," I objected, then stopped, wondering if it had to be.

The lieutenant nodded. "That is the point, isn't it? Your answering machine logged a call, from a voice you recognized as Townsend's, at ten P.M. If we assume the call *did* come from Townsend—and in lieu of evidence to the contrary, we have to—then he was alive at ten."

"Does the medical examiner know about the call?" I asked slowly.

Trey Fortier nodded again, this time with an approving gleam in his eye. "I thought you'd know the right questions to ask. Yes, I told him. And he isn't happy, although officially he's sticking to his estimate. He told me—unofficially—that he believes Townsend was killed earlier. Probably between eight and nine."

"Then stabbed sometime during the next hour. Why on earth was that done? We aren't looking at two killers, are we?"

"That's a little too coincidental for my taste. If, that is, you mean that someone killed him peacefully with drugs, and then someone else came along later and stabbed him before they realized he was already dead."

"It'd be a bitch of a case to prosecute, wouldn't it?"

"Complicated, to say the least."

"So why would the killer peacefully stop his heart and then stab him with a butcher knife?"

"Symbolic, maybe," Fortier offered in a thoughtful tone. "Our resident expert in these matters says it's possible. Or that the killer felt a need to shed blood while at the same time disliking the idea of getting his shoes spattered."

I didn't even wince. "Did your resident expert suggest that it could have been an act of sheer hatred? That killing Townsend with the pills was too easy, and the knife was pure impulse?"

"No, but it makes sense to me."

I brooded a moment, but no blinding flash of revelation came to me, not that I expected it to. "Okay. So we have to assume Townsend was probably killed between eight and . . . say, eleven. Close enough?"

"If we're discounting the idea that Townsend himself made that call to you, yes."

"I don't like the idea that a dead man's voice invited me to visit," I said dryly, "but the M.E.'s uneasiness is good enough to convince me that's probably what I heard. A recording, maybe. But it's awfully fancy."

The lieutenant shook his head slightly. "Not really. This is the electronic age; you could hardly go into a house and not find at least one small recorder. And even though it requires some knowledge, I've known kids to splice together recordings or edit a sound track to suit their purpose."

I had already, of course, provided in my official statement the exact message I'd received, and I remembered it now: *This is Jeffrey Townsend. I have a job for you. Please come to my home at eleven to discuss the matter.*

I sighed. "All right, let's accept, for the moment, that what I heard was some kind of doctored recording. Then why was it later erased?" I held up a hand, realizing. "Of course. That message proved I believed Townsend wanted to hire me, but his own note in the datebook just stated an appointment. Without the recording, my motives for being there could be called into question."

"Exactly."

"And that's why the message was left in the first place.

It looks like I was meant to be a suspect. Or a red herring, at least."

"Indicating that the killer knows you."

I shivered. "Great. But look, I've gone over it in my mind, and I can't come up with anyone—"

"Maybe you don't know them."

"Huh?" That had already occurred to me, but I wanted to hear his thoughts on the subject.

He smiled a little. "Think about it. Suppose Townsend had decided, before that night, to hire you. He could have talked about it to someone. Maybe to someone who had a great deal to lose if you were called in to find—whatever. A possible motive. The killer has to stop Townsend, and your name is right there as a dandy red herring."

It made sense. And it sounded better than my imaginings that everything had happened that night. "Then I have to try to find out why he intended to hire me."

"I'd say so."

I frowned. "But if Townsend himself wrote that note in his datebook—"

"The handwriting expert says it's fifty-fifty. I thought it would be verified, because the handwriting matched that on the earlier entries. Our expert, however, compared the writing to documents we know Townsend wrote. And there are differences. Enough to rule out a positive match."

I was beginning to feel like a long-distance swimmer: out of breath and wondering why the hell I was *doing* this. "But that brings us back to the family. Or was the datebook something Townsend took to his office?"

"He took it to his office. And on trips. And," the lieutenant added dryly, "so far, nobody has admitted to writing in it at all. Everyone says Townsend wrote his own notes of appointments, that it was his habit."

I started to groan in frustration, but then I had one of those blinding flashes of inspiration you read so much about. It caught me off guard, and I didn't trust the damned thing, because I'd never had one before. "That datebook. Can I see it?"

The lieutenant immediately picked up his phone and punched a few numbers. "Rudy, the Townsend evidence. I need the datebook. Right, just that. Thanks." He hung up and gazed at me. "What hit you?"

I wasn't sure I liked being so obvious, but I answered anyway. "A wild idea, probably. I think we both agree this murder had to be planned in advance."

"It looks that way, certainly. So?"

"There are two possibilities for my involvement. Either someone panicked because Townsend was going to hire me, or someone deliberately set me up to look suspicious. Since we don't know yet if Townsend really did want to hire me, let's take the second possibility. If we're assuming I was carefully and deliberately set up, then we can also assume the frame was built to fit. The message that sent me to the estate, the message erased to cast doubt on my motives, and the note in the datebook."

"Yes."

"Then suppose that the killer knew Townsend's handwriting well enough to think he could fake it—*if* that note of my appointment matched the rest of the entries. You yourself said you thought it was Townsend's writing for that very reason. The killer could have assumed that they would be the only samples checked, especially since Townsend is apparently known to write his own appointments in the book."

"A duplicate book," the lieutenant said softly. "With the earlier entries copied sometime in advance. The killer would only have had to add a few entries at most that night—and then the note of your appointment."

"Not such a wild idea?" I ventured.

"You ought to be a cop," he said.

I felt a momentary glow that all too soon vanished. "Well, but that doesn't tell us so much more than we already know. If Townsend took the damned book with him everywhere, God knows how many people could have had access to it. Unless we find the original book stuck under somebody's mattress, I don't see how it helps us."

"Every answer helps us," Trey Fortier said flatly. "We start out with questions, Montana, and every logical answer we find is a piece of the puzzle. If nothing else, this particular answer tells us the killer planned well beforehand. It also tells us something else. In the original book, we might have found the killer's name in an appointment for that night."

I hadn't thought of that. "Damn. I don't suppose evidence that good is generally found under a convenient mattress?"

"Not often, no."

We both looked around as Rudy Flint lumbered into the room. "Here you go, boss," he said, placing a thin leather-bound book on the lieutenant's blotter. "Anything else?"

"Not at the moment. Thanks, Rudy."

"Sure." He lumbered back out.

"Grizzly bear," I muttered.

"What?"

I cleared my throat and tried not to look self-conscious. Stupid, anyway, trying to identify the particular kind of bear the sergeant reminded me of. "Nothing. May I see the book?"

He handed it across the desk.

I looked at it, asking my brain for inspiration. Nothing came this time. It was expensive and looked neither old nor new, but just . . . like a thin leather-bound book. Nothing on the spine except gold embossing, strictly decorative. I opened it and flipped through the pages. The only headings were dates, professionally stamped rather than handwritten, and there were neat entries on the lined pages in a back-slanted writing that was almost printing. It wouldn't have been too terribly difficult to copy, I decided.

"Lieutenant—"

"Trey," he said.

I stared at the page bearing my appointment, wondering what I'd been about to say. "Um. Fine. Trey."

"You were saying?" he prompted.

I cast about wildly. "Oh, just wondering how difficult a book like this would be to find. Buy. And if anyone did."

The lieutenant—Trey—didn't seem to find my dithering confusing. Or, at least, he didn't comment on it.

"I'll have it checked out."

"Good." I set the book on his desk, looking at it instead of him and frowning. Deep in thought. Sure. Actually, I said the first thing I could think of. "The security system. How good was it? I mean, could a stranger have gotten in?"

"We're having it checked out now, but the system looks pretty secure on the surface. Assuming it was active, I seriously doubt a stranger could have gotten in without tripping the alarms."

Silently, I decided to check with Drew about the system; he might be able to tell me more—and quickly. "Okay, we've covered some of this. But there's a lot we haven't talked about. The lack of footprints in the room, for instance."

"You were right. It had been vacuumed. We checked the house vacuum, and there wasn't a print on it. Wiped clean. The bag was missing as well."

"A mess he had to clean up?"

"Maybe. But it's more likely he, like everyone else, has seen enough on television to know that fibers found in carpets often provide forensic evidence. And either he did a good job with the cleaner or else he was being overly cautious. We didn't find a thing out of place."

"The drapery cord," I offered.

"Yes, I noticed it was missing. We didn't find it, and Mrs. Townsend has no idea what happened to it. She says it was in place when she left for New York the day before."

"*Did* she leave for New York?"

"Someone did."

I gave him a sharp look, alerted by something in his voice. "But you don't think it was her?"

He hesitated, then shrugged. "Evidence says she did. A confirmed airline reservation. The seat was used. Hotel room, also made use of. She definitely came back from New York this morning. The police there were telexed a photo, showed it to the hotel staff. They said it looked like the woman who had occupied that particular room. The old school friend she went to visit says she was there."

"But?" I prompted.

"But . . . I don't know that I believe her. She's a very controlled woman, doesn't give anything away. Maybe she flew back home sometime Monday and then caught a plane out of Atlanta that night after she killed her husband; there were half a dozen flights to New York from eleven P.M. on. We didn't find out which hotel she was staying at until early yesterday morning, and it's a big one; the staff might not have noticed her particularly until she checked out even though the room was supposedly occupied. She could have killed him. I just don't know."

After a moment, I nodded. "How about the kids?"

"Jeff was on his college campus, taking a make-up exam from five P.M. until almost eight. He then waited just outside his instructor's office for over an hour while the exam was being graded—in full view of several faculty members. He passed the exam and went out to celebrate. With the instructor and a few of his friends. They carried him back to his dorm at about midnight. The college, by the way, is Duke University."

"No holes anywhere?"

"None that we could find. Samantha was sixty miles away staying with some friends. They had a *hell* of a party that night, with about two hundred people present. Everybody apparently got drunk, but the entire household and all the guests we've managed to question will swear in court that Samantha was there all evening. They're sure of it."

"Can't break that alibi either, then."

"No."

"Um." I thought about it. "She was at a party on a school night?"

"She graduated last spring."

"She's not in college?"

"No."

I couldn't see anything in that. "Have you questioned Luther Dumont?"

Trey didn't seem surprised that I knew of Townsend's sometime partner. "I have an appointment for tomorrow morning."

"Could you manage to let it slip that Townsend had apparently wanted to hire me?"

"I could. Why?"

"He's least accessible to me," I explained. "His partnership with Townsend wasn't an open one, and I wouldn't be likely to know about it unless I'd dug for the information. I don't want to just turn up on his doorstep without something to go on. If he doesn't react to my name, then I'm putting him at the bottom of my list for the time being."

"Instinct?" Trey asked.

"Not really. At least, I don't think so. Just casting out a line here and there. See what bites."

"Another dangerous game," he noted evenly.

He didn't have to tell me that. I wished he hadn't. "I suppose you've ruled out the servants?"

"For now, anyway."

"I guess the butler doesn't do it very often?"

"Not in my experience."

I nodded. "By the way, who inherits?"

Trey didn't have to look at the open file. "Amy Townsend gets one-fourth of the net income of her husband's estate and, if she doesn't marry again, the use of the mansion for the duration of her life; upkeep and servants' salaries come out of the estate separately. The rest is divided equally between the kids and left in trust until they're twenty-five."

"What happens if she does marry again?"

"She loses the house immediately, and the money one year after her wedding day."

I thought about that and mentally put a large question mark beside Amy's name, although it seemed to me that if money was a motivation, she'd gained less by her husband's murder than she might have by divorce, even if she didn't remarry. The courts would surely have given her at least a third, if not half, of Jeffrey's income. I didn't know for sure, though. "What's the estate worth?"

"Millions, easily. Mrs. Townsend can expect to have an income of about a hundred thousand a year, after taxes. If she doesn't marry."

"And nothing if she does."

"Right. The company is under the direction of a board of executives, and that doesn't change. The family attorney, Randal Fane, is executor."

I sighed, tried to think. "The muscle relaxers. How did the killer persuade him to take them?"

"By guile, we think. The stomach contents showed he'd ingested a considerable number of chocolates. It was another habit of his, eating candy."

"Greeks bearing gifts?"

"Looks that way. We didn't find the box in the house. They were the kind of chocolates given on Valentine's Day and other special occasions."

"With the gooey centers. Perfect to hide pills in."

"Yes."

"And the knife? Borrowed from the kitchen?"

"One of a set, obviously missing."

I caught myself chewing on a thumbnail and hastily stopped. "Did he die there on the couch?"

"The M.E. thinks so. No evidence to the contrary."

"Those pills. Does anyone in the house take them?"

"Yes. Mrs. Townsend has a prescription from her doctor because she apparently strained her back several years ago. But the problem flares up only occasionally, and since the last time she had the bottle refilled—over a month ago—she hasn't had to take any. The bottle's full.''

I was running out of questions. "Did—has Mrs. Townsend seen that room since it happened?''

"No. We've got it sealed for the moment. Why?''

"I just had a feeling that there should have been a rug in front of the fireplace when I looked at the room. I don't know why. Maybe I saw a picture in a magazine or something. Anyway, I was wondering if I was right about that and, if so, whether the rug should have been there that night.''

"Why don't you ask Mrs. Townsend?'' he suggested.

It caught me off guard. "Well . . . I thought maybe after the funeral or something . . .''

Trey was shaking his head. "As soon as possible. Today, in fact.''

"But, I don't have a reason to intrude . . . ,'' I fumbled.

"Sure you do.'' He reached into his desk drawer and produced a folded paper, which he pushed across the blotter to me. "Deliver that to Mrs. Townsend.'' He smiled suddenly, a genuine smile, and it lit his face with amusement. "Tell her the brutal police turned you into a lackey after questioning you cruelly.''

I stared at the document and realized that it was official notification that the sealed room could be reopened. It occurred to me that this was probably highly irregular, if not downright illegal, and I looked at him severely. "Can you get into trouble for this?''

"Yes. Don't wave the damned thing around as you pass through the squad room.''

The noble lieutenant risking his job for the lowly P.I. (Well, close enough.) I loved it. "Just like in the books,'' I murmured.

"What?''

"Nothing. Nothing. I suppose—I'd better be going, then. I'll keep in touch.''

"Do that." He rose as I did, though he didn't move around the desk toward me.

I was opening the door when his voice made me turn.

"Montana?"

"Yes?"

"Be careful," he said softly.

I felt an inexplicable lump rise in my throat. "Sure. You just tell your faithful watchdogs to stay close. I'm not that brave."

He watched me until I left the squad room. I could feel it. But maybe he was just worried I'd wave the damned document around and get him fired.

I STOPPED by Jason's loft, having decided to try Drew on the security system. Besides that, my brother's place was on the way, and I knew he'd be intensely curious about what had been happening.

I found him in his studio section and was both surprised and a little unnerved to see what he was working on.

"Why?" I demanded by way of a greeting.

Jase was holding a paintbrush between his teeth and using another on a canvas reposing on an easel. In a perfectly distinct voice despite the brush, he replied, "Because. He has an interesting face."

I looked with disfavor on the interesting face of Trey Fortier that was taking rapid shape on the canvas. "I thought you hated doing portraits without sketches."

"This isn't a portrait. It's a character study. The man's got buckets of it, or didn't you notice?"

I decided to ignore that. "Jase, would Drew know who to ask about security systems?"

"Yes," my brother replied simply.

"Would he, for me?"

"Probably." Jase took the brush from between his teeth and dropped it and its fellow into a coffee can of turpentine. Then he faced me briskly, obviously through with his "character study" for the moment. "Townsend's estate?"

I shrugged. "It's a place to start. The police are checking it out, but the sooner I have a few answers, the sooner this mess just might begin to make sense. If the system was on and had to be deactivated from inside, the number of people who could have done it has to be limited. Townsend and family, maybe somebody he was involved in business with, or else an expert with security systems. I need to find out.''

"Maybe Townsend turned it off because he was expecting you.''

"I thought of that. It's reasonable, I suppose, but it doesn't feel right. Wealthy men are usually cautious; he would have buzzed me through at the gate.''

"Then,'' Jason said, "he would have buzzed the killer through as well. Someone he knew.''

I nodded. "So I have to know how good the system is. Presumably, Townsend buzzed the murderer through, and that's who turned the system off after he killed Jeffrey. So he could get out, maybe. Or so I could get in. The question then becomes, would a stranger have known how to do that? Was the control panel for the system hidden or in plain sight? It must have taken some kind of code for a shutdown; I can't believe there's just an on/off switch. How many people could have shut down the system?''

Jason pursed his lips thoughtfully. "I see the point. And you want me to ask Drew?''

"My escort's still with me. If I go down and spend time with Drew, they'll wonder why. He doesn't need that kind of attention.''

"Right. So I'll go down and ask him—and I'll come back with a couple of soft drinks from Drew's vending machine just to make it look casual.''

When Jason had gone, I wandered into the living room with one of his sketch pads and sat down to draw a diagram of the room Townsend had died in. I'm no artist, but I'm fairly good with floorplans and the like, and I wanted to get that room down while I still remembered it clearly.

I'd gotten most of it, remembering to note the missing drapery cord and lack of footprints, when Jason returned.

"Drew has to make a few calls," he told me cheerfully, handing over a slippery can of Pepsi and popping the tab on his own. "Is that the room?"

I gave the drawing to him and opened my drink. "As well as I remember."

"Umm. Why've you got an oval with a question mark in it at the fireplace?"

"Because there wasn't a rug."

"Should there have been? Not everyone uses hearth rugs."

"I know, but I got the feeling there should have been one there. Maybe I saw the room in a magazine spread, or—"

"Hang on." Jase jumped up and went to an overflowing magazine rack near his wood stove. He found what he wanted quickly and came back to the couch, muttering, "I know they did an article about his house and—here!" He handed the open magazine to me with a grin. "Score one for you, Lanie."

It was Townsend's living room, just as I remembered it from my single visit—and there was a rug. It was one of those fluffy polar-bear conceits and looked out of place in the room, but it was definitely lying before the hearth.

"It sticks out like a sore thumb," Jason said dispassionately. "No wonder you remembered it."

I looked at the date of the magazine and brooded for a moment. "This went into print a couple of months ago, so the photos were probably shot anything up to a year ago."

Jason nodded. "I can't see this helps us any. The rug could have been taken up and moved to another room, or even be out at the cleaners. It's doubtful the murderer carted it away from the scene of his crime because it matched his own decor."

"True. Well, I never really thought of it as a clue anyway. It was just something that bothered me."

"Like the missing drapery cord?" Jason asked, pointing at my scrawled note on the sketch.

"Yeah. Why would anyone take that?"

Jason grinned. "To tie up the bear rug?"

As asinine as it sounded, I couldn't think of a better answer. "God knows." I had to laugh at myself. "It probably fell off and I didn't see it behind that chair. Talk about making mountains out of molehills!"

Abruptly serious, my brother said, "No, I think you're doing fine. You'll have to rule out everything, one item at a time. Like the rug, and the cord, and the security system. And you'll have to talk to everyone involved. Have you decided how you're going to manage that?"

As a matter of fact, I had thought about that all the way to Jason's place; I still didn't like the idea, but since it looked as if I had little choice . . . "Well, the lieutenant gave me an excuse to go to the house; I'm carrying the notification that the police seals have been lifted. That gets me in, I hope. Since Jeffrey wanted to hire me for something apparently—I can't be sure he didn't—that gives me something to talk about. And since I found the body *and* am a suspect, it stands to reason I'd be interested. With a little luck and my friendly smile, I should be able to—"

"Worm your way into the family?"

I winced. "How charmingly you put it. But, yes. And not just the family, Jase. There's a sometime partner of Jeffrey's I need to check. And heaven knows who else'll fall out of the cracks."

In a learned tone, Jason said, "In the vast majority of these cases, a family member, usually the spouse, is guilty. Better find out if Mrs. T has a lover on the side."

"Or if Jeffrey did," I retorted.

"With a jealous husband," Jason elaborated.

I frowned. "No, that doesn't fit. If you'd seen it . . . Jase, except for that big knife, it wasn't a scene of violence. Besides that, when I talked to the lieutenant a few minutes ago, he told me that it turns out Jeffrey wasn't killed with the knife anyway. Somebody apparently fed him enough muscle relaxers—hidden in chocolates—to stop his heart. That means premeditation. It wasn't a hot-blooded murder, an uncontrolled killing in rage. And the killer didn't panic afterward; that room was freshly vacuumed."

Jase frowned. "He was already dead when the knife went in?"

I nodded. "Yes. And, before you ask, I have no idea why the killer would have stabbed a dead man. To make sure he got the job done, because the pills were too easy, because he needed to see blood—I don't know. And neither do the police."

"Umm." Jase shook his head slowly. "That's a definite wrinkle. A relatively peaceful murder given a violent epilogue. Weird. But I see what you mean about the other man/other woman angle. An enraged mistress, husband of mistress, or wife's lover probably would have acted in—for want of a better word—passion. Unless . . . Suppose Mrs. T had a lover, and they planned to knock Jeffrey off. She could give him the security code and then get herself off somewhere distant with a cast-iron alibi. He did the deed, but hated Jeffrey too much not to draw blood, so he stabbed him after the pills took effect."

"I guess there's a possibility in there somewhere," I allowed. "The pills that killed Jeffrey *were* the same kind Amy had for a strained back. But I can't believe she'd be that stupid, and anyway, men don't usually give chocolates to other men. I don't buy it. It seems to me divorce would be less dangerous."

Jason grinned at me. "Practical Lanie. Try to think greedy. Suppose the lover's poor and Mrs. T doesn't want to lose her money and status. Bump off her hubby and—bingo!—she's got the lover and the kitty."

"She doesn't inherit much—just a fourth of the estate's income—and that stops if she marries again. She could have gotten lots more in a divorce. Besides that, conspiracy in a murder case is really rare, Jase."

"I suppose your lieutenant told you that?"

"He didn't have to," I muttered, not liking the possessive pronoun very much.

"Um. But he did tell you quite a lot, didn't he? Sounds to me like he's crawling out on a very long limb."

"He's in a tough spot," I reminded, trying to be fair. "You can bet his superiors have been pressuring him not to rock the social boat unless he has damned strong evidence. And that's something he hasn't got. It's not likely he can get it, either, because you can also bet he has to walk lightly around everyone involved. He as much as told me that."

"So he's depending on you to get the goods for him."

"It's in my best interests."

Jase gave me one of his perceptive looks. I hate those looks.

"Come off it, Lanie."

"What?" I avoided his eyes and concentrated on finishing my soft drink.

"He got to you."

"I don't know what you're talking about." It's hard to sound huffy when you've just swallowed a mouthful of fizzy cola.

"Lieutenant Trey Fortier," Jason said deliberately. "That's what I'm talking about.

"You're out of your mind," I said.

"Am I? Being on the inside looking out as you are, you can't be expected to know what we on the outside see."

I tried to decipher that. "Come again?"

"You've fallen for him," my dear and only brother said in a very precise tone.

"Bullshit."

He gave me one of his intense looks then. I hate those even more than his perceptive ones. It means he's trying to work something out in his mind, and when he does that Jase is like a hungry cat after a mouse.

"He's single," Jason said gently.

"How do you know?" I asked involuntarily.

"I had Drew check him out."

After making a few inarticulate sounds that Jason seemed to enjoy, I sputtered, "What the hell for?"

"Well, if my only sister is going to get involved with a cop, I have to make sure he's a decent sort, don't I?"

I gnashed my teeth. If this kind of thing kept up, I'd wear them down to nubs. "I am not getting involved with a cop. Pay attention to me, Jason. I am not getting involved with Trey Fortier. Got it?"

"You're already involved," Jason said.

"In the case. The *case*. Nothing more."

Ignoring that, Jason said, "I haven't seen you look at anyone the way you look at him. You wore a somewhat similar glazed look back in college whenever Phil was around, but—"

"*Jason,*" I said through gritted teeth.

"Yeah, I know. You lost control then and swore you never would again. That's why your so-called relationships these last ten years have held all the heat of a cold fireplace."

He was jabbing a sore spot, and that was so unlike my brother that it caught me off guard. "I like being alone," I muttered.

"No," Jase corrected calmly. "You like being single. The problem is, you've convinced yourself that passion equals commitment equals disaster."

"After Phil, can you blame me?" I asked, then looked away from those too-perceptive eyes.

"No," Jason answered a little sadly. "I can't. Phil left you with a few scars. But they're only scars, Lanie, not open wounds. And you can't shy away from what looks like a potentially terrific relationship because of those scars."

I was trying to think clearly. "Jase . . . I just met the man. And if that isn't enough, he's a cop and, officially at least, I'm a suspect. In a murder investigation. Even if there was some attraction between us, there'd never be a worse time. But there isn't an attraction. I don't think I even like him. He's arrogant and bossy and . . . and he uses people. Hell, he's using me, and—"

"And when he's around," Jason said, "you can't keep your eyes off him."

"Goddamn it," I whispered.

"Just don't run from it, that's all I'm saying."

I had a sudden clear memory, tucked away, I'd thought, in mothballs and nearly forgotten. A memory of desire that had stolen my breath and my senses, and every last vestige of intelligence; passion that had seemed, then, larger than life. Violent. Overpowering. And, in the end, painfully destructive. And I didn't realize I was speaking aloud until I heard my own voice.

"I won't let that happen again."

"Christ, Lanie, you were in college," Jason said intensely. "Stuffed to the gills with wisdom, wit, intelligence, and idealistic fervor. In other words, you didn't know shit."

My brother. Such a tactful soul. "All right. I was dumb. Emphasis on *was*. But I'm not now, and—"

"You were also," Jason went on inexorably, "at the perfect age to be blinded by the hormonal rites of spring. Since you were frantically casting off inhibitions right and left, it stood to reason virginity had to go. Phil was the one because you'd been going steady since high school, and because you thought you were in love. It was a mistake in judgment—nothing more—because he happened to be a bastard, and you didn't know it."

I barely had a chance for an inner gulp before he was continuing in the same relentless tone.

"So I can understand your being a little bitter and cautious. You fell in love with the wrong guy. What I fail to understand is why a perfectly natural and normal deflowering in the backseat of Phillip Sander's '73 Chevy still consumes you with unresolved emotions ten years later."

"*Jesus*, Jase!" This time, my gulp was audible, and I felt my face redden for the first time since I was ten.

Calmly, Jason said, "I told you then that Phil was a bastard, but what do little brothers know? He bragged, Lanie. He bragged a lot. To hear him tell it, he was the greatest lover since Casanova. Stupid ass didn't know the difference between a lover and a self-glorifying stud. Well?''

Let me be honest here. To hear the first and only great and haunting passion of my life (ending tragically, like all great passions) torn to analytical shreds by my loving brother ten years after its demise couldn't do much for my self-esteem. That relationship had, to some extent, shaped my life in the years since. As Jason had pointed out, I had been in the habit of avoiding anything that looked as if it might shoot sparks. It definitely shook me up. But, after the gulp of shock, I found I could accept it from Jase.

I could even accept it, finally, from myself.

''Well?'' he repeated.

''Well, what?'' I pulled myself together and suddenly voiced an opinion I'd been holding inside for too long. ''All right. Phil was a dyed-in-the-wool son of a bitch, and all the time I was wearing his ring he had duplicate fraternity pins he handed out to girls for a hundred miles. The backseat of that Chevy saw a lot of action, and the glove department held a supply of condoms to shame a drugstore. Satisfied?''

''I just can't believe he duped so many of you,'' Jason said in a dry voice and with a pained look. ''He had to have been a rotten lover; no one that selfish could have been anything else.''

''I really didn't have anything to compare it to,'' I muttered, and quite suddenly, for the first time, I wanted to laugh about it.

''That's my point,'' Jason said gently. ''You committed yourself to him body and soul—and it was a mistake. Just a mistake, Lanie, an error in judgment when you were young and naïve. Since then, you've chosen the safest paths you could find. Nice guys, your occasional flings these last years. Nice guys you didn't mind letting into your life for a little while. Guys you didn't mind saying good-bye to. You never looked at them the way you look at Trey.''

What he was saying finally hit me. "God . . . don't tell me it's that obvious."

"To me. And, judging by the sparks you're getting in return, to him."

"I didn't see them," I managed.

"He hasn't let down his guard yet. I only saw them because I've learned to look beneath the surface. Take a gander at the painting before you leave."

"Jase, it's impossible."

"That's a very final word, Lanie. The timing isn't great, I'll agree, but life rarely arranges things to be neat and pretty and convenient. What is—exists. There's something between you two, and it's a long way from tame. He's got a very elegant pose, our friend the lieutenant, but the hands give him away. When he finally lets go—and he will—I think you'll definitely have something to compare old Phil to."

I couldn't even tell Jase he didn't know what he was talking about. He did. The reason I hate his perceptive looks is because I know only too well the intelligence and insight behind them. A very bright man, my brother, and I've never known him to be wrong.

It was scary as hell.

"But, in the meantime," Jason said dryly. "There's this small matter of murder. Let me know what you find out at the Townsend place."

"Right," I muttered.

FIVE

I LOOKED at the painting before I left. Jason, tactful at last, didn't walk me to the door, but busied himself in the kitchen. I looked at the painting of Trey. The features were all (surprisingly, terrifyingly) familiar, and Jason had captured the somewhat aloof and enigmatic surface that reminded me of a cat. The lieutenant looked back at me with eyes that were alive and a face that was subtly different from any I'd seen the man himself wear; a face stripped of its mask, naked and vulnerable.

"Lanie?" Jason called briskly.

"Yeah?"

"He was looking at you."

I stared at the painting and thought vaguely that Trey wouldn't be comfortable if he saw it, and that he'd hate anyone else to see it.

"Jason?"

"Yeah?"

"Don't show it to him."

"I won't. Not until I know him better."

I thought Jason knew Trey Fortier pretty well already. But I understood what he meant. He wouldn't show Trey this painting until Trey knew *him* better.

My brother can defend himself nicely, but he hates getting punched in the nose.

* * *

I PUSHED the revelation of Jason's painting to the back of my mind as I headed across town. As my brother had said, there was this murder to be dealt with. Besides that, I was feeling more than a little unnerved at the swiftness of my attraction to Trey. It was something that just didn't happen to me.

So I decided not to think about it for a while.

I thought of another question I should have asked Trey as I was turning into the drive of the Townsend estate, but by then I could see the answer for myself. The elderly lady who had seen my car that night couldn't have known whether the gate had stood open before I arrived; her house was the only one across the street, but although she could easily see the beginning of the driveway, the tall brick fence that ran around the estate solidly blocked her view of the iron gate.

There was an intercom set up beside the drive, and I stopped at the closed gate and reached out to punch the call button. Within seconds, a daunting male voice responded.

"Yes?"

I felt suddenly at a loss, realizing that Mrs. Townsend must have been turning away reporters and God only knew who else since her husband had been killed. After a silent gulp, I said, "My name is Lane Montana. I have a . . . document to deliver to Mrs. Townsend from the police."

There was no further word from the intercom but, to my astonishment, the iron gate rolled open majestically. Before anybody could change their mind, I drove my station wagon through and headed up the drive. I was still surprised by the easy acceptance and wondered with a grin what Trey's watchdogs (the unmarked car had stuck close all day) would have to say in their report to him.

To any Yankee visiting in the South, the big house inside those forbidding brick walls would have come as a surprise, mostly because it wasn't Tara. Actually, the Townsend mansion was blatantly Tudor, which is nobody's idea of the Old South. Not surprising, really, since it had been built a scant forty years earlier. Still, it was a lovely place.

I had seen it before, though, and wasn't much interested in exteriors. I was too busy at the moment trying to figure out how to handle this all-important first meeting with Mrs. Townsend. I didn't have much time to think and found myself ringing the doorbell still lacking a clear idea of how to proceed.

Some problems you just have to toss into the wind.

A butler to shame Jeeves opened the door and looked down his nose at me. "Miss Montana?" he inquired, holding the name away from him.

"Yes," I confessed meekly.

"This way, please," he commanded, stepping back to let me in.

I followed, still meek. He led the way to a room across from the scene of the murder; the living room doors were tightly closed and an obvious tag ordered that they weren't to be opened. "Jeeves" didn't look at those doors, rather pointedly, I thought. Offended dignity, I suppose; the best families choose not to air their dirty linen in public.

Melodramatic I know, but he made me think like that.

He opened the other door, which led to a den. "Wait here, please. I will inform Mrs. Townsend."

It occurred to me suddenly as I scurried obediently into the den that there hadn't been a wreath on the front door. Or did Townsend's sort do that? God knew. Jeeves hadn't been wearing an armband, but the funereal black of his suit certainly conveyed the correct mood anyway.

I dismissed those thoughts and began looking around me. I wondered if the entire house was done in pastels. This room was certainly pretty, but hardly original. It was done in shades of yellow and green, everything blending and matching so perfectly that the decorator should have been shot for lack of imagination. Then I remembered that Amy Townsend had herself redecorated the mansion a few years back. Could she possibly be so bland?

I wandered around, too restless to sit, still trying to

come up with a good approach with Amy. If I was going to "worm" my way into the family as Jase had suggested, I'd have to do it carefully. Otherwise, this brief visit to deliver the document would be my only one. Without the goodwill—or at least acceptance—of Amy Townsend, I didn't stand a snowball's chance in hell of getting through the front gate a second time.

So it was definitely important for me to get a handle on Amy as quickly as possible. I could only trust to luck and instinct for that, because there was really no approach, under the circumstances, that could be called "right."

"Miss Montana?"

I turned quickly, storing impressions as fast as my little gray cells could manage. Newspaper and magazine photos hadn't done her justice. She was a beautiful woman and couldn't have been more than a few years older than me. Ash blond hair, worn up. Perfect face, with a model's cheekbones and wide-spaced blue eyes. She had a somewhat frail appearance, a slender figure, graceful carriage. She was wearing a simple black dress, no jewelry except her wedding rings. She came toward me with the kind of walk men watch.

Married at eighteen to a man I was beginning to believe had been something of a bastard, she was the product of a background containing plenty of blue blood but very little in the way of money. *Real* money, I mean, as opposed to what the rest of us have to make do with. Rumor had it that Jeffrey senior had quite literally paid through the nose for the privilege of marrying his son to Miss Amy Bennett, and he'd gotten her straight out of a convent—despite the fact that her family wasn't Catholic. God knew if she'd been given a choice about either the convent or the marriage.

I drew a deep breath and spoke hastily. "Mrs. Townsend. I'm sorry to intrude, but—"

She nodded, her lovely face still and expressionless. "Yes, Lieutenant Fortier phoned to explain your errand."

Which explained my acceptance. And Trey was right;

this woman was very, very controlled. "He . . . he asked me to deliver this to you," I said, holding out the document. She unfolded it, read it. Still no change in expression.

Without looking up, she said calmly, "He also told me that you were the one who found my husband's body."

"Yes." I wondered if that bit of veracity on Trey's part would make it easier on me—or harder.

"The lieutenant seemed to feel that your . . . presence here that night was somewhat questionable."

I debated for a silent moment, then opted to stick as close to the truth as possible. "Mrs. Townsend, your husband called and left a message asking me to come here. He said he had a job for me, but didn't explain. I can't prove that to the police unless I find out what the job was."

Amy Townsend turned away suddenly toward one of the two yellow couches in the room. "Sit down, Miss Montana."

I felt as wary as she probably did, but followed her and sat down on one couch while she took the other one. We looked across at each other for a minute before she finally spoke, and her voice was the same. Even. Expressionless.

"What is it that you do?"

I gave in to popular opinion. "I'm a kind of private investigator, but what I do is very limited. I find things. Everything from runaways and lost pets, to packages that stray in the mail and misplaced jewelry."

"I see. And you have no idea what it was my husband apparently wanted you to find."

"None. Do you—were you aware of any reason he might have wanted to hire me?" I saw something in her eyes then, and I knew she could have answered yes. But I hardly expected it to be that easy.

"No, Miss Montana. But my husband's business dealings were kept apart from our private life."

It wasn't a terribly subtle way of leading me away from thoughts of their private lives, but I followed anyway.

"Who could I talk to? About his business dealings, I mean."

She studied me for a moment in silence. "My husband was a secretive man, particularly regarding his businesses. I really have no idea, Miss Montana."

We seemed to have reached a dead end there, but since she was clearly willing to talk to me, I decided to take advantage of it. "Mrs. Townsend, I saw a photograph of the room—the living room across the hall—a while back, and there was a white bearskin rug in front of the fireplace."

Her delicate lips tightened slightly, and I knew the rug was Jeffrey's taste rather than her own. "Yes. What about it?"

"Was it in the room that night?"

"It was there when I left the day before," she replied. "Isn't it now?"

"No."

"Then perhaps my husband had it removed. I often told him it clashed with the decor."

It was possible, that answer, but I didn't think either of us believed it. If Jeffrey had kept the rug in the face of his wife's opposition, I doubted very much he'd suddenly decided to get rid of it in the hours before he was killed. Too coincidental, and too damned neat. But maybe there was another explanation. Maybe.

The door opened suddenly and Jeeves appeared. In his precise voice, he said, "Pardon, madam, but Mr. Fane is here and wishes to see you."

If I hadn't been looking at Amy, I wouldn't have caught it. Her reaction to the announcement was fleeting, just a slight widening of her eyes, but it was more than enough to alert me. The last thing I wanted to do right now was to politely leave, damn it, but—

"Send him in, Halley," she said, and then looked at me. "Our family attorney, Miss Montana. Perhaps he may be able to answer your questions about my husband's business affairs."

"Thank you," I murmured, wondering if her gesture in introducing me to the lawyer was as magnanimous as it seemed. I told myself to be as observant as possible, and rose along with her as a man strode into the room.

If Trey Fortier resembled a lawyer, then this man was the prototypical image of a middle-aged city cop. He moved with the kind of trundling, flat-footed solidity of too many years of walking a beat, and he carried an extra twenty pounds or so on his big frame; I got the feeling the extra weight was a fairly recent layer of fat over old muscle. He was over six feet tall with wide, sloped shoulders, and the jacket of the conservative business suit he wore couldn't possibly have been buttoned over his belly. His healthy thatch of hair was suspiciously black; his heavy, handsome face a bit florid; and under drooping lids, blue eyes peered out on the world with a kind of startled uncertainty.

I watched speculatively as he crossed the room quickly and took Amy's outstretched hand in his two surprisingly slender ones. He was as controlled as she was, in a different kind of way, but the glow in his eyes when they rested on her couldn't be hidden. Oh, God, I thought, Jason was right. Mrs. T *does* have a lover.

"Amy, I'm sorry to interrupt," he said in a voice that rumbled with a warmth he didn't—or couldn't—hide and which made the apology intimate. "I've made the arrangements for tomorrow, and I thought we should discuss them."

"Certainly, Randal." She gently withdrew her hand, better at hiding her feelings than he was. "This is Miss Montana, who has some questions for you. Miss Montana, our attorney, Randal Fane."

The lawyer turned to me as if I'd been invisible to him until then. Maybe I had been. He shook hands briskly and we all sat down, with Fane taking a place beside Amy on the couch.

"Mr. Fane," I began carefully, "do you know of any reason Mr. Townsend would have wanted to hire me? I'm a private investigator." Before I could add the explanatory rider, Amy murmured a slight explanation of her own.

"She found the . . . the body, Randal."

He looked at her for a moment, then at me. "Jeffrey said nothing to me about hiring an investigator, Miss Montana. And, to be perfectly frank, I can't imagine why he would have needed your services. There are three full-time investigators on the company payroll, all experienced and very good at their jobs."

I hesitated. "Maybe this was something personal. Something he didn't want the company investigators handling."

"Then he kept it to himself," Fane said calmly. "Tell me, Miss Montana, does that unmarked police car parked near the drive belong to you?"

It was a lawyer's trick to turn the tables like that, to begin questioning instead of answering, but since he had provided the opportunity for me to explain my escort, I forgave him.

I managed a faint grimace. "Afraid so. The police are keeping tabs on me. They're as . . . curious about why I was called out here that night as I am."

"And you have no idea?" he probed.

"None. Mr. Townsend just left a message on my answering machine asking me to come here and saying he had a job for me. I'm sure you'll understand how anxious I am to find out what that job was supposed to be."

He shook his head slightly. "I'm afraid I can't help you, Miss Montana. As I said, Jeffrey never mentioned the matter to me."

I decided to be blunt, partly because the utter calm of these two was beginning to grate on me. Control was fine and dandy, but they didn't even seem *curious* about this. "Do you have any idea who might have killed him, Mr. Fane?"

He looked grave. "Wealthy men often make enemies, Miss Montana, and Jeffrey was quite wealthy. However, I have no knowledge of any threats made against him re-

cently, nor am I aware of anyone with such grievances as
would make them prepared to kill.''

"No lawsuits pending?''

"None," he said promptly.

"No disgruntled ex-employees vowing vengeance?''

"Not to my knowledge.''

I looked at them both, two waxworks with pleasant,
know-nothing expressions. Except for Amy's surface con-
ventionality of the black dress, I thought, Jeffrey wasn't
being mourned in this room. It was interesting, but it didn't
get me anywhere. All I had was a hunch which, if I was
right, gave both of them a motive to kill.

I didn't like it a bit. Okay, I'm a sucker for a romance,
I admit it. But I just couldn't see why Amy and/or Fane
would have chosen murder over divorce. He was a lawyer,
for God's sake; he, more than anyone, would know how
slim the chances were of getting away with it. As for Amy,
divorce would probably have netted her more money if she
was greedy, and I couldn't believe that widow's black was
preferable to being a divorcée. I don't care what kind of
upbringing you have or how rigid the social pressures are,
it's a lot less damning to dump a husband than it is to
bump him off. For either or both of them to be the killer
didn't make any sense to me.

I managed a polite smile. "I see. Well, Mrs. Townsend,
Mr. Fane, thank you for your time. I'm very sorry to have
intruded.''

They rose as one.

"I can find my way out,'' I said, and since neither offered to shake hands again, edged toward the door. They
said nothing, and I escaped out into the foyer.

Jeeves—I mean Halley—was standing by a small table
near the stairs, the phone to his ear, and I waved cheerily
at him as I headed for the front door. He seemed to think
I wasn't worth showing out in style, and ignored me as he
set the receiver gently on the table and crossed the hall to
the room I'd just vacated.

I was opening the front door as he reached that other

door, and I found it very interesting that he knocked before entering the den. He hadn't, I remembered, knocked when Amy and I had been alone in there. I was even more interested to catch a glimpse of two people moving hastily apart in the room as he went in.

A RED MERCEDES SPORTS CAR PULLED UP in front of the house in a spray of gravel as I went down the steps toward my own battered station wagon, and I wasn't surprised to see Samantha Townsend climb out. I *was* surprised to see the two huge shopping bags she pulled from the back. Judging by the colorful material spilling out of one of the bags, she hadn't been shopping for funeral clothes.

I decided to take advantage of the opportunity, and waited on the second of the broad steps as she approached. "Hello, Samantha. Remember me? Lane Montana."

"Sure. I remember," she said as she halted on the same step. "Last summer in Daddy's building. Your brother was painting in the lobby." She had a curiously toneless voice and a flat delivery. Her blue eyes were speculative.

She was a lovely girl, but she didn't really resemble her mother. Except for control, maybe, and I couldn't be sure about that. She looked untouched by her father's death. Her soft brown hair, which I remembered as being very long the last time I'd seen her, was cut short now in a halo of permed curls; I caught a whiff of the chemical solution used to coax straight hair and realized she'd just come from having her hair done. The style was a mistake because it made her heart-shaped face look chubby.

She had a pert, upturned nose and cupid lips, and was about my height. She was fairly slender, with just the suggestion of breasts despite her eighteen years, and I wanted to tell her that the push-up bra she was wearing (God, did they still make those things?) didn't compensate for nature's lack of generosity.

She was wearing skintight jeans and a long-sleeved sweater with a plunging V neckline, and her makeup was inexpert and heavy. It surprised me, since most girls learn

how to apply the stuff long before they reach their teens.
I could remember experimenting for hours with my
friends, and I could also remember watching my mother
getting herself ready for dates. Amy's makeup had been
beautifully understated; didn't Samantha watch her
mother?

Maybe a lot of things were different when your family
had millions.

"What are you doing here?" she asked me now.

Nothing ventured . . . And besides, I could see that if
Samantha was grieving, she was hiding it well. "I'm sorry
about your father, Samantha. I came because he apparently wanted to hire me, and I was trying to find out why.
Do you have any idea?"

"No. Jason said you found things."

It was an abrupt comment, but I nodded. "That's right.
Had your father lost anything recently?"

"How would I know?"

The question wasn't so much pugnacious as indifferent,
and I couldn't help wondering if she felt anything at all
about her father's death. I shrugged. "It was worth a try."

She looked at me, still with those reflective eyes. "Are
you a suspect? Do they think you killed Daddy?"

"Why would you ask that?" I said slowly.

Her smile was instant, like a switch being turned on.
"There's a car with two men in it parked on the street, so
I wondered. It wasn't there when I left a couple of hours
ago. Cops, you can always tell. Are you a suspect?"

"Mr. Fane's inside with your mother," I said. "Maybe
they're following him."

Samantha's eyes narrowed for an instant, but she shook
her head and said, "No. He has an alibi for that night. I
heard him and Mother talking about it. Are you a suspect?" she repeated.

I shifted uncomfortably. "Sort of. But I didn't kill your
father, Samantha. I didn't even know him."

She nodded and said, "I expect it was a hit-man. A lot
of people hated Daddy."

I blinked. "Why?"

"Because he was a son of a bitch," she said sweetly. "Mother won't say that out loud, but she was raised in a convent. I think he blackmailed people to make them afraid of him, just the way he blackmailed us."

This was very unnerving, and I felt guilty for pumping an eighteen-year-old, but I'd come too far to try to stop her surprising flow of information. "Did he? Blackmail you, I mean."

"Oh, yes." She nodded once, decisively. "He was always threatening Jeff and me, telling us he'd send us away to school in Europe or put us in a military academy. Both of us. And he wouldn't let Mother do anything at all. He made her wear clothes she hated and smile at men he wanted to impress."

She seemed to have an imperfect grasp of the concept of blackmail, but she was certainly drawing an appalling picture of her father.

"Are the police going to arrest you?" she asked.

"No, because I didn't do it," I said, keeping it simple.

Samantha apparently decided that subject was exhausted. "Your brother's a fox," she said with a faint show of enthusiasm. "Does he have a girlfriend?"

"Lots," I answered dryly.

She lifted a hand to pat her curls in a coquettish gesture that would have been second nature to Scarlett O'Hara but looked ridiculous from a girl wearing jeans. I noticed she had false fingernails like red claws and a Band-Aid on one finger. "He liked me."

I wasn't about to tell her that Jason had needed prompting to remember her name. "I'm sure he did."

Her red lips curved. "Maybe I should commission him to paint my portrait."

I made an absent mental note to warn Jason, although there was really no need. He could easily handle girlish crushes. In fact, he did so adroitly enough to avoid breaking tender, adolescent hearts. And even though Samantha was eighteen and hardly more than ten years separated her

in age from Jason, she was quite definitely still an adolescent.

"See you," she said abruptly, and continued on up the
steps.

I half turned to watch her, wishing someone would tell
her that she didn't have the grace or the style to copy her
mother's walk. Then I went to my car and left the Townsend estate with a good deal of relief.

Some demon possessed me as I was pulling out of the
drive, and I drew my car up beside the one belonging to
my escorts. I recognized them: Darrel Hughes and Link
Carpenter. To those two impassive faces, I said, "I'm finished for the day, guys. Want to visit the McDonald's drive-
through?"

Hughes cleared his throat, offered one of those fantastic
smiles of his, and said, "We'll be going off duty shortly,
Miss Montana." Carpenter looked at his hands bemus-
edly.

I nodded serenely. "Okay. See you tomorrow." I caught
myself giggling as I drove on and couldn't decide if it was
amusement or sheer nerves. The visit to the estate had
shaken me, and realizing that my watchdogs were two
homicide detectives with, I would hope, more important
things to do than watch me hadn't helped. It made me feel
paranoid again. I started to wonder, uneasily, if there was
more against me than Trey had told me about.

Yes, I know. I was innocent, so what did I have to worry
about? Means and opportunity . . . The only thing left was
motive. Did the police believe I had a motive to kill Townsend? It would explain why two homicide detectives were
shadowing me. Maybe whoever was pressuring Trey just
wanted to give me enough rope to hang myself, but I had
the odd feeling that there were things moving all around
me, faster and faster, and I couldn't see them.

Damn.

I visited McDonald's and bought myself a fast-food feast
and a chocolate sundae for Choo, then drove sedately back
to my loft.

My mind was still in high gear, though, and it had a great deal of information to sift through. I lugged my supper up to the loft and greeted Choo, who was annoyed. He's never gotten over the conviction that his person exists to be with him all the time, and he tends to greet me after my absence with a surplus of feline indignation. You've never really heard indignation until it's been voiced by a Siamese cat.

I opened his favorite flavor of Friskies (tuna with eggs) as an apology, put his sundae in the freezer for later, and collapsed on the couch to eat my own supper straight out of the bag.

Choo was eating out of his dish on the coffee table, and I stared at him with my mind elsewhere. "They're lovers, Choo."

He growled in the back of his throat and continued to pick the egg bits out first because he loves them. I ate another french fry and pondered. "They are, I know it. And Jeeves knows it too, because he knocked on the door. But what does that mean? Amy could have gotten a damn sight more by divorcing Townsend, unless . . . maybe he wouldn't give her a divorce?"

Since my busy companion offered no response, I sighed and brooded to myself.

Amy Townsend and the family lawyer, Randal Fane, were lovers. I knew it. But had Jeffrey known it? Judging by what I knew of him, and what I'd been told, if he had known he wouldn't have liked it one little bit. Had Amy asked for a divorce? I wondered (assuming Samantha had been truthful about the matter) if Jeffrey's cruelty to his family had been all mental and emotional, or if he'd thrown a little body language in for spice.

I didn't think I would have liked Jeffrey very much.

NEXT MORNING'S NEWSPAPER (which I read around lunchtime, and which, by the way, was Thursday's paper—if you've lost track, the murder occurred on Monday night) was full of speculation about Townsend's murder and information about his funeral. When I got my eyes open enough to read, I discovered that even his servants were expected to attend—along with the mayor, the police commissioner, and all of city hall.

Somehow, it made me feel . . . rushed. Even though he seemed to be in my corner, I knew damned well that unless something new came to light pretty soon Trey would have to turn whatever he had over to the D.A.—and that meant my name on the arrest warrant.

All right, even though more murderers are convicted on circumstantial evidence than by eyewitnesses, I still wasn't in much danger of being convicted of a crime I hadn't committed. They didn't *have* any circumstantial evidence against me, not really. They could place me on the scene that night, yes, but that was pretty much it. I had a number of points in my favor, including the fact that I'd called the police.

Still, even if you respect the law, you'd be just a mite trusting to assume that the system *always* gets it right. That meant I needed to start digging again.

I debated silently for a moment, and then called the police station. I knew Trey's extension number by now and asked for it. Trey. I was thinking of him as Trey in my mind, but I didn't feel secure enough to address him that way verbally. Instead, I demanded without preamble, ''Is my phone bugged?''

There was a beat of silence, and I waited patiently. I didn't think he'd lie about it, because then I could get him for entrapment later. Couldn't I?

''No,'' he said finally. ''Why?''

''Why did I think it could be? Call me paranoid.'' I thought it was a nice evasion, but Trey wasn't buying it.

''Why are you asking?'' His voice was calm. As usual.

''Because I want to make some private calls,'' I answered huffily. I wondered if I was overdoing the huffiness. I hoped not. Trey wasn't a fool.

''Then feel free to make them,'' he said politely.

''Thank you. That's all I wanted to know.''

"My pleasure."

I hung up and stared at the phone. I wanted to giggle, but wasn't exactly sure why. And I hastily squashed the notion in my mind that Trey could probably be a lot of fun when he wasn't being a cop. I shouldn't be thinking about that, I told myself, and besides, cops were always cops.

Weren't they?

I rang Drew and, while waiting for someone to call him to the phone, sat listening to welders and crashes and bangs and thumps for several moments until Drew came on the line and presumably closed the door of his tiny office.

"Drew, did you find out anything about Townsend's security system?"

"Yep. You want it all?"

"Yeah."

"Okay. First, that place is wired like the White House. The brick wall around the estate has pressure plates along the top; anything heavier than three pounds lands anywhere on that wall and very loud alarms summon the police. Second, come near any window or door and you set off the alarms—and I mean *near*. When the system's on, even the welcome mat is wired; the family knows not to step on the thing."

I gulped silently. "Uh-huh."

"Third, there are two control panels. One's in Townsend's study, and the other's in his bedroom. Both are well-hidden, and supposedly only Townsend himself knew the code."

"Wait a minute," I objected. "What if one of the other members of the family came in late or something?"

"I'm getting to that," Drew told me. "On the box out by the front gate, there's a keypad—"

"I only saw a call button."

"The keypad's hidden under a cover; flip the cover up and it's obvious, but if you don't know it's there you won't spot it. Got it?"

"Yeah."

"Okay. There was a separate security code for the rest of the family. They punched that in, and the gates opened. Then, when they got to the house, each of them had a little remote with only one button on it. Push the button, and the system lets you in one of the doors."

"Christ," I muttered.

Drew chuckled. "It's something, isn't it? The man who designed and installed the system told me he'd advised Townsend to have a couple of dogs patrolling at night, just for the hell of it, but Townsend said no way. He was allergic to dogs, and he didn't like them. Couldn't stand to have one around him."

I thought about it for a moment. "What about now? If Townsend was the only one who knew the code—"

"Mrs. Townsend called their security guy back on the day after her husband bought the farm. Either because she didn't know the old code, or else just a reasonable precaution. He wiped out the old code and reset the system."

"Do you know—?"

"Sorry, Lane. Can't tell you that. He designed the system so that even he wouldn't know. He reset the program, showed Mrs. Townsend what to do, and she picked her own code after he left."

"Great."

Utterly calm, Drew said, "So you can't get in there without an invitation."

"What makes you think—" I began huffily.

Drew laughed.

I decided I'd better work on my huffy routine. It didn't seem to be very effective. "Damn," I muttered. "Drew, what you're telling me is that only Townsend and his family could have gotten past the security system, providing it was active?"

"Unless one of the family gave both their remote and their security code to someone else, yes."

I immediately thought of Randal Fane. Amy could have given him the code and then left town to establish an alibi. But Samantha had said that Fane had an alibi as well.

Drew said, "Townsend could have deactivated the system from inside, of course; realistically, he was the only one who could have. But it's a damned expensive system not to use, so why would he have shut it off? If he was expecting a visitor, all he had to do was answer the call from the gate. By the way, there's a control panel in the foyer that operates the gate—just the gate, though. And if any of the doors are opened from inside, it won't trigger the alarm."

"The gate was open the night . . . Monday night," I said slowly. "Just standing open."

"Then the system was completely off," Drew said. "There's a day and night mode, two separate settings. Night, fully activated. Day, the gate opens when it's told to, and only the pressure plates on the wall are active. When it's completely off, the gates stand open."

I started to ask another question, then suddenly remembered that the gates had opened automatically for me as I was leaving the estate yesterday—which meant pressure plates on the driveway inside the fence. Hell to get in, easy to get out.

"There's no other way onto the estate?" I asked instead.

"You could go over the wall in a few places," Drew said thoughtfully. "If you knew the system was off. There are some trees around near the wall on both sides, but you couldn't avoid touching the top of the wall."

I wanted to cuss.

"That cover everything?" Drew asked.

"Everything I can think of at the moment. Thanks, Drew. I really appreciate it."

"Sure. Um. There's just one more thing, Lane."

I felt wary. "Yeah? What?"

"The place has a trap."

"A trap? What do you mean?"

"I played a hunch," Drew told me. "From the amount of security Townsend had installed at the estate, I wondered it he might have more to protect than his knickknacks. I happened to remember that a trap man did some work in these parts a few years back, so—''

"Trap man? Drew, what are you talking about?''

Patiently, he explained, ''A trap is a very carefully designed and built safe; a trap man installs it. It's an old mob trick, Lane. Trap men used to swear a blood oath that they'd never reveal the existence or location of the traps. If they broke the oath, they usually ended up in the foundation of some building; if they kept the secret, then they were entitled to a percentage of whatever valuables the trap contained when the owner died.''

"And Townsend had one?'' I said slowly.

"Yeah. I got in touch with the trap man. He'd already heard about Townsend, so he knew he could talk. He's retired now, and he isn't hurting for money, so he isn't really interested in what's inside Townsend's trap. Especially since the man was murdered.'' Somewhat casually, Drew added, ''He said, by the way, that if it's needed, he'll contact the police and tell them about the trap.''

I thought about that. ''And who tells him if it's needed?''

"Me. After you tell me.''

I felt both amused and warmed by Drew's faith in me, but left it at that. ''What kinds of things usually go in traps?''

"Very valuable things. And very damaging things. In the old days, it was whatever the mob boys were dumb enough to put on paper. Records of bribes and payoffs, things like that. You don't have a trap installed to protect your jewelry or bonds, Lane. And Townsend probably wouldn't have told a soul about his, or left any indication that the thing existed.''

"Okay. Did the trap man tell you where it was?''

"Yeah. It's in Townsend's bathroom—the one off his bedroom. There's a Jacuzzi, with a separate shower stall. The trap's in the drain of the shower. Just put your fingers through the grate and give it a quarter counterclockwise turn; the grate'll come up. Reach down into the drain and press against the pipe toward the faucets. You'll feel a slight depression just big enough to get a couple of fingers in; pull straight up, and the trap'll open.''

"Wow," I muttered.

"Cute, isn't it?"

"Now how the hell am I going to . . . ?"

Drew sighed. "The thing might be empty. Or it might hold something that would give somebody a very strong motive to have killed Townsend."

After a moment, I began to realize what Drew was telling me. "You think I should see it before the police do. Why?"

Bluntly, Drew said, "Because two homicide detectives are tailing you, and I can guarantee it's not because they think you're cute. Jase told me the story, Lane, and it stinks. Sounds like somebody went to a lot of trouble to frame you. If there's evidence of a motive in that trap, you'd better make sure it doesn't point at you.''

SIX

I FELT SHAKEN. "How could it? You said nobody but Townsend would know about the trap, and he wouldn't have framed me for his own murder!"

"Want to take the chance?"

I decided that I didn't. "I see your point. Thanks, Drew. Thanks very much."

"No problem. Watch yourself, Lane."

"Sure. Bye." I hung up the phone and stared at it. I was doing a lot of that lately. And I was getting more paranoid by the minute—except that it wasn't paranoia, because somebody really *was* after me. With a vengeance. Damn, damn, damn. I looked at my watch. The funeral should be getting under way shortly, I decided. And I thought Jeffrey's would probably last a good long time.

The Townsend house would be empty. No widow, no kids, no servants, and no reason for the cops to guard the place that I could think of.

There'll never be a better time.

When that thought breezed through my mind, I almost choked on a swallow of coffee. Was I really even considering—? Damn it, I *was* considering, and this from a woman who sometimes has trouble getting into her own loft with a key. I thought I needed my head examined.

By an expert.

Immediately.

I brooded for a few moments, then called Trey again. "Listen, are you going to the funeral?" I asked.

"No." As before, he wasn't shaken off balance by my abruptness. "I have a couple of people going just to see who turns up."

"I don't suppose we could count on a mafia hit man watching his victim get buried?"

"It's doubtful."

I cleared my throat. "And I don't suppose you could give me a few hours off for good behavior?"

There was a moment of silence, and then Trey said, "I'm not calling off your watchdogs, if that's what you mean."

"They're crowding me," I complained, trying to sound merely annoyed about it.

"What do you have in mind?"

I hesitated. "Is this call being recorded?"

"You *are* paranoid." He sighed. "Montana, in case you didn't notice, we have a few hundred phones in this building. The only calls we record are emergency calls. Now, what do you have in mind?"

I stared at the ragged edge of my thumbnail. Had I been chewing on the damn thing again? "Ummm. Well, I wanted to walk around the outside of the Townsend estate. The wall, you know."

"Why?"

"Just to look. I, uh, I understand that someone could have gone over the wall if they knew the system was off. And since that lady across the street didn't see another car . . ."

"Come to the station," he said after a moment.

Alarmed, I said, "That isn't necessary. I mean, just tell me I can't, or—"

"Montana, just come to the station, all right?"

I swallowed. "All right."

A few minutes later, driving to the station with my escorts dutifully following, I felt very nervous. I wasn't worried about being arrested for murder because, rationally speaking, I couldn't see that I'd said or done anything recently to suddenly bring that on. So there was no reason for me to be nervous, no reason at all.

Sure.

I parked in a visitor's space and went into the station, knowing the way to Trey's office by now. The building wasn't, by the way, the kind of grungy, violent place you saw on "Hill Street Blues." It was a modern facility, and fairly tranquil, or at least it had been during my visits. I hadn't even seen anybody wearing handcuffs. Yet.

I went up to Trey's floor and picked my way through the squad room, which hummed with the muted energy of busy people. I felt glances that were filled with the instant, almost unconscious wariness of cops who sense an outsider in their orbit. It was unnerving.

The door to Trey's office was open, and as soon as I walked in, I said, "God, that's unnerving."

He looked up and rose in one motion. "What?"

I nodded my head back toward the squad room. "That. I felt like I was walking through a cage full of tigers, and they weren't sure they wanted company."

"Guilty conscience, Montana?"

I frowned at him. "Very funny."

He came around the desk. "Let's go."

"Go? Go where?"

"The Townsend place."

He got his coat as he passed the wooden coat tree, then came to me.

I felt my arm being taken. And when I say I felt it, I mean I *felt* it. Even though I was wearing a sweater, I could feel the strength of his big hand and vaguely imagined the rough skin of his palm warm against my arm. My tongue glued itself to the roof of my mouth, and I stared down to watch my feet walk as we went back through the squad room. And the only tiger I felt was the one holding my arm and walking beside me.

For Christ's sake . . .

I'm not susceptible, really. I've never much favored men

with intensity, especially the hidden kind which is far more dangerous. My tastes run to fair men with easy charm and uncomplicated natures. I go a long way to avoid tigers, believe me.

But if Jason was right, I was already in trouble. Even so, the timing *was* all wrong, and hidden intensity scared me. The last thing I wanted was to get involved with Trey Fortier. He made me nervous and unsure of myself, which is a hell of a thing to happen to a mature, independent woman past thirty.

He didn't speak again until he'd put me in the Mercedes and got in behind the wheel. I still felt the hand that was no longer on my arm. Talk about unnerving.

"Nothing to say?" He started the car and headed in the direction of the Townsend estate.

I cleared my throat. "Not really. Except, why are we going there?"

"You said you wanted to."

I stole a glance at him and saw that he was paying attention to his driving. As always, he was impossible to read. "Oh. But I can't go alone, huh?"

"I'd rather you didn't."

I didn't have to look behind us to know that the unmarked car wasn't following. "What did you tell my watchdogs?"

"To work on some of their other cases for a while. We do have other cases, you know."

"Well, I wondered. It's kind of a waste of your best manpower to have them following me, isn't it?" I wanted to sound casual.

"Some of my superiors don't think so," he murmured.

I shot him another glance. "Uh-*huh*. They're hoping I might hang myself, given enough rope?"

"Something like that."

There didn't seem to be much I could say about the subject that I hadn't already said. But I didn't like a silence between us; there were things floating around in it that made me wary. Clearing my throat, I said, "Did you see Luther Dumont this morning?"

"Yes."

I looked back at him quickly, and this time I kept looking. "You didn't like him."

Trey frowned slightly. "Am I that transparent?"

"It was in your voice," I said vaguely, somewhat pleased to realize that I could read his voice, at least. "Why didn't you like Dumont? Does he have an alibi?"

"Everyone has an alibi," he said. "Dumont was playing poker with several friends from seven until after midnight. They verified it."

"Why don't you like him?" I persisted.

"Call it a clash of personalities."

I decided I'd better stop pressing, because his calm voice had a definite edge in it now. "Oh. Did you tell him about me?"

"Yes."

"How did he react?"

"As far as I could tell, he didn't react at all. He just said he knew of no reason why Townsend would have wanted to hire you."

I shrugged. "If he doesn't try to get in touch with me, then we can assume he was telling the truth."

Trey was frowning again, but he said nothing. The silence started to prickle again, and I broke it a bit nervously. "How about Randal Fane? Does he have an alibi?"

"Why should he come into it?" Trey asked, shooting me a glance that was very sharp. A cop's eyes, suddenly. "He's the family attorney."

"Did you interview him?"

"Yes. About the Townsends' legal affairs. Routinely, I asked him where he was Monday night. He said he was working at home; he has an office there. There are no servants who live in, but it's a reasonable enough thing for him to be doing. He often works at home."

"Then he doesn't have an alibi," I muttered, wondering

what, exactly, Samantha had overheard between Fane and her mother. Talk about the lack of an alibi, maybe?

Trey pulled the car suddenly off the road and into a parking lot. We were at a restaurant where the lunchtime crowd had already cleared out. He stopped the car and half turned toward me, and the cop's eyes were sharp enough to cut.

"Montana, why do you think Fane comes into it at all?"

I looked at him warily. "I don't have any proof."

"Never mind proof for now. What makes you think Fane comes into the case?"

"Look, it's just an impression I got—"

"Tell me."

I had the oddest feeling that he was touching me, even though he wasn't. That his hands were on my shoulders, holding me trapped in place with a kind of strength I couldn't fight. The car was suddenly way too small, and he was too close, and I couldn't seem to breathe. And I didn't like the feeling, because . . . because he wasn't looking at me as a woman in that moment, or even as a person. He was looking at me as a source of needed information. He *wanted* that information, and he meant to get it.

I had almost forgotten he was a cop.

In a voice that I knew sounded shaken, I said, "I think— I got the impression that Amy Townsend and Randal Fane are lovers."

"Damn," Trey said softly. "We missed that."

"I told you, it's just an impression. I could be wrong. Easily. And it doesn't help us anyway."

Trey looked at me, the sharpness leaving his luminous eyes. And when he responded to my objection, it was gone from his voice as well. "You know better than that. It gives him a possible motive, and a pretty strong one at that. It wouldn't be the first time an inconvenient husband had been shoved out of the picture."

"Assuming he was stupid enough in the first place to

commit a murder, Fane would have given himself a better alibi," I objected. "He's a lawyer—"

"Yes. And maybe he's a smart enough lawyer not to give himself too good an alibi. He can't prove it, but the prosecution would have a hell of a time disproving it. And it's the kind of alibi juries believe, Montana."

"Divorce is easier," I said stubbornly. I wasn't sure why I was fighting the idea, but it just didn't feel right to me. That's what I told myself, anyway.

"Maybe Townsend refused to divorce her."

I tried not to remember my conviction that Townsend had been the kind of man to very likely threaten his wife, especially if she wanted to drag him to court. "So what? She could have left him whether or not he liked it. The kids are beyond a custody fight; both of them are of age. Why would she stay with him if she didn't want to?"

"Money. Social position."

"She won't benefit from his murder," I protested. "Not enough to warrant the risk, anyway. Fane has to be pulling down big bucks, surely enough to support her in style, and she'd probably have gotten more in a divorce settlement than she'll inherit. Why murder Townsend? In her social circles, a second marriage wouldn't raise an eyebrow, but living in sin would, so she's bound to marry Fane. Her income stops after she marries again, and she loses the house. Killing her husband doesn't make sense."

"You're talking about Amy Townsend murdering her husband. I'm talking about Randal Fane committing the murder," Trey said softly.

"Same points," I said. "From any angle you like, divorce is easier. Fane's not an idiot; he wouldn't have risked murder."

"Crimes of passion are never reasonable."

"This wasn't a crime of passion, and you know it. It was planned, carefully." Remembering suddenly, I said, "Besides, why on earth would Fane bring Townsend chocolates?"

Trey blinked, then smiled. "That is a point."

I didn't feel very much like smiling, because I'd realized something else. "And it points . . . to a woman, doesn't it? Men don't bring candy to other men. Not that kind, at least. But a woman might."

After a moment, Trey turned back to his driving and continued on toward the Townsend place. "That brings us back to Amy."

"It's all speculation," I said.

"Yes. I suppose the murderer could have merely delivered the candy, claiming it was from someone else. It's a reasonable possibility. But if Amy Townsend and Fane are lovers, the relationship gives both of them a possible motive to kill Townsend. And it gives us something else to follow up."

I sighed. "Motel registrations? They wouldn't. Not the style for either of them."

"Agreed. So they'd have to be meeting somewhere else. His house, maybe. Or the lake house that belonged to the Townsends." His mouth twisted in a kind of pained amusement, but he didn't explain the reasons behind that. "If it's been going on very long, someone's bound to have seen them together. We'll check."

I was beginning to feel like one of those sleazy detectives who burst into motel rooms to take damning pictures for divorce actions: dirty. I wanted a shower. I wanted to squirm on the fine leather of the Mercedes's seat, but held myself still with an effort. I stared straight ahead, wishing I hadn't allowed myself to be seduced by a chocolate voice on my answering machine. *Chocolate.* God.

"You don't like this," Trey said quietly.

I didn't look at him. "Not much, no. Did you expect me to like it?"

He seemed about to respond; I could see him stir slightly from the corner of my eye, but he said nothing.

When the silence started to grow again, I cast about in my mind for something to break it with. When I found it, I was dimly surprised the question was only now occurring

ring to me. "Your people checked the outside of the wall, didn't they?"

"Yes."

"And found nothing. You could have told me that and saved us this trip."

I saw his powerful, ugly hands tighten on the wheel, but his voice remained calm. "You wanted to see inside the house with the family absent. Didn't you?"

I didn't bother to deny it. "The security system will be on, won't it?"

"Not for a few hours."

"Why not? The house'll be empty, and the newspapers reported that everyone would be at the funeral; it'd be a perfect time for burglars to come calling."

After a moment, Trey said, "A few hours ago, a transformer in the area blew. Power's out all over the neighborhood. Work crews are on the job, but they estimate it'll take them about six hours to restore power. Amy Townsend was worried about security, since the estate doesn't have an independent power source. I told her I'd post a man at the gate until the family returned."

"Rudy?" I guessed.

He nodded once.

I decided not to ask if that blown transformer was legit. "The house'll be locked."

"I have a key."

"Do you have a warrant?"

"No."

"You do like to walk the edge, don't you?" I said.

"Yes," he said.

I KNOW. Right now, you're asking yourself why on earth Lieutenant Trey Fortier was about to do something downright unethical and (debatably, since he had a key) illegal. I was wondering too. Easy enough to say he was still crawling out on that limb because he thought I could help him catch a killer. Too easy. There was something else here, something I couldn't really put my finger on.

Drew had hinted that the police had something I didn't know about, some piece of evidence that might give me a motive for the murder. But, how on earth *could* they have something like that? Damn it, I didn't *have* a motive!

Was it possible to have a motive to kill someone if you didn't know you had a motive?

But if there *was* something against me that I didn't know about, was Trey taking the risk of giving me a chance to clear myself before I could be formally charged?

Or was he the one holding that rope I was going to hang myself with?

The remainder of the drive to the Townsend place was silent. I had stopped feeling paranoid; now I was feeling hunted. Even so, I was conscious of things still moving in the silence, slow and heavy now, like water under ice. I remembered the cop's sharpness in Trey's voice and eyes, and reminded myself over and over that he might well be the one who would snap the handcuffs on me unless I could find out who had killed Townsend.

It didn't help.

The Mercedes turned into the drive at last, and Trey didn't stop beside the unmarked car parked at the end; he merely nodded to Rudy Flint and went on through the opened gates. At the house, we both got out and, still silent, walked up to the wide porch. Trey unlocked the front door, and we went inside.

I stood there for a minute just looking around. In forty years, how much violence had this lovely house known? Amy had fallen down those stairs and lost her unborn child more than twenty years ago; her husband had been murdered in that room just off to the right. Only God knew what else had gone on inside these walls.

"Where do you want to start?" Trey asked.

I almost said, "The trap, of course." But as hunted as I felt, total honesty wasn't easy. It probably wasn't prudent, either. I managed a shrug. "I just want to get a . . . a feeling for these people. Would you mind if I wandered around upstairs for a while? By myself?"

He looked at me for a long moment, his face expressionless. "All right," he said finally. "At most, we've got a couple of hours before the family could return; I want to be out of here in one."

"Right." I crossed the hall and began climbing the stairs, feeling his gaze on me. Trying to move casually. Ever tried to do that? It's hell.

It's also hell to have a guilty conscience. Which I did. I very badly wanted to turn around and say, "Look, there's a trap up here, and it might have something important in it; come with me and we'll find out." But I didn't.

Instead, once I was in the upstairs hallway and out of Trey's sight, I moved very quickly. The hallway branched into two wings, and I turned right even before I could flip a mental coin. The doors were all open, so a glance was all I needed as I passed each room. I'd read in Jason's magazine that the Townsend house had eight bedrooms on the second floor, and I'd automatically assumed that meant four in each wing—probably because I was thinking of space being divided evenly.

I was wrong. The right-hand hallway had six bedrooms and four baths. Four of the bedrooms were obviously for guests; they were decorated in bland pastels and had the look of rarely being used. The fifth bedroom was, I guessed, Samantha's; it was pink and white and the walls were covered with posters of rock stars. The sixth bedroom was Jeff III's; blue-and-green plaid with models of cars and planes on shelves and a couple of college pennants on the walls.

At the end of the hallway was a walk-in linen closet.

I scurried back toward the left-hand wing as fast as possible, wondering how much time I'd have before Trey came looking for me. There were only two doors on this hall—on opposite sides. The right-hand door opened into a picture-perfect bedroom (with a bath off it) that was utterly feminine. From the ruffled print bedspread on the king-sized bed (matching drapes) to the satin-covered boudoir chairs and fresh flowers in crystal vases on the night-stands, this was a woman's bedroom.

Somehow, it didn't surprise me that Jeffrey and Amy had separate bedrooms.

I crossed the hall and found myself in Jeffrey's bedroom. One glance told me that Jeffrey had fancied himself *mucho macho*. The color scheme (Amy could have done it only at his direction and under protest, I decided) was an aggressive and unquestionably opulent black and scarlet. The bed, dresser, and chest of drawers were heavy, dark wood, vaguely Oriental in style; the red carpet was plush, and all the fabrics were velvet, silk, and satin.

Oddly enough, it was a beautiful room, yet an utterly masculine one. It was also sensual, and I had to believe that had been Jeffrey's intention. The fabrics used were the most tactile possible, the colors bold and vibrant. Even the (somewhat abstract) prints and oils hanging on the walls were decidedly erotic.

I couldn't spot the security panel, but since Drew had said it was well-hidden, that didn't surprise me. I wasn't much interested anyway; I just wanted to get a quick feel for the room and the man who'd slept here.

There were no mirrors, which I thought was odd—until I went into the adjoining bathroom. The mirrors were there. On every wall, including the inside of the shower stall and the back of the door.

I blinked at assorted images of me, which were all extremely bright and clear due to three skylights in the ceiling. It was like being momentarily hypnotized. I stood there for a minute feeling disoriented, then shook off the sensation and forced myself to look around quickly.

The color scheme of the bath was a stark black—the floor (black marble) and the fixtures: a long, marble-topped vanity with one sink and a sunken tub (excuse me—a Jacuzzi).

The shower stall was as large as some bedrooms, with two clear glass walls (one of which was divided into a set of double doors), two mirrored walls, and a black marble floor.

Even the towels hanging on stark silver racks were black.

The room was very unsettling, but I didn't have much time to ponder why. Ignoring the shifting images from every mirrored wall, I opened the shower doors and knelt on the floor beside the circular drain.

Even though I was conscious of a sense of urgency, I debated for a moment. Fingerprints? Damn it, I didn't have a handkerchief with me, and if I used a towel over my fingers they wouldn't fit through the grate. I'd have to risk it.

The grate didn't turn easily, but it finally gave a quarter counterclockwise lurch and I was able to lift it out and set it aside. The inside of the drain wasn't black, but I couldn't see into it very well. I slipped my hand down along the pipe toward the faucets and felt the narrow notch.

"What are you doing, Montana?"

The question was almost conversational, but it cut through the silence like the roar of a crowd. I wondered vaguely, even as I slowly withdrew my hand and sat back on my heels, if I had just provided the rope that would hang me. I looked up at him.

He was standing at the door of the shower stall, hands in the pockets of his coat. I thought he was a little pale; I didn't know why. I knew I was pale, because I'd felt the blood rush out of my face as if a plug had been pulled. Have you ever felt pale? It's a disturbing feeling, an insubstantial feeling.

Beyond him were infinite reflections, jarringly sharp. His back, his sides, odd angles providing peculiar pieces of him. It was like being enclosed by facets of a man, blinded by the myriad parts of him, triggering an overload of the senses. For an instant I felt disoriented again, confronted by the images surrounding me, trapped by illusion. Then the disquieting sensation passed.

"What are you doing?" he repeated, his voice still quiet but unusually flat.

I didn't have to debate my answer. There are certain points of stupidity that, having been passed, leave few options but the truth. So that's what I told him.

"I had a friend of mine check out this house's security system. In doing that, he discovered that Townsend had had a trap installed. I want to see what's in it."

"Why didn't you tell me?"

When caught in a lie (or a bit of duplicity, whatever) it's quite easy to get mad about it. And, truthfully, I was tired of jumping like a guilty schoolgirl over this *mess*. I hadn't killed Townsend, damn it!

I scrambled up, because it's hard to work up a good head of steam when you're at a man's feet. "Maybe I would have," I told him tightly. "If you'd been honest with me."

"What are you talking about?" he demanded in a voice not quite so controlled as before.

"I'm talking about two homicide detectives tailing me. And don't give that guff about your superiors hoping I'll hang myself. As you said, there's no evidence against me. Unless you're keeping something to yourself."

"And what would that be?"

Until then, I hadn't really believed there *was* something. But there was, I could see it in his eyes. There *couldn't* be, I thought dazedly. Means and opportunity . . . It had to be motive. They'd found something that possibly gave me a motive? It had to be something they couldn't be 100 percent positive about, otherwise I'd be in jail.

"I didn't kill him!" I practically wailed.

He was a bit disconcerted by that. Not the denial, the volume of it. I'd been told before that when I raised my voice the windows tended to rattle. I've never noticed myself. You don't notice things when there's a red haze in front of your eyes, and I never yelled unless there *was*.

The haze cleared quickly, though, because, damn it, there really *wasn't* a reason for me to have killed Jeffrey Townsend.

In my normal voice, I said, "What have you got? What makes you think I killed him?"

"I don't," he said quickly.

"But somebody might? What is it?"

Trey hesitated for a moment, his hard eyes holding mine. Then, slowly, he said, "Even though he wasn't killed there, we searched Townsend's study the day after the murder. We didn't find anything surprising. Except this." He reached into the inner pocket of his coat and produced a photograph wrapped in clear plastic, which he handed to me. "We've identified the background; this was taken in one of the bedrooms of the Townsend lake house."

That was when I understood Trey's earlier pained amusement. If Amy and Fane were using the lake house for their trysts, they weren't the only ones.

The photograph was of Jeffrey Townsend—and he wasn't alone. It appeared to have been taken from above the foot of a bed and probably by a camera with a timer (unless Townsend had gone in for threesomes or liked people watching him, which was possible). Or maybe it was a still from a video of some kind. I didn't know. I didn't really care.

Townsend lay on his back, stark naked. And he was, to put it as politely as possible, engaging in an intimate act with the lady who was crouching on top of him. His wrists were tied to the brass bedstead with velvet ropes (one of the gentler forms of bondage, I understand), and judging from the strained look on his flushed, perspiring face, Jeffrey was on the very edge of experiencing what the French so aptly call "the little death."

His partner was not Amy Townsend. It was a rear view, showing little of the face except for a slice of cheek and one earlobe; she had obviously been in motion when the photo was snapped and was somewhat blurred—but it wasn't Amy. This woman was obviously shorter than Amy and not so reed-slender.

She also possessed a mop of short, tousled black hair.

I studied the photo for a long moment, then handed it

back to Trey. "It isn't me, if that's what you think," I said.

He didn't glance at the photo. He just returned it to his pocket and kept looking at me. "It could be you," he said.

I was feeling very relieved and no doubt looked it. Cheerfully, I said, "I can give you courtroom proof it isn't me—testimony from any doctor you'd care to choose."

"To what would the doctor testify?" Trey asked.

"If it comes to that," I said, "I suppose I'd even strip down in court myself. The tabloids would love it."

"Montana." But he had relaxed.

I grinned at him, then turned my back and lifted the hem of my sweater up several inches. "It would be fairly obvious in the photo, don't you think? And I've had it for twenty years; my family doctor would testify to that."

As I've mentioned, I tan easily. And my skin isn't pale at any time of the year, even in the areas almost always covered by clothing. Cherokee blood? Mother says yes, but then, she would. The scar was pale, and it showed up starkly against the surrounding skin.

There was a moment of silence, and then I felt a light touch on my lower back, to the right of my spine and just above the waistband of my jeans. It tickled, but I wasn't tempted to laugh. I was conscious of a peculiar breathlessness as his fingers traced the curving scar to the point where it disappeared under my jeans.

"What happened?" he asked.

"I was thrown by a horse. There was a piece of crumpled tin on the ground with a sharp edge, and I landed on it." I tried to sound matter-of-fact, but it was almost impossible once I noticed Trey's reflection in the mirrored wall of the shower stall. He was looking down at my scar, still touching it, and for an instant—just a moment—I saw the softened, naked face in Jason's painting.

Then he looked up, caught me watching him, and his

face closed down instantly. He returned his hand to his pocket.

I dropped my sweater and turned back around. And I managed to keep my voice calm. "I always hated that scar, because I couldn't wear a two-piece bathing suit. I never thought it'd save my neck one day."

"Do scars bother you so much?" he asked impersonally.

I lifted an eyebrow at him. "When you're a teenage girl, you don't particularly want all the boys leering and making remarks about an S-shaped scar directly above your right buttock. Just think of all the words that begin with an *S.*"

Trey's lips twitched. "I see your point."

"I thought you would. Now—and for the last time—are we clear on the fact that I didn't murder Townsend?"

"Is that the royal plural?"

"Answer the question, Trey." It didn't hit me until I saw his eyes flicker that it was the first time I'd casually used his first name.

"We're clear," he said. "You didn't kill Townsend. Unless, that is, we find another photo in that trap—of a lady with an interesting scar."

"Very funny." I knelt back down on the floor of the stall and, as he followed suit, added, "I thought about fingerprints, but I don't have any gloves."

"Neither do I," he said, "Wait, use this." He produced a snowy handkerchief.

I draped the linen over my fingers and stuck my hand back down inside the drain, sliding it over the places I'd already touched. No need to leave prints if I could help it. "There's a notch . . ." I inserted two fingers into the notch and pulled upward. We both heard a soft click, and a kind of drawer, hinged at the bottom, popped open just below the notch. In the drawer was a cylinder about eight inches long and ten inches in circumference. I managed to get my linen-covered fingers around it and pull it free of the trap.

Trey didn't take the cylinder, but examined it carefully

as I set it on the black marble beside the drain. "Looks like the lid screws on," he said.

Gingerly, I moved the cylinder until it was trapped between my knees, then unscrewed the lid and set it aside. "What was that you said about another photo?" I murmured, reaching inside. It was hell with the handkerchief over my fingers, but I managed to get hold of a stiff photo and folded envelope and pull them out.

Trey took them from me, being careful to keep the handkerchief in place. He placed the photo on top of the cylinder's lid so we could both see it without having to hold it, then opened the envelope and glanced at the contents.

"Negatives. More of the same, I'd guess."

I was staring at the photo, feeling a little sick. Like the picture in Trey's pocket, this was another sexual encounter captured on film.

"Do you recognize him?" I asked.

"Yes. Luther Dumont."

Jeffrey Townsend's "silent partner" was naked in the photo. And he was very busy. He was on his knees on a tumbled bed, with his hands holding the hips of a girl facing away from him who was also on her knees. Hands and knees, in her case. It was a side view, but the girl's face was clear because it was turned as if she were looking back at him. Dumont had the same look I'd seen moments ago on Townsend's photographed face, that anguished look of near completion.

The girl, though—and I'm using that word literally: she wasn't more than twelve years old, if that—the expression on her pretty face had nothing to do with passion. Those were real tears on her cheeks, and there was real pain in her eyes.

I had to look away from those haunted eyes.

The room, from what I could make out, looked very ordinary. It was just a bedroom, as impersonal as a hotel. No photographs were on the part of the dresser that was visible; nothing on the nightstand, except a lamp. I could see the edge of a curtained window, but not enough to tell if the picture had been taken during the night or day.

"I'm sorry," Trey said softly.

I looked up to find him watching me, and I knew that my feelings had shown plainly. Like I said, I'm a lousy poker player. And he was too close—I couldn't think for a moment. Then I pulled my gaze away from his and looked at the photo.

"Blackmail, obviously."

"It looks that way," he agreed.

"But Dumont has an alibi, you said."

"Yes. He does."

I forced myself to study the photo with detachment. The man was in profile, and it was difficult to get a clear idea of how his features would look when they weren't distorted by lust, but he looked younger than I'd expected. I'd assumed that Jeffrey's silent partner would be about his own age; this man didn't look much past thirty.

"Do you think this is a recent picture?" I asked.

"No," Trey said immediately. "Dumont's in his forties. And every year shows."

I thought about that. "According to what I've managed to piece together, Dumont's been Townsend's silent partner for roughly ten years." I looked at Trey. "About right?"

He nodded, gazing at the photo. "About. So we can speculate that Dumont became a partner under duress. Possibly because Townsend decided to involve himself in unscrupulous deals without getting his hands dirty and wanted someone to front for him."

SEVEN

"A STRONG MOTIVE for murder," I noted.

"Yes. Ten years is a long time to wait, though."

"Maybe it took him that long to figure a way into this fortress, *and* to work out an alibi for himself."

"Maybe."

My knees were beginning to ache from the hardness of the marble floor, and I was feeling depressed. Blackmail is one of the worst crimes, in my opinion. And these damned photographs . . .

Mind you, I'm not narrow-minded when it comes to sex. To each his own. So what if Jeffrey liked being tied up in bed? But it was another piece of his personality which, added to the rest, was beginning to make up a dark and murky picture.

I liked Jeffrey less and less.

And then there was Luther Dumont. To each his own, as I said, but using a virtual baby for sexual "pleasure" was nauseating. He had hurt her, you could see that. God, her haunted eyes . . . I tried to detach myself, tried to listen to the nagging voice telling me that there was something familiar about the picture. The girl? Dumont? The room? *Something.*

Thankfully, the picture was removed from my sight as Trey returned it and the envelope of negatives to the cylinder. He picked up the lid—using his handkerchief—and began screwing it back in place. I found myself staring at that big, powerful, ugly hand, so close to me because the cylinder was still between my knees. I heard myself talking in a distant voice.

"Rules of evidence. I'll get word to the man who installed the trap. He'll come forward, since the news of Townsend's murder reached him. You can get a court order to open the trap."

Trey was silent while he replaced the cylinder in its hiding place and closed the drawer. I had to put the grate back in place over the drain, because his fingers wouldn't fit. I thought for a minute that he was going to say something about having previous knowledge of the trap and how that could make the evidence tainted, but he didn't.

I guess he *did* like to walk the edge.

"Get word to him as soon as possible," Trey said.

"Right." I scrambled up and got out of the shower stall very quickly. And out of the bathroom. And out of the bedroom. I was conscious of him following me. "How much time do we have left?" I asked as we stood in the hallway.

He glanced at his watch. "Half an hour at most."

I went across to Amy's bedroom and inside. I stood in the middle of the room, looking around and trying to get some sense of that very controlled woman. "Pretty," I commented to Trey, who was standing in the doorway watching me.

"You don't like it," he noted.

The truth was I didn't. It was too frilly, *too* feminine, as if Amy had been trying too hard. This bedroom and Jeffrey's had only one thing in common: they were both stark statements of gender. This room said, I am a woman; Jeffrey's room said, I am a man.

I wondered if they'd shared a bit of confusion as to what their roles were supposed to be.

An armchair shrink—that's me.

Without responding to Trey's comment, I located the closet and opened it. A walk-in, of course. A place for everything and everything in its place. High rods for long gowns and dresses; lower rods for skirts and blouses and jackets and pants; neat cubbyhole shelves for shoes; racks for belts and other accessories. On a high shelf running around all three walls was an assortment of hatboxes and half a dozen wigs on stands.

Wigs. That surprised me, since Amy had such beautiful hair. But apparently Jeffrey liked variety. (I couldn't believe Amy did; her home was too bland.) There wasn't a blond wig in the bunch. There were two coal-black wigs, one long and straight and the other short; two red wigs, also long and short and of different shades; and two medium-brunette ones—again, long and short. I studied the wig made up of short black curls and decided that it didn't match the hairstyle of the woman in the photo with Jeffrey.

There was a built-in chest of drawers on the end wall, and I opened the top drawer. Nighties. Babydoll pajamas. Teddies. They were of all colors, fashioned of delicate silk and lace, the trappings of a woman bent on seduction. The other drawers held more of the same, and all were scanty and sexy.

I thought of Amy, so controlled and seemingly fragile. I wondered if, before the advent of Randal Fane, she had tried to hold the attention of a husband who liked sensuous fabrics and colors and women with different hairstyles— and being tied up in bed.

I got out of the closet, closing the doors as I'd found them. Trey was still waiting in the doorway of the bedroom. I was trying to keep my face expressionless, but I was hating this. I felt more and more like a sleazy detective. I wanted to go home and take a shower. A long, hot one.

"Find anything?" Trey asked. He stepped back out into the hall as I left the bedroom.

"No. I want to look at the kids' bedrooms."

"They have alibis," he said, following me.

"*Everybody* has an alibi. It's just too damned pat," I

muttered irritably. I always get irritable when I'm feeling like a sleazy detective.

"What do you mean by that?" he asked.

I went into Samantha's room and began looking around, trying not to think about him standing in the doorway. Watching me. I replied to him without really considering my own words—sort of a stream-of-consciousness response, if you know what I mean.

"It just is. Everybody has a nice, tight alibi. Except Randal Fane, that is—but maybe the killer thought he wouldn't come into the case. And he *wouldn't* have if I hadn't seen him in a clinch with Amy. Dumont was playing poker with witnesses, Amy was in New York, Sam was at a party with a couple hundred people as witnesses, and Jeff was in another state, also with witnesses. Damn it, maybe somebody hired a hit man. That's what Sam thinks."

"Does she?"

"That's what she told me."

Her bedroom was a typical teenage sanctuary, pictures of rock stars and makeup, and lots of clothes and records. There was a phone (pink), a stereo (latest Japanese model), and a television set (color), and stuffed animals lining shelves. Books, hardback and paper, on another set of shelves; I glanced at some of the titles and found a few old friends of mine as well as some of the recent potboilers.

Her dressing table was overflowing with bottles and jars and little mirrored cases. Most of the makeup looked new and barely used, and I thought that was probably why Sam had been made-up so inexpertly. Jeffrey had no doubt refused to let his daughter wear the stuff when he was alive.

Her closet was crammed full of clothes, as disorganized as her mother's had been neat. Jeffrey obviously hadn't wanted her to dress like a teenager, either, because while the newer stuff (some still tagged) was ultrateenage, the stuff pushed to the back and dropped carelessly on the floor was pink-and-white, pretty and feminine, with lots of ruffles and bows.

Without saying a word to Trey, I went on to Jeff's bedroom and studied it quickly. Another television and phone, an extensive stereo set, more records and books on shelves. The room was neat, probably because its occupant had been away at college. The closet was sparse, holding mostly the kind of more formal clothing that a kid wouldn't take to school.

Nothing. I'd gotten virtually nothing from poking into closets and corners.

I felt more irritable.

As soon as we got back downstairs, I said, "Do we have time to check his study?"

Trey glanced at his watch. "If you make it quick. Down the hall there, second door on the left."

I don't know what I expected. It was a typical home office, with a desk and phone and a couple of wood-grain filing cabinets. The desktop was clear, not even a blotter; there was just the phone and an answering machine.

"The picture was all you found?" I asked Trey as he stood just inside the room and watched me.

"Yes. In the top left-hand drawer."

"Just lying there?"

"No. Wedged in at the back, as if it had been overlooked."

As if. Was the photo a bit of carelessness on Jeffrey's part? Or had the murderer somehow found it and then planted it where the police couldn't have failed to find it—either because that woman could have been me or merely to confuse the case further?

"Were there any fingerprints on it?" I asked.

"No." Somewhat dryly, he added, "Which would have been a good argument for the defense."

I looked at him. "Is that why you decided to give me the benefit of the doubt? Because it looked like a plant?"

"Partly."

I decided not to ask for his other reasons. "Where's the security panel?"

Trey nodded to his right. "Behind the door. Your friend was thorough."

Without commenting on that, I went over and looked behind the door. It took me a minute to spot the panel, because it was cunningly hidden. This wall was covered in heavily molded wooden paneling, and the seams of the security panel blended right in. I didn't try to open it; I wouldn't have known what I was looking at anyway.

I turned back to the room and stared around. Something was nagging at me again, damn it, but I couldn't figure out what it was.

"Seen enough?" Trey asked.

I nodded and followed him from the room. Minutes later, we were in the Mercedes and pulling out of the Townsend driveway. I half expected Trey to show some sign of relief once we were out of there, since he'd taken a hell of a chance with this visit. But he didn't.

Talk about controlled people. Then again, maybe it wasn't control. Maybe the man just didn't have any nerves to speak of. It was an interesting thought. People with no nerves didn't mind walking the edge, or even going out on limbs.

Unfortunately, I have my nerves and a couple of other people's as well.

"Something was bothering you in Townsend's study," he said as we left the estate behind.

I didn't much like the way he was waltzing in and out of my mind so easily, but he seemed to have acquired the knack of it.

"Something," I agreed. "But I don't know what it was."

"Something you saw? Or didn't see?"

"I don't know." I felt his glance, but he didn't say anything else about the study. Instead, he changed the subject. Slightly.

"I'd like to hear your thoughts on all this," he said. "Why don't we have a cup of coffee and talk about it?"

"Fine," I said.

Well. Would *you* refuse such a harmless suggestion? Of course not. Especially after being so relieved that you weren't the girl in a smutty piece of evidence. There was certainly no more to it than that.

Sure.

Half an hour later, we were sitting in a small café, across from each other in a booth with the coffee on the table. Neither of us had said much to that point. I was still trying to figure out what was nagging at me. I don't know why Trey was so silent, and I told myself it was useless to speculate about it. Jason had been right about one thing: the man wouldn't give away anything he didn't want known.

"You've met the suspects, with the exception of Townsend's son and Dumont," he said finally. "What do you think of them?"

I pushed away whatever was bothering me; I knew it would come to me eventually. "I don't think it was a happy family," I said dryly.

"Because Mrs. Townsend was probably having an affair?"

"That's part of it. Have you met Townsend's son?"

"Briefly, when he arrived home."

"Was he . . . upset?"

Trey seemed to consider that. "He was shocked by his father's death. I don't know that he was grieving very much, if that's what you mean."

I nodded. "None of them are. Amy's wearing conventional mourning, but . . . I don't know. Samantha isn't grieving, and she didn't waste any time before telling me her father was a son of a bitch. Jeffrey's bedroom looked like something out of a Turkish harem. I don't suppose you found any whips or chains?"

"No. Not at the estate."

"What about their lake house?"

"I can't get a warrant without cause. That picture isn't enough. So far, there's nothing to indicate the lake house is important to the case."

"That woman in the picture with Townsend," I said. "A mistress? Any sign of that?"

"Except for the picture, no."

"Only one of those involved has a really strong motive," I said. "Are you sure Dumont was playing poker? If Townsend was blackmailing him, he has a hell of a motive."

"Three other men confirmed it, and I don't believe any of them were lying."

"He couldn't have slipped out for an hour?"

"He didn't. He wasn't out of sight of those men for more than five minutes at any one time."

Trips to the john, I thought, but didn't say so. *"Somebody* killed Townsend," I said, stating the obvious. "And unless we're missing a suspect, it was either a family member, Fane, or Dumont."

"Fane seems most likely."

"He's the only one without an alibi," I admitted. "But I can't see him bringing Townsend chocolates. Or stabbing him after he was already dead. It doesn't make any sense." A sudden thought occurred to me. "Where was the vacuum cleaner kept?"

"A storage closet off the kitchen."

"Would Fane have known that? No," I said, answering myself. "It's a big house, and a visitor wouldn't have had the faintest idea where the cleaning things were kept. He'd have had to look for it, wasting time. And what about the rug and drapery tie? What happened to them?"

"We don't know they were removed from the house that night," Trey said.

I looked at him. "Do you want to assume they weren't?"

"No."

Resisting an impulse to chew on my thumbnail, I thought for a minute to try to get everything straight.

"Okay. Townsend was killed sometime between six and midnight."

"Right."

"The cleaning service left around six. When did the butler and cook leave?"

"At six."

I frowned. "Is that usual?"

"On the nights the Townsends didn't entertain, yes."

"When did Townsend eat dinner?"

"He didn't. It was left in the oven for him."

"So, the drug took effect more quickly with nothing but chocolates in his stomach."

"According to the medical examiner, yes."

"And the medical examiner thinks—unofficially—that Townsend died closer to eight than ten?"

"Yes. Say between eight and nine."

I felt like I was trying to gather all the threads someone had unpicked from a tapestry. There were too many threads, too many different colors, and I didn't have the key to weave them back into place.

Find the key. It was there, I knew it. One fact, one bit of information that would bring everything else into focus.

"What?" Trey asked.

I looked at him, realizing only then that I'd spoken aloud. "The key," I said. "There has to be one. Something we've overlooked."

"Is that what's bothering you?"

"I don't know." I took a breath and tried once more to get it straight. "Townsend died sometime between eight and nine, probably, and was stabbed in the next hour. At ten, the call was placed to me. Have you verified that?"

"Yes. The call was placed from Townsend's study."

"His study . . ." I jumped suddenly as a high-pitched beeping sound erupted. "What the hell—?"

Trey produced a pocket pager and shut it off. "Sorry. I have to call the office. Excuse me."

I watched him rise and walk toward a pay phone over near a corner, feeling embarrassed at my extreme reaction to his beeper. God, I was jumping at everything! Then, watching as Trey called his office, I realized something, and I knew what had nagged at me in Townsend's study. The hell of it was that it seemed to produce more questions than answers.

By the time Trey returned to the booth a couple of minutes later, I was chewing on my thumbnail and scowling.

"What?" he asked the moment he sat down.

I took my thumb out of my mouth. "Oh, nothing. Except that I've realized what bothered me about his study."

"Is it important?"

"Beats the hell out of me. It's his answering machine, Trey. It's the same one I have."

Trey frowned very slightly. "I don't see the point."

"I didn't either, until your beeper went off. It reminded me of something I'd totally forgotten. If the killer knew I had the same machine as Townsend, and knew how it worked, then he didn't have to be in my loft later that night to erase the message he'd left. He could have done it from any push-button phone."

Trey sat back and looked at me for a long moment. "Isn't there some kind of personal code?"

"You can set it up that way, but I never did. When my machine answers, you just push the asterisk on the phone's keypad; that signals the machine to replay all messages on the tape. If no other button is pressed, the machine resets itself at the end of the last message. If you want to rewind the tape to the beginning—erasing all the messages—you just push the pound sign after you've heard the messages."

"Which means," Trey said slowly, "that if the killer knew your machine, he—or she—could have been safely back where they were supposed to be well before midnight."

"And called from there," I agreed. "But it doesn't narrow the possibilities that I can see. Everyone with an alibi was covered all evening. I suppose Dumont could have killed Townsend before his poker game got started—

maybe—but he couldn't have been in Townsend's study at ten. Jeff couldn't possibly have been there; he was just too far away. Samantha had witnesses all evening. And Amy—''

''Was seemingly in New York.''

''You have to accept her alibi, don't you? Since her friend swears she was there and everything else meshes?''

Trey nodded. ''Unless someone comes forward and places her near here, which isn't likely. Or unless we get lucky questioning airline employees and find out that she came back here just long enough to kill her husband.''

''Are you doing that? Questioning employees, I mean?''

''Yes. Amy Townsend wasn't listed on any flight during the right times, but she could have flown under another name. We're showing her picture to the employees who were on duty.''

At, I thought, Hartsfield International Airport, one of the busiest in the world. At least nine national airlines and half a dozen commuter airlines. God knew how many employees. And, given the times involved, the police were probably having to question two shifts just to be sure; those that had come on around four that afternoon, and the third shift at midnight. It sounded like a hopeless task.

''So it comes down to Fane again.'' I shook my head. ''I don't think the D.A. would go for it. You said Fane had the kind of alibi juries believe, and even if he is having an affair with Amy, you have absolutely no evidence tying him to the murder scene.''

With a somewhat twisted smile, Trey said, ''There are a couple more things. When you went upstairs at the Townsend house, I called my office and had someone ask a few more questions. I just got the answers.''

''And?''

''Randal Fane's only car was being repaired from Monday afternoon until Tuesday morning; the garage verified it. I'm having the cabs checked out, but you can bet none of them will be able to say they picked up a fare answering his description.''

"So he has a sort of alibi?"

"He could argue that. And unless I could show a means for him to get to the Townsend estate that night . . ."

"It must have been a hit man," I said tiredly. "Maybe someone had the chocolates delivered and then showed up later to stick a knife in his dead victim's chest."

"The security system was fully active when the servants left. Why would Townsend have turned it off?"

"He wouldn't have. It isn't reasonable."

"Then how did your hit man bypass security, assuming that the chocolates arrived before him? If Townsend was already dead and couldn't have let him in?"

"The deliveryman was the assassin," I speculated, just about half-serious. "He delivered the chocolates, but then didn't really leave. He waited inside the fence, and when Townsend was dead, he sneaked in through a conveniently open window and stabbed him."

"Why stab him?"

"That's not a fair question. It applies to whoever the murderer was. Stabbing Townsend after he was already dead doesn't make sense no matter who did it."

Trey half nodded. "Granted. It's a nice theory, but if a deliveryman did it, we haven't been able to discover a trace of him. There were no official deliveries to the estate that night. More importantly, if a relative stranger killed Townsend, how did he know the shutdown code for the security system? Even if he got in through an open window, the system *was* shut down."

"Blind luck?" I guessed.

"You're beginning to get discouraged," Trey observed quietly.

I put my elbows on the table and rested my chin in my hands, silently (and automatically) discounting my mother's teachings. "Of course I'm getting discouraged. Everybody involved has an alibi except Fane, and *he* has one more or less by default. The murder scene was neat as a pin except for a missing bearskin rug and drapery tie. The suspect with the perfect motive is Dumont, who was apparently being blackmailed, but *he* has an airtight alibi verified by three witnesses. Damn.''

"And so?"

"Why don't you lock me up now and save wear and tear on my nerves?"

"You didn't kill him," Trey said.

That unequivocal statement should have made me feel better. It didn't. I'd certainly be able to prove I wasn't the woman in the smutty picture with Townsend, but I was the only one involved who had indisputably *been* there the night of the murder. And even though no actual physical evidence tied me to the crime, that could be said of everybody else as well.

If I were the D.A., I knew who I'd pick.

"Montana?"

Yeah.

I realized I'd been rubbing my face with both hands, the way I do whenever I'm at the end of my rope. I stopped and looked across the table at him. In a steady voice, I said, "According to what I've read, if a murder isn't solved within the first forty-eight hours, it isn't likely to be."

"Unlikely, maybe. Not impossible. You said there was a key, something we've overlooked. What could it be, Montana?"

He didn't lean toward me, but it felt as if he did. I couldn't look away from him, and I had the odd feeling that the room was pushing in at me, shrinking until he was too close and I couldn't breathe.

"I don't know," I managed to say.

"Think." His voice was quiet, insistent. "Something you've seen? Something you've heard?"

That cop's sharpness was suddenly in his eyes, making them hard even though his voice was soft. I sat back jerkily and looked away from him. "I don't know. I don't remember."

He didn't say anything for a long minute, and then he asked quietly, "What happened just then?"

"I don't know what you mean." My answer was too quick, and I knew it.

"Yes, you do. You were suddenly uncomfortable. Why?"

Somewhat warily, I met his gaze. Luminous eyes, nothing sharp or hard. I wasn't at all sure I should explain this, but I figured he wouldn't give up until he knew.

"Why?" he repeated. "It's the second time that's happened. The first time, we were in my car, talking about Fane."

"No. Not talking about him. You were questioning me."

He got it instantly, and a frown drew his flying brows together.

I took a breath. "Maybe that's just a part of being a cop, I don't know. Maybe it's what they teach in Interrogation 101. Pin the suspect in place until he—or she—squirms. But I'm not supposed to be a suspect, am I? That's what you keep saying. And you . . . you don't look at me like a cop. Except during those odd moments when you're trying to get something out of me."

"I'm sorry. It wasn't intentional."

Somehow, I thought that made it worse. I felt unglued, depressed, and more than a little miserable. "Can we go now, please?"

"You've seen inside the Townsend house," he said, his voice formal now. "And you've met everyone involved except Townsend's son and Dumont. What do you plan to do next?"

"Meet Dumont."

"Even if he doesn't contact you first?"

I slid out of the booth and stood up. "Even if. I don't have any time to waste."

Under the neat mustache, his mouth hardened. But he didn't try to reassure me on that point; we both knew it would have been a waste of breath. Instead, he left the booth and walked beside me as far as the cashier's stand.

I went out while he was paying for the coffee, and was already in his car when he rejoined me.

"I'll take you back to the station," he said, "so you can get your car."

"And my escort," I said. "Don't forget my escort."

I always get sarcastic when I'm feeling unglued, depressed, and miserable.

Trey didn't comment on the sarcasm. He just radioed ahead to make sure my watchdogs would be ready to pick up the trail again. Neither of us said anything during the drive to the station.

We didn't even say good-bye.

ALL RIGHT, maybe I was being unfair. If you're trained to get information a certain way, sheer habit would make you tend to stick to that method; maybe to a cop, every source of information was, at least potentially, a suspect. So for Trey to look at me like that wasn't terribly surprising, and it was hardly something I should take offense over.

But.

Have you ever, say, encountered a teacher years after you'd grown up and left school? Wasn't it hard to relate to him or her, as one adult to another? Sure it was. If you meet one of your teachers as an adult, your own maturity clashes head-on with memories. You feel disoriented, because what you remember, what your experience of that adult person consists of, is a child/adult relationship. You don't know *how* to relate to your teacher as an adult yourself.

The problem I was struggling over with Trey was something like that, only in reverse. Our relationship had, from virtually the beginning, been undefined. At first, he was a cop and I was a suspect. Clear enough, that. But then, very quickly, the lines started to blur. He pulled me halfway over the line and made me an active participant in an attempt to solve the case, even though I was still officially a suspect. And then something else entered the picture, something that was distinctly man/woman but couldn't be defined because neither of us was willing to give it a name.

One moment we were discussing the case as pseudo partners, the next he was looking at me as a man—or as a cop.

It wasn't working. I couldn't see him as a cop the way I should have, because I saw him too often as a very attractive and intriguing man. Which means that I was horribly shaken every time this attractive man's beautiful eyes hardened with a cop's intent, demanding stare. And equally shaken when, while I was busy reminding myself that he was a cop, he'd look at me as a man who wasn't likely to refuse an invitation for breakfast in bed.

See what I mean?

I'd never been particularly sold on the idea that it wasn't wise to mix business with pleasure, but I knew damn well it wasn't at all smart to contemplate a personal relationship with a cop when he was investigating a murder and I looked like the prime suspect—something neither of us could forget for very long.

Problem was, I couldn't seem to be smart about it. I was too conscious of Trey, and I thought he was having the same difficulty. He'd controlled whatever unprofessional impulses he had better than I did (except for when he had touched my scar in the shower stall), but given his growing ability to read my face, it was just a matter of time before one of those sparks I was sending his way ignited something.

It was a scary thought.

I forced it out of my mind as I drove back to the loft. It wasn't easy, but I knew it wasn't something that could be resolved with this murder hanging over me.

My announcement about seeing Dumont had been made on impulse, but I knew I had to do it. He had the best motive, and it was still remotely possible that he'd hired someone to kill Townsend after discovering a way onto the estate.

Besides that, I was suspicious of airtight alibis on principle, and this case was full of them. I had the vague feeing that too much of this had been planned; people just don't usually have alibis. I mean, think about it.

The murder happened on a Monday night. Not a weekend, when people tended to party or make other plans outside their homes. It happened during the hours when most of us are taking it easy after the first workday of the week, when we're watching television or planning the week ahead. Can you recall what you did last Monday evening? Probably, it was nothing unusual, if you can even remember.

But in this case, all the family members as well as the suspect with the strongest motive had good, tight alibis. Yet Randal Fane, who had a motive virtually guaranteed to come to light under investigation of the family, had the flimsiest—and most likely—alibi of the lot.

I didn't like Fane for the murder, mainly because I thought he was too smart for it. Also, try as I might, I couldn't figure out what on earth he'd want with a bearskin rug and drapery tie. That last was true no matter who was the killer, of course; I had the feeling that if I could just figure out why those things had been taken, I'd be a lot closer to understanding what had happened that night.

In any case, what I was left with was the idea that at least one of those airtight alibis had been fabricated. And all I had to convince me of that was this vague feeling of being led around by the nose. And the fact, of course, that I knew *I* hadn't done it.

I had to take a very close look at these alibis. And since Dumont had the strongest motive, I wanted to start with him.

So I drove back to the loft trying to think of some way of seeing and talking to Dumont without giving away what I knew about him. I went inside the building and up to my door, still thinking. When I got inside, I sent an automatic glance toward my desk.

The light on the machine was blinking. I approached it warily, making a mental note to see about getting an answering service, and jumped a foot when Choo landed on the desktop, glaring at me.

"Don't do that," I told him. "And don't glare at me."

Choo snorted and sat down, washing a forepaw with supreme indifference. I reached around him and punched at the machine. It began whirring as the tape rewound, the LED indicator flashing at me. A message had come in about an hour before.

"Miss Montana, this is Luther Dumont. I was involved in several business ventures with Jeffrey Townsend. I would like to talk to you, either at my office or your own. Please call me at your convenience." He left a number.

A good voice. But not a chocolate one.

I glanced at my watch. A little before five. Well, damn it, I *didn't* have time to waste. So I called the number. A nasal voice, presumably a secretary's, took my name and put me on hold for a few seconds. When she came back on the line, she reported that Mr. Dumont was in a meeting that was scheduled to break up in the next ten minutes or so. Could I possibly come to his office today? I could.

Since I had no idea how long I'd be gone, I took the precaution of feeding Choo his supper before I left. I wasn't very hungry myself. The secretary had given me detailed directions to Dumont's office, and I had no problem finding it. My escort, of course, stuck close.

Luther Dumont's office was out toward Marietta—a suburb of Atlanta. It was a small building, one of those undistinguished places that's probably been everything from a restaurant to a boutique in its time. Today it was simply a small place with one floor and limited parking. The discreet sign above the door proclaimed Dumont Enterprises, which could have meant anything at all.

From what I'd gathered, Dumont was a dabbler. He dabbled in the stock market, in real estate, in used cars. With Jeffrey Townsend, he'd dabbled in a number of businesses that had appeared and disappeared so quickly they *had* to be shady. Nothing blatantly illegal, though.

I parked my car at the side and went around to the front

of the building. The unmarked sedan containing my watchdogs had pulled over to the curb half a block away; I started to wave at them, but decided not to. I didn't feel very playful.

I pushed open the front door and stepped into a reception area, which consisted of a desk, a few chairs; uninspired prints on the walls. The room was empty. Presumably, the secretary had gone home since it was after five. There'd been no bell on the door, at least not one that I'd heard, so my arrival may well have gone unnoticed.

I stepped to a doorway on the right and found myself gazing down a hallway with a few doors along it, some open and some closed. I was about to call out when I realized that I should make the most of the opportunity.

Retreating from the doorway, I went to the secretary's desk and looked it over quickly. I didn't waste time with the Rolodex; there was an appointment book, so I began flipping the pages quickly. What was I looking for? I don't know. A name I recognized, I suppose. And I found one—but it wasn't what I expected. After an instant's thought, I checked back over the previous three months and found the same name on the same days each month.

I didn't dare take any more time. Leaving the desk, I returned to the open doorway and called out, "Mr. Dumont?"

"First door on your right," he called back immediately.

About now, you may be wondering why I was walking innocently into a meeting—alone—with a possible murderer (never mind the alibi). I wasn't. Not innocently, I mean. I wasn't keen on being alone with Dumont, even if he wasn't the one who'd killed Jeffrey, because child molesters turn my stomach and I *knew* Dumont was that. But, you may remember, I was running out of options.

So I went into his office.

He rose from behind a modern glass-and-chrome desk and came toward me. I don't know what I'd expected Luther Dumont to be, but he certainly was something different. From the moment I walked in, I felt the effect of him. It was like being in a room with an electrical charge bouncing off the walls. My skin tingled, my legs felt weak, and I was suddenly hot all over. He moved with the kind of grace God meant only for cats, and the kind of sheer, raw virility reserved for stallions.

"Miss Montana?" He smiled, hand outstretched.

I didn't want to touch his hand, but forced myself to. It was surprisingly hot, but very dry, and his grip was firm. He was a big man, the kind that filled doorways. The kind that filled rooms.

"Mr. Dumont," I said.

EIGHT

HE WAVED me to a seat, and I sat down gratefully. He went back around the desk and sat down himself. The solid glass-and-chrome object between us should have felt like a barrier. It didn't.

Though I was only half conscious of the animal analogies then, I realized later how apt they were. The man literally gave off an aura so powerfully—almost brutally— sexual, that it was like walking into the den of some feral creature where the scent of aeons of mating had been absorbed by the very earth.

Yes, I know it sounds weird. That's nothing compared to how it felt. I'm not usually conscious of a man's sexuality—not overly conscious, I mean. And most especially not when I know that a man gets his kicks abusing little girls. But I had never encountered a man who made me instantly and starkly aware of the most basic and primitive functions of my body.

But I want you to understand something: whatever it was that I felt, it was in no sense an attraction. It was more an instinctive fascination, like being unable to take your eyes off a snake.

No wonder Trey hadn't liked him. I had the feeling that Dumont's peculiar aura would be as obvious to another man as to a woman, and not many men would feel comfortable if they were conscious of it. Maybe that was why Jeffrey Townsend had chosen this man as his partner.

Maybe it was another indication of Jeffrey's need to feel macho.

God knows.

"You're probably wondering why I asked you to come here, Miss Montana," he said in a deep, velvety voice.

I had planned to play dumb, but didn't think I could pull it off now. So I shook my head slightly and managed a rueful smile. "I think I can guess. The police must have told you that Jeffrey Townsend had wanted to hire me. Or at least," I added dryly, "that I *say* he wanted to hire me. They obviously don't believe me, since they've put a tail on me." I offered that last bit of information deliberately, because I wanted to see his reaction. As far as I could tell, he didn't react.

"Why did Jeff want to hire you?" he asked.

"He never got the chance to tell me."

Dumont studied me for a moment, his expression grave. And, for the first time, I realized that the man wasn't only not good-looking—he was actually ugly. His dark face was too wide across the forehead and his cheekbones, too narrow at the chin. His thick eyebrows knit together over the bridge of his wide, flat nose, and his eyes were so heavy lidded it was hard to tell they were a yellowish green. His mouth was thin lipped, and his hair was so blond it was nearly white.

He was ugly, and it had taken me several minutes to see it. Talk about having an impact.

"According to your ad in the phone book," Dumont said, "you find things. True?"

"That's right. I naturally assumed that Mr. Townsend had lost something. Do you have any idea what that could have been?"

"Jeffrey Townsend," Dumont said calmly, "was not a man to lose things. He kept a . . . very tight grip on what belonged to him."

"Meaning?"

Dumont smiled easily. "Why, I don't know, Miss Montana. I suppose that could mean anything."

"Mr. Dumont—"

"Luther," he suggested.

I hoped my distaste didn't show on my face. "Mr. Dumont," I repeated deliberately, "your remark seemed a bit suggestive, and I think you intended it to be. Do you have an alibi for that night?"

"Yes."

I shrugged. "Then you stand in no danger by telling me what you know or suspect. I, on the other hand, have a number of marks against me, which means that I badly want to find out who killed Townsend."

"I can understand that," he murmured.

"Good. Then tell me what you meant by saying that Townsend kept a tight grip on what belonged to him."

Dumont studied me for a moment, then shrugged. "He was a possessive, manipulative man who enjoyed controlling things. And people. If he said jump, he expected people to ask how high only on the way up. And that included his family as well as his business associates."

"You?"

"I was a business associate. And, to be perfectly honest, Miss Montana, I resented Jeff's determination to control every aspect of our ventures. But that was hardly a reason to kill him, was it?"

I wanted to say that blackmail was a very good reason, but I didn't want to give that bit of knowledge away just yet. Instead, I said, "How did Townsend exert control over his family? To your knowledge, I mean."

Dumont shrugged. "I was never inside their home, Miss Montana. I . . . infer my knowledge of his control over his family by what Jeff said in my presence, and the way he treated his wife in public. He boasted more than once that he provided strict guidance in all areas of his children's lives. And his wife was expected to be the perfect wife."

"Perfect in what way?" I asked.

"In every way. And I do mean perfect, especially in the physical sense. His image, you know. He told me that he'd sent Amy to a plastic surgeon a year or so ago to have a few crow's-feet removed from her eyes and to have her breasts lifted. They'd started to sag, he complained.''

After a moment, I said, ''He had that done against her will?''

''He said she begged him not to make her go. She was terrified of surgery, you see. He laughed about it. He said next time he'd have her ass tightened. That's a direct quote, by the way.'' His gaze dropped, as if in embarrassment, and then flicked upward. To gauge my reaction.

Jeffrey hadn't been a nice man but neither was Dumont. He'd enjoyed telling me about Amy's surgery, and not only because it reflected badly on Jeffrey. He'd enjoyed picturing Amy's desperate pleas in his mind, enjoyed the thought of her being controlled like that. It was obvious in that quick upward dart of his eyes and the intentness in them. He almost licked his lips.

I felt queasy, and I knew he saw it.

In a gently reflective tone, Dumont went on. ''Jeff set very high standards for his public image. His wife had to be the most beautiful woman in the room, the sexiest. And Amy almost always was, you know. He made sure she never gained a pound and was never seen looking less than her best. In public, he was always courteous and affectionate toward her, touching her, hugging her. And yet, Miss Montana, in ten years, I've never heard him talk about her as if she were anything to him but a beautiful possession he wore on his arm. Just like his Rolex.''

Did I believe everything Dumont was telling me? Not necessarily; I knew he had a hell of a grudge against Jeffrey Townsend. And yet, it meshed with the mental image I'd been drawing of Townsend. It also fit, in a crazy kind of way, the blackmail. Maybe Jeffrey had needed someone he could trust absolutely to boast to and confide in, and Dumont had had too much to lose himself to risk betraying the confidences.

Until now, anyway. And now Dumont was thoroughly enjoying his opportunity to finally talk.

"He had a mistress," Dumont said abruptly.

"Did he tell you that?"

"No. But he complained that Amy bored him in bed. She wasn't adventurous enough to suit him. He said that he'd trained her right—his phrase—since he'd gotten her . . . fresh out of a convent when she was barely a woman. He taught her all his favorite games, so she didn't, according to him, mind wearing slinky things or wigs for a bit of variety. Still, he said he was tired of her, bored with her. He told me that years ago."

"Do you think he would have divorced her?"

"If he could have blamed her for it, yes."

"What do you mean?" I asked slowly.

Dumont laced his fingers together over his stomach and leaned back in his chair, frowning a bit. "He had to have the perfect wife, Miss Montana. A beautiful wife so other men would envy him. He liked seeing lust in the eyes of men watching his wife. But we all age, don't we? Unfortunately, though a man can be considered handsome well into old age, a woman rarely is. Jeff wouldn't have wanted an old wife. Eventually, the plastic surgery to lift and tighten and enhance wouldn't have . . . improved her enough.

"But Jeff wouldn't have dumped his wife because she was looking too worn. That would have been a bad move for the public image. He would have found a way to be the injured party himself, and he wouldn't have waited much longer, I think. It would have been easy enough to do. Pay some handsome boy to seduce Amy."

I frowned a little. "I got the impression Jeffrey's pillar-of-the-community public image wasn't the only one important to him. He didn't strike me as the kind of man who would like being seen as a cuckold."

"Perceptive of you," Dumont murmured. "But you have to understand Jeffrey's priorities. He was strongly, frankly sexual; he had no doubts whatsoever of his masculinity. And since he was certain of that, his public image as a good man was the one he felt a need to protect. Being wronged by one's beautiful, heartless wife would inspire sympathy; dumping an aging wife because of a few crow's-feet would invite scorn.''

I could see the reasoning clearly enough. And what the results would have been. Jeffrey Townsend, the wronged husband, publicly shattered by his adored wife's infidelity. (He'd been known for his pious speeches about the sanctity of home and family.) Poor Amy, humiliated and disgraced.

If you or I play around outside marriage vows, it generally stays in the family, so to speak. But let a married woman in the Townsend's set get caught in bed with a lover and she might as well wear a scarlet letter.

I considered and rejected the notion that Townsend might have pushed Amy toward Fane's bed; as Dumont had said, much easier to pay some handsome young stranger to get the job done. I thought Amy had gotten Fane on her own, and entirely without her husband's knowledge.

What really bothered me was the realization that if Dumont knew how Townsend's mind worked (assuming he was being truthful), then Amy must have, too. She would have known Jeffrey was thinking along the lines of replacing her, and she would have known how he'd go about it. Hell, he might have told her so himself. He'd been enough of a bastard to do that.

And, to my mind, that strengthened Amy's motive to murder her husband. An amicable ending to a marriage was one thing, and perfectly acceptable, but Jeffrey's version of a tidy divorce would have ruined her socially. It wouldn't have mattered to some women; was Amy the type to choose murder over social disgrace? I just didn't know, but I had to consider the possibility. She could have decided to make herself a respectable widow before Jeffrey could drag her through the mud.

But she had an alibi . . .

I looked up to find Dumont watching me and forced

myself to think clearly. "You said he had a mistress. But he didn't tell you so?"

"No, but, as I said, Jeffrey considered himself something of a stud. If he was bored with Amy, you can bet he didn't waste any time finding himself a fresh new piece."

It occurred to me that Dumont was going out of his way to lace his conversation with blunt sexual phrases—unless he talked like this all the time. Whatever the reason, it only made me feel a little sick and definitely in need of a bath. I tried to turn the conversation in another direction. "You hated him, didn't you?"

He smiled. "Miss Montana, I hated his guts."

Boldly, I said, "Then why were you in business with him?"

"Profit conquers all."

I let him think I accepted that. "I see. Still, it's a good thing you have that alibi. Lucky, I mean."

"Luckier than you know," he said dryly.

"Why?"

"Any other week," Luther Dumont said, "I wouldn't have had an alibi."

I felt a prickling sensation in my head, the way you do when your subconscious is jabbing at you. Slowly, I said, "What do you mean by that?"

He shrugged. "The poker game I enjoy with my friends is a weekly event. We always play on Tuesday night."

"Then why Monday night this week?"

Dumont smiled and said gently, "No, Miss Montana, I didn't change nights to give myself an alibi. It wasn't my idea at all. One of my friends had a vacation planned and needed Tuesday night to get ready for it. He suggested we play on Monday night, and the rest of us agreed."

"When was the change decided on?"

"Monday afternoon. Luckily, we were all able to play that night."

So, I thought, the most likely person to have killed Townsend had an alibi more or less by accident. Habits . . .

Suddenly, I said, "What do you usually do on Monday night?"

"Watch football. Alone."

I wondered how many people had known that. But I didn't ask. I had a lot to think about. But I did have one final question for Dumont.

"Why were you curious about my involvement, Mr. Dumont?"

With what sounded like perfectly honest sincerity, Dumont replied, "Jeff had a rather nasty habit of using levers against people; I was curious if that was the reason he'd wanted to hire you. We were considering a venture in partnership with a local businessman who hasn't a mark against him. I thought Jeff might perhaps have wanted you to dig up a little dirt, assuming any could be found."

I didn't comment on Dumont's assumption that I would have been willing to take on such a job. "So he'd have a lever. To use how?"

"Oh, Jeff wasn't greedy." Dumont smiled unpleasantly. "He'd likely have demanded sixty percent of the profits rather than fifty. He just liked to know other people's secrets, Miss Montana. It gave him a sense of power."

"Did he know your secrets?"

"I don't have any secrets," he replied placidly.

Well, I'd hardly expected him to volunteer the fact that a certain photo and negatives existed. I got to my feet and edged toward the door. "Well, thanks for your time, Mr. Dumont—"

"We could have dinner," he suggested in a silky voice, rising behind the desk. "Maybe if we talked about it, I could help you find out why Jeff wanted to hire you."

"Thanks all the same," I managed to say, "but I have to get home."

"Another time, then."

I didn't tell him not to count on it. God help me, it was always possible I'd have to see him again. I wasn't sure if I couldn't stand him because of the picture I'd seen or because of that peculiar sexual aura he exuded, but whichever it was, I knew my reaction to him was too strong to allow me to pretend I enjoyed the man's company. One of these days, I'm going to have to find someone to teach me how to play poker.

I escaped as quickly as possible without bolting and drove home without making a stop; I was hungry, but there was also a bad taste in my mouth.

Jason's black Cougar was parked at my place. I parked beside it and went up to the loft. He was in the kitchen area cooking something that smelled good. (In addition to getting gold flecks in his eyes, Jason also got whatever culinary talents my family could boast.)

He waved a knife at me. "I wanted to—"

Ignoring him, I went into the bathroom and brushed my teeth. Thoroughly.

"—find out what you've been up to. You haven't told me what you found out yesterday *or* today," he finished as I returned.

"What're you cooking?" I asked, absently patting Choo as I leaned against the breakfast bar. My cat was sitting on the bar, needing only a few rings on his tail to be the image of the royal felines of Siam. (If you don't know the story, legend has it that a princess entrusted her valuable rings to her Siamese cat whenever she went in bathing; she'd slide them over the cat's tail for safekeeping. But one day the cat allowed the rings to fall into the water, and the enraged princess tied a knot in his tail the next time she let him guard them. Which is why, to this day, all purebred Siamese cats have a kink in their tails. Or something like that.)

"Steaks and salad," Jason replied briskly, chopping various vegetables and tossing them into my big wooden salad bowl. "Did you just brush your teeth?"

"Yes."

"Why?"

"I want healthy teeth."

He lifted an eyebrow at me. "Sure. Why, Lanie?"

"Because I just came from meeting Luther Dumont,

that's why," I said. "Between the man himself and what he had to tell me, I got a very bad taste in my mouth."

"The man himself? What's wrong with him? Rumor has it he's a bit shady, but—"

"I forgot you didn't know." I shook my head. "God, this has been a long day. Jase, Drew found out that Townsend had a trap installed. That's a—"

"I know what it is. Drew told me. So you managed to get a look at what was inside?"

"Um, yes." I explained my trip to the estate with Trey, keeping it brief. I also explained the pictures—the one that could have been me as well as the one of Dumont.

Jason was silent for a moment while he turned the steaks under the broiler, then straightened and looked at me seriously. "So the police did have something they believed gave you a motive. And now?"

I shrugged. "It isn't much better now. Sure, I can prove I'm not the woman in that picture. But I'm still the only one the police can place on the estate that night."

"Trey doesn't think you did it?"

"No. But he'll have to turn what he has over to the D.A. eventually. In default of a better suspect, yours truly is likely to be wearing the handcuffs."

"You don't really believe that?"

"To be on the safe side, I think I'd better."

"Um. See your point."

"I thought you would. So I have *got* to figure out who really did it."

"Dumont has the best motive," Jason observed.

"And an airtight alibi. Which he wasn't supposed to have."

"Huh?"

I explained what Dumont had told me, finishing with, "He wouldn't have offered that bit to me if it wasn't true. On any other week, Dumont would have been alone in his house watching television on Monday night. But this week, a lucky fluke provided him with an alibi."

"Not a planned lucky fluke?"

"I don't think so. Trey believes those other men weren't lying, and they say that Dumont wasn't out of their sight for more than five minutes at a time. I doubt very much that three men conspired to give him an alibi for murder. It just isn't practical. He couldn't have killed Townsend."

Jason thought about that while I pushed Choo to the other end of the bar and began setting out plates and silverware for us. Putting a hand on my cat's solid belly distracted me, and I said, "Did you feed him?"

"He devoured a pound of shrimp," Jason said absently.

"Damn. I fed him before I left. The vet wants him to lose at least a few pounds."

"I would have waited until you came," Jason explained, "but Choo greeted me at the door with all the air of a neglected, abandoned, and starving specimen of cathood."

"He's good at that," I agreed, eyeing Choo irritably. "I thought cats were supposed to be dignified."

"Yours isn't. Listen, Lanie, if Dumont didn't do it, then who did? You said the rest of them had solid alibis."

"Yes, except for Fane."

"Who?"

"Randal Fane, the family lawyer."

"He's a suspect?"

I grimaced. "Mrs. T. *does* have a lover on the side. At least, I think so. I saw them in a clinch yesterday at the house. And if Dumont was telling me the truth about Townsend, I don't blame Amy a bit, because—"

"Wait." Jason held up a hand. "I've got two days of your sleuthing to catch up on, and I'd rather hear about it in order. Tell me while we eat."

So, while we sat at the bar and ate supper, I filled my brother in on what had been happening.

"So," Jason said when I had paused for breath, "Fane *might* have done it, but you don't think he did?"

"No. If he made sure everybody else had an alibi, it's a lead-pipe cinch he'd have one himself."

Jason stared at me. "Did you hear what you just said?"

I was baffled. "What?"

"Lanie . . . do you think all these alibis were planned? That the murderer made sure everybody'd be covered?"

I opened my mouth, and then closed it for a few beats while I thought. "You know . . . I think I do believe that. It's been bothering me all along. Everyone was nicely out of the way, except for Fane—and me. I was obviously meant to be a suspect; Dumont was *probably* meant to be a suspect unless the killer knew he'd switched his poker night, and I doubt that, since they'd only decided that afternoon."

"What about Fane?"

"Maybe he was supposed to have an alibi." I looked at my brother, trying to make it come clear. "If he *was*, then this whole thing was planned to . . . to protect everyone involved, except for me and Dumont."

"How do you figure?"

"Well . . . Look, Jase, suppose you were going to murder someone. Would you be worried about alibis other than your own?"

"Probably not," he admitted. "Unless—"

"Unless someone you cared about was likely to become a suspect."

"You don't think Townsend was killed Monday night just because he happened to be alone; you think he was killed then because everyone involved had an alibi. What makes you so sure of that?"

"The fact that all the alibis are too good, too tight. That just isn't reasonable. And if I find out that Fane was *supposed* to have an alibi, I'll be sure."

Jason whistled softly. "Okay, you've sold me. The killer knew about Dumont being blackmailed, do we assume that?"

"For now, let's assume it."

"Right. So the killer maybe watches Dumont long enough to know he spends his Monday nights alone; and maybe he also knows that you tend to be at large in the evenings. Anyway, he's going to get you out to the estate by a faked message, which puts you neatly on the spot with murky motives, plenty of means and opportunity. The time of death is bound to be a little vague, because it always is. You're a suspect. The killer is reasonably sure that Dumont's very shady reputation and—supposed—lack of an alibi will work against him, so it's likely he'll be a suspect as well, even if the police don't discover the blackmail. And everybody else is very neatly accounted for.''

"Except for Fane. If *he* did it, I'd expect him to have a better alibi. He's no fool; just to be on the safe side, he would have assumed the police would find out about him and Amy. And once they knew, it gave Fane a good motive.''

"But is it good enough?'' Jason mused. "Like you said, divorce is easier. And even if Amy had to take the blame for the divorce, Fane isn't poor, so he wouldn't give a damn if she brought nothing but herself out of that marriage.''

"Remember what Dumont told me? Jeffrey would have ruined Amy in a divorce, just to make himself an object of sympathy. If Fane knew that and believed she'd be destroyed by it . . . That's a motive I could believe for him.''

"But can you believe that stuff Dumont told you?''

I thought about it. "My impulse is to say yes, because I think Jeffrey was a bastard. But it isn't only that. Jase, I saw the wigs and sexy underwear Amy has, and I don't think she bought them for herself because she isn't the type; the fact that she has them backs up what Dumont said about Jeffrey liking variety. Dumont said he'd never been inside the house, and I believe that, because it would be too easy to prove otherwise. But how else would he know about the wigs? Amy doesn't wear them in public, that I know.

"Also, I saw the picture of Jeffrey tied up in bed with a woman who wasn't Amy, which is fair evidence that he didn't think much of his marriage vows. And I saw the picture and negatives he must have been using to black-

mail Dumont, which makes it clear that he liked controlling people.

"I've also studied the family history. As far as I could
tell, Jeffrey was always something of a bad boy. His wife
isn't mourning him noticeably, nor are his children, and
Dumont couldn't wait to vent some of *his* spleen."

"So you think that what Dumont told you about Townsend fits?"

"I think so. I mean, granted, he had every reason to
want to kill Jeffrey. He could have been pointing me toward Amy as a suspect to turn suspicion away from himself, but why would he? His alibi is solid as a rock, and
Amy never did him any harm that I can see."

"But what he told you *does* make it look bad for Amy."

"And Fane," I agreed. "I don't think it would have
bothered Fane very much if Jeffrey had opted to make his
wife look the guilty party in a messy divorce. But I'm
afraid it would have bothered Amy a lot, and Fane
wouldn't have liked that. There is one very large question,
though. If we suppose that Amy wanted out of the marriage—and I don't see why she'd have wanted to stay with
Jeffrey—then I would have expected Fane to tell Jeffrey to
plead no contest to a divorce or risk seeing his own reputation dragged through the mud."

"Tales of his cruelty to Amy?"

"Why not? Fane wasn't some gigolo hired to seduce
Amy; he's clearly in love with her. He's a man with a good
reputation, and people would listen to him. So, why didn't
he do that? The only way I could see Fane's risking a
murder is if Jeffrey had something on *him.*"

"Something worth murder?"

"Yeah. I mean, threats only work if there's no counterbalance. If Jeffrey had something really dirty on Fane,
then it wouldn't do Fane any good to threaten him without
taking a big risk himself—murder might have been the
only way out for Fane as well as Amy."

Jason got up to get more coffee, frowning thoughtfully.

When he sat down again, he said, "You think Jeffrey really liked to blackmail people, don't you?"

"I think he did. But I also think that he usually didn't take it very far. What Dumont said about that rang true, that Jeffrey liked to know people's secrets because it gave him a sense of power. But if he'd been *actively* blackmailing anybody but Dumont, there would have been a few more things in the trap. So I don't think he had anything on Fane."

"Which," Jason said, "removes Fane from the role of First Murderer."

"I'd say so. Especially if I find out that he *should* have had an alibi."

"And that leaves you with the family—all of whom have nice, solid alibis—or a stranger, unknown to us at this point, who managed to bypass a hell of a security system."

Jason left me to brood about that while he efficiently cleaned up the kitchen. He's good about doing things like that; Mother believes firmly in equality between the sexes, so Jason was expected to do his share from an early age. That's why he can cook. (I have no excuse for not being able to.)

Finished, he said, "So what're you going to do next?"

"Tomorrow's Friday. I think I'll try to talk to a few of the people in Jeffrey's life."

"To confirm what Dumont said about him?"

"Yeah. If all that was true, Amy's got a pretty strong motive aside from her affair with Fane. I need to be more sure of that."

"And then?"

Feeling more than a little daunted, I said, "And then I've got to take a closer look at those damned alibis. One of them *must* have been fabricated, and the seams have got to show somewhere."

"I think it's Amy," Jason said reflectively. "She tied up the bearskin rug and took it away because she hated the thing. You said she hated it, didn't you?"

"I got that impression. But she wouldn't have used a drapery tie to bundle up the rug. It left the window looking crooked."

Jason blinked. "She'd worry about that in the middle of a murder?"

"Yes."

"I've got to meet her," he muttered.

"Never mind. Thanks for cooking supper, Jase."

"Don't mention it." He leaned against the bar and folded his arms, smiling gently. "I'm not leaving yet, though. There's one more thing we haven't discussed."

I should have known.

"I've had a very long day. Good night, Jase."

"Trey Fortier. He took you into the Townsend house, where neither of you had any business being with the family absent. He allowed you to open a hidden trap, which brings to mind the phrase 'tainted evidence,' and he just happened to have with him a piece of evidence that looked rather damning against you."

"So?" I said weakly.

"Looks to me like he's risking his job to cover your ass."

I had a sudden (entirely unwanted) sensual image fill my mind, and I felt my face get hot. For those of you without a dirty mind, the phrase 'cover your ass' was the basis of the image.

The mind plays tricks on us all.

"He knows I didn't kill Jeffrey," I said in some confusion. "He thinks I can help him find out who did. That's all."

"Uh-huh. Running, Lanie?"

I retreated from the bar and curled up on the couch, hugging a pillow. (All right, I was feeling insecure again!) Of course, Jason followed me and sat on my coffee table with the patient expression of a man waiting to have things explained to him.

"You don't understand," I said with great originality.

Jason looked pained. "No? Then make me."

"He confuses me, damn it. Sometimes he's a cop—and then he's not a cop. He waltzes in and out of my mind like it has swinging doors, and *his* is about as open as a bank vault. I doubt that we have anything at all in common—except that he's a cat person and we're both involved in this murder. Hell, Jase, he may be the one to arrest me!"

"Seems to me he's bending over backward to *not* be the one," Jason said.

"That makes it worse." I hugged the pillow tighter. "Don't you see? I'd know how to react to a cop. And I'd know how to react to a man."

"But in this situation," Jason said softly, "you don't know how to react to both."

"I'm a suspect, I can't forget that. He can't either, even though he knows I'm innocent. And then there's everything going on around us. This case . . . the more I find out about Townsend, the dirtier it gets. I feel—I feel dirty myself. I don't like this, Jase. I never wanted to be this kind of detective."

"You just wanted to find lost things," Jason murmured. "I wonder if you even know why."

"Because there's nothing else I'm good at," I said irritably.

Jason smiled a little, but rose to his feet. "Well, I can't see any shortcuts for you. If you're lucky, this murder will be resolved before you and Trey have to thrash out what's between you. It should be easier to . . . react to him then."

I frowned up at him. "And what if I'm not lucky?"

"Then," my dear and only brother said gently, "a suspect and a cop will have to do the best they can."

"That's what I'm afraid of," I said miserably.

"You don't suspect his motives, do you?"

I hesitated, then shrugged. "I think that's part of it. When he looks at me like a cop, I wonder if he's not just using me as a means to an end." I could feel my lips twist in a faint grimace. "I think I'll try to stay out of his way for a few days and think it through. If I have a few days, that is.''

And that was the question.

After Jase had left, I called Drew to ask him to contact the trap man, and he told me the man would be in Atlanta by the following afternoon. Then, tired and worried, I went to bed earlier than usual.

WHEN I WOKE UP the next morning, it was with the sense of something having just flitted through my mind. You know what I mean? It's like hearing three notes of a tune and it sounds so familiar that it drives you nuts trying to remember the rest of the song.

I groped my way to the kitchen, fed Choo, and put the coffee on, then stood under the shower trying to get the damned tune. What was it? The murder, of course; I wasn't thinking about much else these days. But what about it? Whatever it was, it floated just out of reach maddeningly.

When I got out of the shower I was a bit more awake, but thirsting for coffee. I dressed in one of those nifty all-purpose (except for exercise) sweat suits, which is about as close as I willingly get to chic. This one was beautifully color coordinated in shades of green and perfectly matched the stripes on my running shoes. A clotheshorse, that's me. The shoes were a bit scuffed, but other than saying "Damn," I didn't do anything about them.

I ate a Pop-Tart and drank my first cup of coffee, which cleared the cobwebs somewhat. By the time I was halfway through the second cup, that tune danced through my mind again, and this time I grabbed it by the toe.

Patterns.

Now, what the hell did that mean?

"Patterns," I said experimentally to Choo, who was sitting companionably on the bar.

"Hroo," he said, blinking.

"You're a lot of help," I said.

I thought about it. Patterns in events. Patterns in . . .

behavior. Things that matched other things. A reaction to an action or event. A response that was habitual.

"What if Dumont really did think Townsend had wanted to hire me to dig up dirt?" Choo blinked at me again, and I stared at him intensely. "What if that was a habit of Jeffrey's? And if he couldn't find any dirt . . . what if he manufactured it?"

I felt my eyes beginning to cross and hastily looked away from my cat. There was something in what I'd just said, but I wasn't sure what it was.

In general, dirt doesn't stick to innocent people. I mean, in order to be blackmailed, you pretty much have to have a secret you don't want to be made public. But . . . I supposed you could be framed so that it *looked* like you had a secret; if the circumstances were damning enough and your public image precious to you, that could be enough to make you bow to blackmail.

Patterns. Jeffrey had liked controlling people. Patterns. Jeffrey had apparently been blackmailing his partner for years in order to have the upper hand. Patterns. Jeffrey would have planned to be the injured party whenever he decided to dump Amy. Patterns.

Okay, I thought, but that still wasn't right. That wasn't what I'd been trying to make come clear in my mind. Something that somebody had said, something that had reminded me of a pattern.

Damn it, what *was* it?

There was, somewhere in all this, a pattern. There had to be. A logical sequence of events that had led to a man being murdered. For every action, there is an equal and opposite reaction . . . Eliminate the impossible; whatever remains, however improbable, must be truth . . .

I sat with my eyes half-closed and just let the jumbled thoughts flit through my mind, not trying to catch any of them now. Disparate images and ideas, half-focused pictures, half-remembered words and phrases.

As far as I could tell, the only result was to give me a headache. Abandoning the effort, I tried to concentrate on what my next step should be. I'd told Jason that I wanted to talk to a few of the people in Jeffrey's life, but I wasn't sure now that it would get me anywhere. With his murder still being investigated, it was highly unlikely that anyone in his company would be willing to talk to me, and I knew very well that anyone I hadn't already talked to in his personal life would probably be uncooperative.

So . . . what?

The damned alibis, that was what.

I was still determined to avoid Trey for a while, so I wasn't very willing to drive to the station and ask to see everyone's statement. I knew I needed to do that, because I hadn't actually *seen* the statements with my own eyes and I wanted to, for whatever good it would do.

However, in the meantime . . .

NINE

I SPENT the early part of the afternoon going back over the research I'd collected on the Townsend family. Did I expect to find anything new? No. Did I find anything new? No.

A couple more questions occurred to me, and after making a few calls I had at least one answer. But it didn't seem to get me any closer to finding out who had killed Jeffrey Townsend, and I was feeling a combination of frustration, confusion, and distaste about the whole thing.

At three o'clock, I called Marc Dennison.

Marc had been, in the words of my brother, one of those "nice guys" I'd been involved with. Divorced (relatively painlessly, he said) and definitely not in the market for ties, Marc had suited me just fine a couple of years ago. He was blond and fair and casually charming. We had enjoyed one another's company without feeling any need to move in together or otherwise deepen the relationship.

To be honest, sleeping with Marc had been rather like spending time with a buddy who made you feel good: pleasant enough that you looked forward to the visits, but out of sight, out of mind, if you know what I mean. He had spent much of our six-month relationship trying to convince me that I needed a computer and had, after we ended it amiably, gotten me one at cost from a friend of his. An IBM PC, if you're wondering.

Marc wasn't as obsessed with his computers as some

hackers seemed to be, but it was definitely more than a hobby with him. Since he was an investment broker, he often worked on his system at home, and I guess it had been natural for him to learn more and more about how computers worked. At any rate, he was the smartest person I knew when it came to gathering data on just about anything.

He had also (and I'd never asked how) managed to rig his system so that he could get into virtually any data bank he wanted. He once told me that he'd figured out a scheme to bilk a fortune from banks and bemoaned the fact that he was too honest to do it.

Anyway.

Marc was at home when I called, and he sounded mildly pleased to hear from me.

"Lane, hi. What's up? Need a fourth for bridge?"

He knew I hated card games.

"Do I only call you when I want something?" I asked, feeling a bit guilty.

"Usually." He chuckled. "Don't worry about it. You take things too much to heart. What do you need? Another rundown of a license plate?"

"No, not this time." Marc was my unofficial link to the DMV. "Something a bit more complicated."

"Shoot."

"I have some names, and I'd like to know anything you can dig up about them. Especially any records of the property they own, even if they've run the titles through holding companies."

"Okay, give me the names."

I gave him the names of Jeffrey Townsend, Amy Townsend (on the slim chance that she owned property on her own), Randal Fane, and Luther Dumont. Just for the hell of it, I also asked if he could access the school records of Jeff III and Samantha.

"I'll see what I can do," Marc said, blessedly (and typically) incurious about either the names or my reasons for wanting the information. "Get your system ready and leave it on-line; I'll send the stuff via modem, so you can make a hard copy."

I was glad he couldn't see my wince; I had promised him I'd use the system, but it took up so much room on my desk . . . "Great. I really appreciate this, Marc."

"I'll make you buy me dinner one night," he returned cheerfully.

"Just say when."

After I hung up, I reflected that there was at least one plus to getting involved with nice guys; they tended to stay friends after it was over.

I went to a closet and hauled out the computer and printer, and all the other paraphernalia, telling myself somewhat guiltily that I really should use the stuff more often; even at cost, it hadn't been cheap. I'd toyed once or twice with the idea of installing some kind of minidesk in the corner and making a computer station there, but I use the thing so rarely that it hardly seemed worthwhile.

Anyway, I cleared off my desk and started connecting cables and plugs, hoping I was doing it the right way and wondering ruefully what I hoped to gain by this. I doubted that Marc could get me any information the police weren't already in possession of, and I didn't even know what I was looking for. At least, not really.

A pattern, I supposed. The problem was, there was so much information in my head now that I was worried I wouldn't see a pattern even if it was marked out in red ink.

I got everything connected, fed the first sheet of a stack of that nifty fanfold computer paper into the printer, and then sat down and turned the beasties on. The printer signaled that it was ready with a beep and then hummed neutrally as it waited for input; the computer automatically loaded its operating system from the hard disk and then waited politely for me to tell it what program I wanted.

Realizing that my mind was blank, I hunted in the desk until I found the instructions Marc had written down for me, then followed them scrupulously. Within minutes, I was ready to receive data. The computer had been given its instructions to instruct the printer to print whatever came in; the modem was hooked up and ready; everything was in a standby mode, including me.

Now all I had to do was wait for the phone to ring.

BY SEVEN O'CLOCK, I was listening to the printer work busily and contemplating my choices for supper. They weren't promising. Fast food, remember? I had a few frozen dinners, a few canned dinners, and a few boxed dinners. What on earth did people do before microwaves and McDonald's?

Luckily, Jason arrived with Chinese takeout.

"Your phone was busy, so I took a chance," he said as I let him in.

I trailed along after him to the kitchen, enticed by those little white boxes like a donkey by a carrot. "You're a superior brother," I told him gratefully. "I was going to microwave something."

"I hope Trey can cook," Jason murmured.

I ignored that. "You did get egg rolls, didn't you?"

"Yes. What're you printing over there?"

"God knows. I called Marc and asked him to do some digging for me. I thought I'd wait until it's all in before I start sifting through it."

"Faithful Marc."

I didn't say anything in response until we were sitting at the bar with our feast. Then, trying to keep my voice casual, I said, "Don't snipe at Marc."

"I wouldn't think of it."

"He's a nice guy."

"Oh, definitely."

I gritted my teeth and counted silently to ten. What had gotten into Jason these days? He wasn't sarcastic by nature, and he had never in our lives needled me the way he had lately. Fixing my attention on my sweet and sour pork, I muttered, "If you have something to say, damn it, say it."

Jason ate silently for a few moments, then contemplated his chopsticks with detached interest. "Useful things, chopsticks. I don't know why we think forks are better."

I speared a piece of pork. "Because some of us can't use chopsticks, that's why." Me, for one. "Is that what you wanted to say?"

Mildly, my brother said, "I wonder why we always have these momentous discussions over food."

"Food for the body *and* the mind, I suppose." I remained patient with effort; Jason was going to take his own sweet time getting to whatever he wanted to say.

"Mother called this afternoon," he said.

As bombshells went, it wasn't as bad as it could have been. But close enough. "Oh, yeah?" I kept my voice casual. "Any particular reason?"

Jason gave me a look. "Lanie, you know our mother. There's always a reason."

"What is it this time?" I could have guessed.

"She's getting married."

I would have guessed correctly.

"Anybody we know?"

"Not yet. They'll honeymoon in Europe for a few weeks, she said. His name's Adam Rowland."

You may be wondering why I reacted so apathetically to the news. I had conjured a bit of enthusiasm the first time. In fact, I'd been reasonably enthusiastic the first three times. But when I tell you that this Adam Rowland would be stepfather number seven, you may understand why the news barely moved me at all.

Our mother likes getting married. Not staying married, mind you, just getting married. Don't get me wrong—she always marries for love. Always. And she's always genuinely heartbroken when she discovers her love doesn't last.

I could write the scenario word for word after nearly twenty years of practice. Mother would be glowing and happy, delightedly embracing whatever offspring her new spouse had produced to date (I have stepsiblings all over the world, many of whom I've never met). That stage would last about six months. Next would come a burst of restlessness, during which her new husband would try anxiously to please her (Men always try to please Mother. Always.) while she redecorated madly or took up a new hobby or something.

After three or four months of that, Mother would discover that the blush had left the rose. She'd try to save the marriage. Some kind of therapy if her husband was amenable, endless emotional discussions between the two of them if he wasn't.

Less than a year from her wedding day, Mother would be divorced again. She'd descend on Jase and me, having come to the conclusion that only her loving children could be her anchor in an unstable universe.

Am I mocking her? No.

I took a sip of my iced tea, then said to Jase, "Well, maybe she'll strike gold this time."

"We're invited to the wedding."

We always were. "Where?"

"London. Next week."

Neither of us would go. We'd stopped attending Mother's nuptials after stepfather number three. We would wire flowers and congratulations; with luck, we might even get to meet this one before he became an ex.

"Lanie . . . you don't have to be like her."

Jason had finally gotten to the point.

"No? Look at the last ten years, Jase. The only difference is that Mother gets married and I don't."

He shook his head sharply. "No. The difference is that Mother's always looking for love and you're terrified of finding it."

"Why would I be—?"

"You know as well as I do. A number of reasons, but I'll name just one: you thought you'd found love with Phil. And when that blew up in your face, you decided not to take the chance—of finding or losing it—again. Jesus, Lanie, look at . . . Marc, for instance. One of your lame dogs."

"What?" I was honestly bewildered.

Jason laughed oddly. "You've never noticed the pattern, have you? They're always hurting, wounded. Marc had just been divorced. So had Steve. And Tim had a history of rocky relationships behind him. You took them in, just the way you'd take in a hungry dog or a bird with a broken wing. Took them in and offered companionship and peace. No violent emotions, no wild highs or lows—just a stable calm. And when they healed, you booted them very gently out of your bed. But not out of your life. They're all good friends now."

"What's your point?" I asked tightly.

"Lanie . . . you aren't like Mother. She needs to be loved, constantly. We both know that. You need to be *needed*. You need to be important to somebody, but you aren't willing to risk your own emotions. So, the lame dogs. Take them in, heal them, and then push them away before they start to need more from you than just peace."

Have you ever entered a room and unexpectedly come face-to-face with your own reflection in a mirror? If so, you've probably felt that odd, disoriented "Is that me?" feeling. A split-second of looking at a stranger and wondering how it could ever be you. I felt like that now.

Was my brother right? It was something to think about.

I drew a deep breath. "You know, it seems that lately I get knocked on my ass every time I see you."

He smiled a little. "The last time Mother got married," he said dryly, "you went on a cleaning spree that lasted two weeks. Hell, you even cleaned *my* loft. And you only do that when you're trying to work through your emotions."

Finally, I realized what he was trying to do. "I see. So you didn't want the news of Mother's latest wedding to be the final straw on my back."

"Something like that. You're under a great deal of stress at the moment. I was afraid you'd get it into your head—despite all my rational arguments—that the apple really doesn't fall very far from the tree. You *aren't* Mother,

Lanie. In fact, you're almost totally opposite. Mother's made a habit of marrying in haste, but you'd never do that. You're so damned cautious about relationships that you aren't willing to even risk being wrong.''

The printer stopped just then, and in the sudden silence of the loft, I said, "Okay. Point taken. But knowing all that doesn't really help, Jase."

He nodded. "I know."

"Trey . . . isn't a lame dog."

"Far from it. If you find out that he does need you, I doubt it'll be anything tame. And I don't think that he'd meekly let you boot him out of your life. I warned you once, Lanie: Don't let the elegant pose fool you. He's a fighter."

It occurred to me then (all right, so I'm slow on the uptake) that Jason was hellbent to get me involved with Trey. I suppose I should have been indignant about it, but I was, more than anything else, curious. Jason had met Trey once—just once—and had apparently made up his mind that this was *it*.

"What did you see?" I asked suddenly. "When you looked at Trey, what was it?"

For an instant, he looked surprised, even disconcerted. Then, slowly, he said, "I don't know, Lanie. Any more than you know how you find things."

I didn't press him. I wasn't entirely sure that I wanted the answer. We finished eating, and then I went over to the computer while he cleared the leftovers. I turned off the machines and unhooked the modem, then gathered a daunting stack of paper from the printer and carried it to the couch.

"If you're not doing anything tonight," I said, "stay and help me go through this. I'm so addled by now that if I saw a confession written out in words of one syllable I'd probably miss the importance of it."

Jason brought coffee over and sat down, looking at the stack of paper with a lifted brow. "Marc was thorough, I see. What'd you ask him to find?"

"Whatever's on record." I divided the stack and handed half to him. "I don't know what I'm looking for. Just . . . something. A pattern. An answer instead of another damned question."

"Do my best," Jason said, and began reading.

But I was the one who found it. I'd waded through pages of Townsend properties and investments (none in Amy's name), years of Jeff III and Samantha's school courses and grades, and too many flash-in-the-pan business deals between Luther Dumont and Townsend. Jase and I had each finished our stack and had exchanged them.

Jason couldn't be blamed for not seeing it, because I hadn't known what I was looking for until a bell went off in my head and I remembered something Trey had said. He'd said that if Amy and Randal Fane were having an affair, they had to be meeting somewhere. We had both dismissed the idea of hotels or motels, and I couldn't see them meeting at either of their homes—or the lake house, for that matter—because of the risk of Jeffrey finding out.

"Damn," I said.

Looking up, Jason said, "What? Find something?"

"Among his many other investments, Randal Fane owns a very large apartment complex."

"A love nest?" Jase suggested after a moment.

"Maybe."

"Won't the police have checked it out?"

"I don't think so. Marc apparently found this more or less by accident. Look. You can see he was listing the investments of record; then he took each of these companies and broke them down, because I specifically asked him to look for holding companies. The apartment complex is officially owned by a subsidiary of a company that Fane owns stock in, but he's used the subsidiary as a holding company. If the police run down Fane's investments, all they're going to see is that he owns stock in this company; why would they take it a step farther and find out what the *company* owns?"

Jason was studying the printout intently. "For a man

with nothing to hide," he said, "Fane sure covered his tracks."

"It's just a way of hiding assets," I said, dismissing that because it wasn't what was bothering me. "Jase, look at the number of units in the complex."

"Forty-seven. Big place."

"Bigger than you think. There are forty-eight units."

He blinked. "How do you know?"

"One of my clients lived there. The damned place is so big that I got lost. You know how I am with numbers; they were on little brass plaques to the left of the doors. Anyway, my client lived in the last block, in apartment number forty-six. When I finally found the right block, I found myself counting backward. And I started with forty-eight."

"So you think that last apartment isn't listed as rental property because Fane uses it himself?"

I half closed my eyes as I tried to visualize the place. "It's the last unit, a private entrance, screened from the road by a hedge. The parking is about as secluded as you can get in that neighborhood. And it's located just about halfway between Fane's house and the Townsend estate."

"So what're you going to do?"

I drank the remainder of my cooling coffee before I answered. "I'll go over there tomorrow. Talk to some of the tenants and find out if anyone saw anything."

"Before you tell Trey about this?"

"I—I want to check it out myself first."

Jason went to get more coffee and then returned to the couch and handed my cup back to me. "Are you looking for confirmation of the affair?" he asked curiously.

"No. I'm looking for someone who saw Amy Townsend here in Atlanta on Monday."

"I thought she was in New York."

"She apparently went to New York on Sunday. Checked into a hotel and saw an old school friend. And the police certainly located her there on Tuesday. The hotel staff says she was there; she didn't check out. But it's a big hotel."

Jason frowned at me. "You think she would have flown all the way to New York, then flown back here on the qt Monday just to spend time with Fane?"

I was beginning to feel like a voyeur, and it made me very uncomfortable. How much would I have to find out about these peoples' private lives before this mess started to make sense? Too much, I thought. Too many closets and dark corners and secrets.

"Lanie?"

I made myself concentrate. "I think . . . that fear would make her very, very cautious. If Jeffrey kept a tight rein on Amy, maybe she had to resort to elaborate schemes."

"Or maybe," Jason suggested, "the trip to New York was just to provide her with an alibi."

"Maybe." I didn't like saying it.

He frowned again. "You expect to find out she was here, don't you? Why? Fane could have killed Townsend, and Amy didn't have to come anywhere near; she has a solid alibi, he has a believable one, and Townsend is dead."

"Chocolates," I said.

After a moment, Jason said, "Right, men don't bring candy to other men."

"You have to admit it's unlikely. I know conspiracy is rare in murder cases, but if one of them did it, I think they were both in on it; I don't think Fane would have brought the candy, and I can't see Amy sticking a knife in her dead husband's chest. Maybe she showed up unexpectedly with a box of candy for Jeffrey, and then let Fane in later and he used the knife just to make sure."

"Maybe they both had to kill him," Jason said. "Like in that Agatha Christie story—I forget which one. Where several people conspired to kill a man, and each of them stabbed him; technically, they all killed him, but how in hell do you prove who stabbed a dead man and who stabbed a live one?"

I shook my head. "In this case, the muscle relaxers in the chocolates definitely killed him; he was stabbed after he was dead. So it isn't a matter of deciding which . . . blow got the job done.''

"Then, like you said, he was stabbed just to make sure.''

"Could be.''

Jason studied me for a moment. "But?''

"But. Aside from the fact that I don't believe Fane would risk murder if he had any other choice, there are just too many ends left dangling. The rug and drapery tie, the message on my machine, the datebook. What did Fane do—pull my name out of a hat, or stick a pin in the yellow pages? It doesn't make sense.''

"Unless he knew beforehand that Townsend had intended to hire you.''

"The more I think about that, the more unlikely it seems. I made a few calls this afternoon. I owe a few favors I'm not looking forward to paying back, but I did find out that Jeffrey *had* hired outside investigators in the past. But only those he could control.''

"What do you mean?''

"I mean he had something on them. Some knowledge that made them inclined to watch their step with him. Two of the investigators I called admitted it, though they wouldn't get specific. The third just said he hoped Jeffrey was roasting in hell, which indicates a few bruised sensibilities.''

"Um. And he hired these guys to . . . ?''

"Dig up dirt on business associates.''

Jason thought about that for a few moments. "So . . . since he couldn't have had anything on you, you don't believe he would have wanted to hire you.''

"Unless somebody convinces me otherwise, that's what I'm thinking. But what makes you so sure he couldn't have had anything on me?''

"Did he?''

"No.''

"That's what I thought. You're too honest for your own good,'' Jason said absently.

I wondered why that observation depressed me. "Well, anyway, I don't believe Jeffrey wanted to hire me. Which means that I was set up, not because I posed a threat to somebody, but just because I happened to be handy."

"Why were you handy?"

"That's the question I haven't figured out yet. Whoever killed Jeffrey must have been in my loft at some time, because how else would they know my machine is the same model as his?"

"Trial and error? Look, Lanie, suppose the killer planned to set you up—for whatever reason. He calls here, maybe just to find out if you have a machine or a service; most businesses do. He gets the machine and, because he knows how the things work, he leaves an unidentifiable message and then calls back to try to erase it. When it works fine, he knows he can carry out his plan."

"It's as reasonable as anything else in this damned case," I admitted. "A possibility. But it doesn't help answer any of the questions that I can see."

"True. Sorry, Lanie."

"Never mind." I leaned forward to drop my half of the printout onto the coffee table. "I'll just keep trying to make sense of it. Tomorrow's Saturday. I should be able to find some of the tenants at home at the apartment complex. Maybe I can find an answer or two."

"Good luck."

After my brother had gone, I went to my desk and turned the computer back on. This time, I loaded the word-processing program and then began typing everything I knew or speculated about the case in a loose summary-type format. My monitor was a color one, so I amused myself by assigning each suspect a particular color and listing the facts relating to them in their own color.

It was a vivid hodgepodge.

When my head started to ache, I saved the summary on the hard disk and then shut the system down. It was still early (for me, anyway) and I felt too restless to sleep. I took a shower and put on one of those loose, zip-up robes, then watched an old movie on cable. *The Thin Man.*

It turned out that the channel was having an all-night mystery marathon. I watched another of the movies with the vague idea of learning something from my fictional counterparts. Halfway through it, I wondered why it was so damned easy to spot the murderer in a book or movie, and so hard in real life.

I finally realized that books and movies don't generally have the room to put in a lot of extraneous stuff. When you watch a mystery movie and the camera pans across a particular section of a room, you *know* there's something important there, so you look carefully. And when suspect A says wildly that suspect B had it in for him, you can be fairly sure that's important as well. You could also be positive that *one* of the suspects was the killer, and if a character was taking up space without any valid reason, it was probably him.

(I've been known to drive Jase crazy by figuring out who the killer is early on in a movie. When he asks why I picked on that particular character, I always answer, "Well, why else is he *there?*" It almost always works.)

But, in real life, you aren't limited by budget or time considerations—and extraneous stuff is all over the place. There's no intently pointing camera to show where to look for the important bits, and no guarantee that one of the people suspected is actually the killer.

Just because I stumbled over secrets—Jeffrey's kinky sexual needs, Amy's affair with Fane, and the apparent blackmail of Luther Dumont because he liked little girls, for instance—didn't mean any of them were important to the case. Oh, sure, the blackmail gave Dumont a strong motive, but he had an alibi. The affair gave both Amy and Fane a motive, but they, too, had alibis (until proven otherwise). Jeffrey's kinky tastes didn't seem to fit anywhere except as an indication of the kind of man he had been.

Were the missing rug and drapery tie important? God knew. The fact that the message had been erased from my answering machine? Again, God knew. Jeffrey's apparent habit of blackmailing people? Luther Dumont's peculiar sexual aura? Samantha's red Mercedes? Jeff III's record collection? Amy's bland decorating?

I went to bed.

Sleep, some say, often brings counsel. If my subconscious counseled me that night, it forgot to tell my conscious to remember the advice in the morning.

I staggered through the last couple of hours of morning in my usual fashion, feeding Choo, putting on coffee, trying to shower away the cobwebs. I put on my spiffiest jogging outfit, ate a Pop-Tart, and drank coffee.

When I called the police station, Rudy Flint answered Trey's phone.

"The lieutenant's off today, Lane, but he'll be in tomorrow. Can I help?"

I was vaguely surprised that Trey took time off. "Probably, I imagine. Do you know if Randal Fane had some kind of appointment on Monday night that happened to fall through at the last minute?"

"Hold on a second."

I sat at my desk waiting patiently through several empty minutes, wondering absently which I preferred—the buzzing of a hold circuit or the elevator music some companies subject you to.

"Lane? Nobody thought to ask Fane that question. Is it important?"

"Damned if I know, Rudy." I sighed.

"If you want to call back later, I'll have an answer for you," Rudy said.

"Okay, fine. See you."

"Bye, Lane."

I chewed on my thumbnail for a while and thought about it. Would the answer to my question help me? No, I decided, not really. It would confirm my earlier theory of this whole thing's being carefully orchestrated—*if* Fane had an appointment and didn't cancel it himself because he knew he was going to meet Amy. If someone else had believed he had an alibi for that night, and hadn't known it had fallen through.

But if Fane had intended all along to meet Amy at the apartment, whether he had made an appointment for that night didn't really matter. Or, did it?

I wished I had a director panning a camera at the important stuff.

I got my car keys and stuffed my billfold in one pocket (I seldom carry a purse), then left. My escort fell dutifully in behind me, and I was interested to observe that there was only one man, and that he was totally unfamiliar to me. Though I couldn't be sure about it, I wondered if my role as a suspect had lessened dramatically after I had proven to Trey that I wasn't the girl in the smutty picture.

I thought about that, weighing the risks of losing this tail. Yes, I know—it sounds stupid in the extreme. But if this guy followed me to the apartment complex, he'd report where I'd gone, and the police would probably fix their attention there and wonder why. Granted, I didn't know for sure that I'd find a witness who could place Amy Townsend here in Atlanta on Monday evening, or who could place Randal Fane at the apartment rather than his house.

But if I *did,* and the police found out, I knew damned well one or both of them would be charged with murder.

I didn't want anybody arrested while I was fumbling around just trying to get my questions answered. Everybody was too tense about this case, too hungry for a killer. If I was going to provide evidence that would lock someone up, I damned well wanted to be sure it was the right evidence. (Remember how reluctant I'd been to tell Trey I'd seen Amy and Fane in a clinch.)

Losing my escort was relatively easy, and I didn't waste time heading to the apartment complex. I figured that my car might become hot pretty fast, so the less time I spent driving around the better. I parked in the semisecluded lot as far from the road as I could get.

I'd remembered the place fairly well. It was a complex

of town-house apartments, designed so that each block contained six units. Behind each unit was a postage-stamp-sized yard enclosed by a redwood fence, and in front was the parking. The first two blocks faced one another across a parking lot (also the private road leading into the complex), but the remaining six blocks faced in pairs, back-to-back, in a kind of fan shape.

Confusing, I know. That was why I'd gotten lost the first time I came here. Never mind trying to figure it out. All you have to know is that apartments thirty-seven through forty-eight faced across their backyards.

I believe in luck only when I fall into it. And it wasn't lucky for me to have begun with apartment thirty-seven, which was directly across from apartment forty-eight; that was just common sense and wishful thinking. What was lucky was that the occupant of number thirty-seven was Mrs. Anna Miller, and she was bored.

She was also thrilled to be visited by a real live detective.

Mrs. Miller was a widow with a cat and a parakeet (who eyed each other the entire time I was there), and she loved to talk. It was almost fifteen minutes before I could guide the conversation away from "Magnum P.I.", "Remington Steele", "Moonlighting", and various other fictional detective shows, and by then I had heard "You just don't *look* like a detective!" about three times too many.

"Mrs. Miller, do you have any idea who lives in the apartment across your yard? Number forty-eight?"

"There, now!" she said in a satisfied tone. "I knew there was something fishy about those two."

"Two?"

"That couple. He can say they both travel on business as often as he wants, what I say is that you never see either of them there unless the other is. You'd think he might spend a night or two alone, or she would, but that's not the way it is. Never just one, and I've yet to see them there more than a few hours at a time, and her looking as skittish as my cat during a storm. I'd bet my pension those two are married—and not to each other!"

"You've talked to them?"

"Just him. Said he was a salesman, but he looks like a cop to me. He also said his name was Smith. Can you believe that? Men are such fools when it comes to affairs. Don't you agree?"

I decided not to venture an opinion. "Um . . . can you describe them to me?"

An inquisitive nature has its uses; Anna Miller described Randal Fane and Amy Townsend beautifully.

I thought my informant probably spent a great deal of time looking out her upstairs windows. Deciding not to ask her that point-blank, I posed the next question as delicately as possible. "Mrs. Miller, did you happen to notice if they were there last Monday evening?"

"Is it a divorce case?" she asked eagerly.

"Something like that. Were they in the apartment?"

"On Monday? Yes, they were. Tell you the truth, I thought it was odd, because they're mostly here during the day. Business hours, I guess, while their spouses are working. She came in fairly early, before six, but then she left again. They both came back around seven, together."

"You're sure it was Monday night?"

"Oh, yes. I usually watch my Monday night programs on the portable in my bedroom." She blushed faintly. "I kept looking out the window, because it seemed so odd, and their lights were on."

"How long were they there, Mrs. Miller?"

She frowned. "Now that I couldn't say. Sometime around eight, the lights went out, and I didn't see a sign of those two again. They could have left by the front door, you know, and I couldn't have seen them." Her eagerness returned. "Will I be called to testify, Miss Montana?"

I felt very tired. "You might, Mrs. Miller. You might."

TEN

I DROVE directly to the police station, which wasn't very far away from the apartment complex. The cops in the squad room must have been getting used to me, because I didn't feel quite so many tiger gazes on me as I went through.

Rudy was in Trey's office on the phone, and as I came in, he looked up, grimaced, and said, "She just walked in. Yeah. All right."

I sat down in the visitor's chair as he cradled the phone, and said brightly, "Am I in trouble?"

He gave a tug on his left earlobe, staring at me. "If you hadn't come in, we would have put out an A.P.B."

I blinked. "Isn't that a little drastic? I thought I'd convinced your boss that I was innocent."

Rudy rested his elbows on the desk, covered his face with both huge hands, and rubbed slowly. I wondered if he did that when he was at the end of his rope like me. He put his hands down and stared at me again.

"Lane, why do I get the feeling you'd play with matches in a munitions dump?"

"I can't imagine." I tried to stare him down, finally gave up, and shrugged.

He sighed. "The boss knows damned well you didn't kill Townsend. Now, where the hell have you been?"

"I'd rather not say right now."

"Why not?"

"May I read all the statements? It occurred to me that I hadn't actually read them."

Rudy bore the expression of a man who was silently counting to ten. Or twenty. "We don't use thumbscrews or rubber hoses anymore, Lane. But you know as well as I do that the boss is going to want that answer. And he usually gets answers."

"I'll give it to him willingly. When I'm ready." I wondered if I could manage to withstand Trey's determination and hoped my doubts didn't show on my face.

Shaking his head, Rudy said dryly, "Guess I'll let the boss worry about that. In the meantime, he said to show you the photos we had developed from the negatives at Townsend's place."

"Anything surprising?" I asked warily.

"You tell me." He opened a file on the blotter and pushed it across the desk to me.

There were six photographs, all eight-by-tens. Four were in living color, two in black and white. Two of the color pics were more in the great adventures of Luther Dumont; same little girl but two more poses. The third color shot was of Amy Townsend going into a motel room—with Luther Dumont; he had one hand on her bottom, and it looked more like a grope than a friendly pat. The fourth shot had obviously been taken through a window and captured Amy and Dumont in bed together (It's amazing what you can see through an inch or so gap in venetian blinds).

The two black-and-white shots weren't of sexual adventures, but they were quite likely every bit as damning. One showed Randal Fane and another man in a restaurant of some kind; Fane was handing the man an envelope, it looked like. Or had just been handed one himself. The second showed Fane talking seriously to a man I recognized; he'd been convicted on a racketeering charge about a year ago.

When I turned the photos over, the first one had a date of about four years ago, Fane's name, a name that I didn't recognize, and a third name, boldly underscored: Reynold. The second photo had Fane's name and the other one's, also block printed neatly, along with a date of nearly two years ago.

When I turned them back over, Rudy reached across to stab a finger at the restaurant photo and the man Fane was sitting across from. "We haven't identified this guy yet, but the computer kicked out the name Reynold quick enough. The Reynold trial made pretty big headlines, and Fane's law firm was handling the defense. It looked like they were going to lose. They didn't."

"Jury tampering," I muttered, taking a guess and hoping I was wrong. "Great."

"The other shot could be equally damning," Rudy continued in an impersonal tone. "I think you recognized his companion; so did we. Fane's never been mixed up with any of the underworld figures, but that meeting looks cozy."

I closed the file and shoved it back across the desk. Damn. The counterbalance I had hoped not to find. Randal Fane couldn't have threatened Townsend to get a divorce for Amy, not if Townsend had been holding this stuff over him. He'd had too much to lose himself.

I'd been convinced that Fane wouldn't have killed Jeffrey if he'd had any other choice. But it began to look as if that was the case.

Oddly enough, I hadn't felt much surprise at seeing the shots of Amy with Luther Dumont. At a guess, they'd been taken several years ago. It struck me as the kind of thing Dumont would have done out of sheer spite; it wouldn't have been much risk to him personally since his reputation wasn't all that great anyway, and he would have gotten a kick out of seducing the wife of the man who was blackmailing him.

If it came to that, Jeffrey could have asked Dumont to seduce Amy—for future use in a divorce or just to humiliate her. I had a feeling, though, that although Jeffrey could well have nudged Dumont toward Amy, he probably hadn't told him about the pictures. I could have been wrong, of course, but everything I'd learned about Jeffrey told me that he had filed those shots away for future need—maybe in case he'd wanted more pressure against Dumont. (Bad enough that he abused little girls; he also stole other men's wives. Something like that.) He might have told Amy about them, though. That would have been just his style.

I looked at Rudy, trying to keep my face blank. "How did Mrs. Townsend react to the existence of the trap?"

"She was surprised," Rudy answered promptly and with certainty. "But not too surprised. And she looked at it like it was a bomb about to go off in her face. We haven't shown the photos to either her or Fane."

"What does Trey say about the pictures?"

"Plenty of motive. And the D.A. agrees. If we can place either Amy Townsend or Randal Fane anywhere near the estate that night, we'll make an arrest."

"They weren't supposed to know the shutdown code for the security system," I objected, saying the first thing I could think of.

Rudy smiled. "Yeah, well, we can make a good argument for the possibility that they didn't have to."

"What?"

"Mrs. Townsend, apparently realizing that the problem of access to the house was ruling out all but family and friends, came forward this morning to tell us that her husband had a habit of turning the system off. Seems she was the one who insisted on having it installed, and he went along because—according to other sources—he thought of it as a status symbol. Electronic security is the thing these days. If I was reading Mrs. Townsend right, she thinks he got in the habit of turning the system off just to spite her; he had the codes, naturally, and so kept control of it. Anyway, we have verification from the servants and a number of visitors to the house. It's entirely possible that the security system wasn't active that night."

To say that I felt disgruntled about that tardy bit of knowledge would be grossly understating the matter. All that time and energy wasted worrying about the goddamned security system, and the thing probably hadn't even been on.

I got hold of myself. "But that—pardon the pun—opens the door wide for a stranger. If anybody could have gotten in, I mean—"

"A stranger didn't kill Townsend, Lane, and we both know it."

The hell of it was, I did know it. "Well, but you still don't have any physical evidence tying Amy or Fane to the murder."

"The pills Townsend was given," Rudy reminded me flatly, "were the same kind Amy Townsend used."

Damn. I'd forgotten about that. But I still didn't think they'd done it. It just didn't feel right.

"Rudy, can I have a look at the statements?"

"The boss said okay. Wait here."

The fact that Rudy brought the file back and handed it to me openly, without bothering to shut the door or the blinds or anything, was pretty conclusive proof that Trey had convinced his superiors I was no longer a suspect. Did that make me feel better? Yes. And no.

I'd gone from being the one looking at the hangman's noose to the one *holding* it. All I had to do was give the police Anna Miller's name, and they'd have their two suspects within a five-minute drive of the Townsend estate on the night he was killed.

So why didn't I? I was fed up to my back teeth with this case, after all. I could give the police the witness's name and retire intact from the whole mess. It would have been the smart thing to do, the sane thing.

I'd looked at this case from several perspectives since it began, less than a week ago: as an innocent bystander who landed in the wrong place at the wrong time; as a suspect myself with the shattering feeling of having been framed like a watercolor and wondering whose toes I had inadvertently stepped on; as a detective trying to piece a puzzle together, first because it looked like I had to save my own neck, and then later, because I just had to know what had really happened that night.

I wanted to let go now. Let the system decide if Randal Fane and/or Amy Townsend had killed her husband. But I couldn't. There were still too many things dangling, still too many things I didn't understand. And because I was now the one holding the rope, I couldn't just walk away. If either or both those people went to trial because of me, I *had* to be sure they were the right ones.

So, with Rudy watching unemotionally, I blanked my mind as best I could and began reading the statements of everyone involved. Even mine. I read them through quickly the first time, then again more slowly and carefully. Somewhere during the process, I felt that mental nagging that told me I'd overlooked something, but I couldn't even figure out which statement had prompted the feeling.

It would come to me. God, I hoped it would.

"Seen enough?" Rudy asked.

I returned the file to him. "I guess. I don't even know what I was looking for. But, thanks, Rudy."

"Sure. Oh, and Lane?" He rose as I did, smiling in that unthreatening way of his. "The boss told me to tell you that you won't get another warning. Until we make an arrest, your watchdog is going to stick to you like a burr. Don't try to lose him again."

"Okay, okay. Who is it, by the way? I didn't recognize him."

"He's just out of uniform." Rudy's smile deepened suddenly. "And you gave him his first lesson in the pitfalls of complacency. It'll probably be good for him."

I couldn't help grinning a little. "Can I help it if I don't look dangerous?"

"It's the ace up your sleeve, and you know it," he retorted.

I waved. "Bye, Rudy."

He wiggled his fingers at me. "Bye, Lane."

But I wasn't feeling very cheerful as I made my way out of the building. I've already told you why. The thought of being more or less responsible for someone else's fate affected me so strongly that I actually felt physically ill. Queasy, you know, and cold.

Maybe it's a character flaw, but I've been like that for most of my life. And maybe that's why I chose this specialized area of the investigation field; you're unlikely to affect someone's future adversely by finding something they've lost. Not if they want it found, anyway.

It's easy enough to get involved in something if you don't think of consequences. And, until today, I hadn't thought much about what would happen *after* the murderer or murderers were caught.

I was thinking about it now, and that was probably why I didn't see the patrol car cut in front of me in the parking lot until I was almost on top of it. Fifteen years of driving leaves you with reflexes, if nothing else. I jammed on the brakes instantly.

And found out I didn't have any.

Neither car was going very fast and it wasn't, thank God, a head-on collision, but even so the impact was jarring enough to bang my head against the steering wheel. I could hear curses in angry voices, but just sat there for a minute conscious of the most amazing clarity of mind. I wanted to savor it, because I had the notion that a very important thing had just occurred to me. Unfortunately, one of the angry voices approached my car and shattered the instant of lucidity.

"Are you blind, lady?"

IT WAS my young watchdog (who had been following so close we nearly locked bumpers) who slid underneath my car and discovered that the brake line had been cut. Until then, neither of the two patrolmen had been disposed to believe my assertion of innocence.

My watchdog introduced himself as Kevin West, then escorted me back inside the station. The lieutenant, he said gravely, would want to know about this. And not to worry about my car; it would be taken to the police garage and inspected thoroughly. He barely gave me the chance to remove the car key from my key ring so I could take the rest with me.

Rudy heard the news with a grim face and immediately called Trey. I didn't listen to the conversation; I was staring at my key ring and trying to recapture that moment of clarity.

"He's on his way," Rudy said, hanging up the phone.

"It's his day off," I protested.

Ignoring that, Rudy said, "Wait here," and then left me alone in Trey's office while he and Kevin went out.

I gave up trying to recapture my earlier thoughts and settled for trying to create a poker face from scratch. I knew I was going to need it.

Let's be realistic here. First, brake lines don't generally sever themselves. Second, it was doubtful that anyone had crawled underneath my car while my watchdog was faithfully observing me or while the car was parked at the police station. And, third, Trey was going to want to know exactly where I'd been sans watchdog.

The brake line must have been cut while I was parked at the apartment complex. I hadn't driven very far after that, or used the brakes much, and I was reasonably sure I could have gone that distance with brake fluid trickling out.

Somebody thought I was getting too close.

Another mark against Randal Fane? Maybe. Or maybe somebody had been keeping an eye on me and just waiting for an opportunity to discourage me.

I wasn't ready to tell Trey where I'd been, and that was why I badly needed the poker face. So I worked hard at stiffening my resolve. I even practiced a surly curl to my lip.

And then the son of a bitch didn't even *ask*.

He came in about half an hour later, looked me over with his usual impassivity, and said quite mildly, "Montana. Rudy said he showed you the photographs. What do you think?"

"I think Jeffrey Townsend was a bastard," I replied, eyeing him somewhat warily. I was more than a little disconcerted, and not only because he hadn't asked the right question.

"I agree," he said calmly. "Do you like Italian food?"

I automatically looked at my watch. It was later than I'd realized. "Yes."

"Good. Let's go."

I got up. He took my arm and led me out of the station. And it was the same as before, except that this time the tiger's stripes were showing.

Maybe I'd expected him to show up in his usual suit and tie even though it was his day off, I don't know. He was wearing jeans, running shoes, and a black leather jacket over a T-shirt. It definitely made a difference. He looked casual, unnervingly approachable.

And when we got outside, he put me into one of those hulking four-wheel-drive things. A Bronco or a Blazer or something; I was too addled to really be sure.

"The Mercedes goes with the other clothes?" I asked as he got in and started it up.

"Something like that," he answered.

This unexpected aspect of his personality intrigued me so much that I started forgetting again that he was a cop.

"Why?" I asked curiously. "I mean, do you compartmentalize your life?"

After a moment, he said, "When I get away from the job, I get away. Completely. On my days off, I help a friend train horses on his ranch. The Mercedes would look a bit out of place there. So would a suit and tie."

I felt a pang of guilt. "Oh. Sorry to bring you back to the job on your day off."

"I wouldn't have come if I hadn't wanted to."

Deciding not to explore that comment, I let myself be distracted by a whispering under the dashboard. A police radio, of course. Had he been wearing his beeper when Rudy called him? Probably. He had the kind of job he could never really escape, even when he spent his free time doing something radically different.

"Why did you become a cop?" I heard myself asking.

"Because I hate waste," he said.

It made sense to me. His job dealt with waste. Wasted lives, wasted energies, wasted hates. I guessed that, like many cops, he felt the need to attempt to impose some kind of control on chaos. It was a losing battle, and I wondered if the people who took up arms willingly were courageous or just incurably optimistic.

I thought I knew which Trey was.

"Why do you find things?" he asked.

"Because they're lost." It was the only answer I had.

Trey half nodded, as if that made sense to him. I didn't have the nerve to ask why it did.

He stopped the Blazer (I'd found the logo by then) at a small Italian restaurant, and we went in. It was the kind of place, so rare these days, where nobody dresses up and the food is wonderful.

And I'll admit I let my guard down. We didn't talk about the case, or about policemen or detectives. We talked about likes and dislikes, disagreed amiably over politics, and joined forces in ruthlessly dissecting the latest best-seller. By the time we finished eating and left, my earlier tension was totally gone and I wasn't thinking very much at all.

Until, that is, I realized that we weren't heading toward my loft. I didn't comment on it until we entered a very nice residential section and the Blazer turned into what was obviously a private driveway.

"Um . . . where are we going?"

"I have a spare room. I don't want you going back to the loft tonight."

A number of things flitted through my mind. I caught one, and said, "My cat. I didn't feed Choo." It was dark by then, and I couldn't see Trey's expression, but he sounded amused.

"Jason's going to feed him."

"You told Jason I was going to spend the night at your place?"

"Yes. Before I picked you up at the station."

He was an arrogant bastard.

"You're an arrogant bastard," I said.

"I have to be," he said, "when dealing with reckless ladies who find more than is good for them."

"You started me looking," I reminded him.

"Yes. I know."

I couldn't quite pin down his voice on that one, but whatever was there bothered me.

An automatic garage door opener clipped to the visor was obedient to his touch, and he pulled the Blazer into its half of the two-car garage beside the Mercedes. Then we went into the house.

ALL RIGHT, I know what you're thinking. For somebody who'd been protesting like mad, I was certainly complacent about going into the tiger's lair.

I could give you lots of logical reasons. The severed brake line on my car made me nervous about being alone, for instance. Or how about: I was totally comfortable with his role as a protective cop and mine as a potential victim, and none of that man-woman nonsense was troubling me any longer?

No?

Can't fool you.

Truth is never simple, because we wrap it in reasons. We always say that something is the truth *because* . . . whatever. So even while I was silently arguing a number of reasons for my acceptance of this situation, I was actually avoiding the truth at the core of all of them.

I was where I wanted to be. Period.

Unfortunately, it would be a long time before I faced that complex truth.

I ASKED for the nickel tour and he showed me around his home, as casual as he'd been all evening. It was a beautiful place, a big colonial with a lot of antiques inside and the warm patina of age and care. Not a showplace, though; books and magazines were stacked here and there, a pair of Western boots reposed on the last tread of the stairs, and one of the downstairs rooms was in the cluttered process of being turned into a sun-room.

"Do you have a housekeeper?" I asked as we returned to the den.

"During the week." He glanced at me as he knelt to kindle a fire in the big brick fireplace. "Like you, I inherited a few investments."

I was relieved to hear it, though not really surprised. I sat down on the couch (which blended in well but wasn't an antique; it had been chosen for comfort) and tried to remember all my nice, rational reasons for being here. He had taken off his jacket, and underneath the T-shirt his muscles rippled as he moved.

I was starting not to believe in any of my rational reasons.

Trey rose to his feet, absently brushing his hands together. "Coffee? A drink?"

"No, thanks."

He came to the couch and sat down about a foot away, half turning to look at me. Quietly, he said, "Are you ready to tell me where you went today?"

Damn him; he was too good at getting people off their guard. Me, anyway. I stared at the fire. "No. Not yet."

"Montana, someone tried to stop you today. Maybe even to kill you."

"I know."

"Because you found something? Because you got too close?"

He wasn't using his cop's voice, and I was glad of that. I kept my gaze on the bright fire.

"You're a stubborn woman."

I swallowed hard, something in his voice getting to me. Keeping my voice as even as I could, I said, "I served on a jury a few years ago. From the time I got the notice until

I was actually in the courtroom, I worried that it might be a murder trial. The thought of having such a definite say in someone's fate scared me. What if I made a mistake? What if I looked at the evidence the wrong way, misinterpreted it? What if I helped to condemn somebody . . . and I was *wrong?*"

"Was it a murder trial?" he asked quietly.

"Yes."

"What happened?"

"I—we—found him guilty. A judge in the appellate court overturned the verdict."

"On a technicality?"

I managed a smile. "Sort of. It turned out that one of the key witnesses had perjured himself; the proof of that was unquestionable. The real murderer was caught later."

Trey drew a short breath. "I see."

"Do you?" I looked at him finally. "I thought he was guilty, Trey. In spite of all my doubts going in, I really believed that man had killed. And I was wrong."

"Montana . . . the system works. The error was caught and corrected."

"But what if it hadn't been? That's what I could never forget. What if it hadn't been? I have to be sure. It's hard enough to condemn another human being when you're sure."

"And you aren't sure." He hesitated for a moment, then said, "I'm sorry."

I didn't ask why he was sorry. All my tension had returned, and I got up because I had to move, had to ease the pressure somehow. I went over to the big bay window that looked out on the dark backyard and stood there staring blindly into the night, wishing I had a few answers instead of so many damned questions.

He followed me—I could feel him. I knew that I was too raw to be here with him, too exposed and susceptible. There were things moving between us again, slow and heavy, like water under ice; things that couldn't be changed or controlled because they were too old and primitive.

We were a man and a woman. It was a terrifying combination.

"Why can't answers be simple?" I murmured, more to myself than to him.

"Because questions aren't," he said.

I was glad he knew that. It had taken me most of my life to figure it out. And part of me longed to return to a time when I'd believed answers were simple, because the questions hadn't hurt so much.

Now even desire hurt; it was a question too, filled with possibilities and pain; the beginning of a path that would lead . . . somewhere. Maybe to answers. Maybe to more questions.

I knew he wanted me. Does that sound vain? It isn't, not the way I mean it. There was that mutual awareness, thick and languid, and yet as sharp and unnerving as the smell of lightning when it's struck too close.

I felt it, and Trey felt it, and we both knew it.

"Montana . . ."

I was too old to still believe that sex was simple, and every instinct I could lay claim to warned that any kind of relationship would be as complicated as Trey and me; a tangle of emotions, senses, beliefs, and God only knew what else.

But there was this thing we couldn't, it seemed, ignore any longer. Because Trey was looking at me with those luminous eyes, and it was like electricity arcing between us.

"What are we going to do about this?" he asked suddenly.

I didn't pretend to misunderstand; that was rather beyond me at the moment. "I don't know."

His mouth twisted a little. "Goddamn it, Montana, we're both involved in this case. There'll never be a worse time."

It felt as if all my insides had turned to liquid. I couldn't look away from him. "I know. We're—we're being stupid even talking about it. I should go find that spare bedroom of yours.''

''Yes, you should.'' He came closer, his mouth still twisted. ''But you aren't going to. Are you?''

In that instant, I remembered my tiger-behind-a-door analogy when I'd first seen him, and I fully understood for the first time what I had glimpsed—because I could see it clearly now. Jason had been right in saying that Trey's hands gave him away. I could see that those incongruously powerful hands weren't as incongruous as I had thought, and that they, much more than his elegant exterior, revealed something that he normally kept hidden away. But it was leaping from his eyes now.

''No.'' I could hardly speak, because I knew I wasn't going anywhere at all.

It wasn't a kiss. It was a . . . a *melding*. I can't explain it any better than that. I won't even try.

His mouth on mine. His mouth on me.

Heat. There was so much heat. Like a fire, like steam. We were burning out of control, and the race to put out the flames was frantic, driven. I don't remember going upstairs to his bedroom; I don't know where the clothing went, who took off what. That was happening on another plane of existence, apart from the rest. Hunger. We couldn't get enough, couldn't possibly, ever, get enough, couldn't be sated. The sensations were overwhelming: his big, ugly hands on me, their strength reined, moving me in a way I'd never felt before, never even imagined was possible, their knowledge of what would please expert and absolute; his mouth caressing; his body, powerful, fluid, graceful, muscles rippling under bronze skin, under my fingers; his luminous eyes, hooded, fierce, fixed on me until I felt that I'd never been seen before, not like this, not ever like this. The intensity was violence barely tempered, breaking over us both in waves, shock and pleasure coexisting in a strange, dizzying resonance. The sounds we made were smothered, urgent, primitive. We were lost in each other, joined, merged.

And then it happened again, sometime in the night, but slow this time, so slow I could feel myself dissolving, like sugar being melted for candy. He was lazy, teasing in silence, his touch lingering until my flesh was so sensitized a mere brush of his lips made me quiver from the bones out, until need was a compulsive, greedy thing, until it couldn't be slow anymore.

DON'T TELL ME it was just sex. It wasn't *just* anything.

Based on my few aborted relationships in the past ten years, I had evolved something of a theory. The theory, simply stated, is that humans go out of their way to build an emotional relationship around sex. Think about it. The entire point of the exercise is, after all, purely biological. Propagation of the race. Nice and simple, a requirement of nature. Animals do it all the time, and you don't notice *them* agonizing about tender feelings along the way.

However, somewhere in our two million years of evolution we learned to verbalize our emotions, and that quickly got us into trouble. We started looking for emotional satisfaction and, being herd animals of a kind, we looked for it in one another. And maybe nature set things up to be boy/girl, even though there were naturally a few girl/girl and boy/boy combinations along the way; that's beside the point.

The point being that this nice, simple, and definitely pleasurable biological function of ours became vastly important to us whether it propagated the race or not. And since the function was designed for two (although I understand a combination of several can be interesting), couples became the order of the day. And that's when we started looking for and even inventing reasons to be part of a couple.

In case you've forgotten, I said that the above *had* been my theory. It was shot to hell now.

Were the emotions a result of the sex—or had the sex been the result of the emotions? All I knew for certain was that I would never be complacent about my stupid theories again.

I didn't have to look for emotions to attach to the wonderful sex—they existed. Too many of them, and all of them confusing. I didn't have to look for ways to bond Trey and me into a relationship—we had one. There was no defining the blasted thing, no way to label it or neatly pigeonhole it—it just *was*.

Like truth.

And I think I knew, even during that incredible night with him, that it would require a balancing act worthy of the greatest high-wire team in the world to find a way for us to live with this thing between us. I think we both knew. Maybe that was where the sense of desperation came from.

Hindsight is great. Maybe if I'd known then, that what was between Trey and me was fire rather than simple sparks—maybe if I'd known that, I would have run like a thief. But by the time I realized it, there was nowhere to run.

I DON'T KNOW if I've mentioned it, but I hate waking up. Choo has me trained to wake up and feed him, mainly because he walks on me until I can't ignore him any longer. Trey, of course, was much more polite than that. If he tried to wake me the next morning, he was too gentle to be effective.

I was vaguely aware of movement, of the distant sound of a shower running. I smelled coffee, but was too pleasantly exhausted to respond to the lure of it. I think he kissed me on the back of my neck before he left; it was the only place really accessible to him, since my face was buried in the pillow. I felt something warm touch me there, at any rate, but by the time I got my elbows under me and hoisted myself up to look blearily around, the bedroom was empty.

I almost went back to sleep, but then Choo's training penetrated. He couldn't walk on me because he wasn't here, but his spirit persisted. Breakfast. My cat would be wanting his breakfast about now. In an empty loft. After having been abandoned all night.

Choo was not going to be happy with me.

I wondered if Trey had asked Jason to feed my cat this morning as well as last night.

It was several minutes before my eyes would focus, and when they did it was on something my system craved to start the day. Coffee. Trey had left one of those insulated pots on the nightstand, along with a handy cup. I slithered across the king-sized bed like an eel.

I saw the note and key ring after my first swallow and thought about them idly. A key ring. Ah, yes, I was temporarily without wheels. The Mercedes? No, I decided, the Blazer. Trey had to work today, which meant he'd be in his professional persona of suit and tie and Mercedes.

He was a fascinating man.

With my cup half-empty, I reached for the note and unfolded it. I was obscurely pleased that he wrote instead of printed; most men print for some reason. The note was brief and to the point: Take the Blazer and be careful. We'll talk later.

Talk later. Was that a promise, or a threat? Professional or personal? It was too early in the morning for my mind to be working with any clarity, and I felt too good (all right, sated) physically to worry much about anything. The future, I decided, would take care of itself.

I finished my coffee and then crawled out of the bed and padded into the master bath. On the verge of turning on the water for a shower, I turned to the large mirror over the vanity and studied my face instead.

During some long-ago part of my life I had been fascinated by particular scenes in a movie. I forget which one. Anyway, in this movie, the heroine had a habit of spending minutes looking at herself in a mirror whenever something unexpected or momentous had happened in her life. At the time, I could never figure out what she was looking for.

I knew now. She had been looking for changes, just as I was. Marks in the flesh, signs of . . . passage. There had to be changes, after all. Something so fundamental had to leave tracks as it passed.

But there weren't any tracks. No marks or signs. My face looked, as always, semifamiliar. But no different from last night, last week, last year.

I got into the shower, not certain if I was disappointed or reassured by my outwardly unchanged self. A little of both, I supposed. Human relationships were like that. It was interesting, I thought idly, this process of connecting two people. Interesting and scary. The physical connection was the simple one, but the emotional—

My blissful mood vanished with the suddenness of a soap bubble. I went still, hardly aware of the shampoo getting in my eyes, a clear, cold realization in my mind as vivid as a neon sign in a dark window.

The key.

Oh, goddamn it . . .

It had been there all along, right in front of me, such an obvious thing I had noticed it only in passing, according it no importance at all.

A tree lost in the forest. One question lost among so many puzzling ones.

When you come out of a dreamy state into reality, the landing can be brutal. I felt the shock of it from my heels to the top of my head. And it wasn't just that I was so close to finding the answers that could condemn someone. It was also the hollow realization that, if I was right, Jeffrey Townsend and his murderer had made victims of us all.

ELEVEN

WHEN I BACKED the Blazer out of Trey's garage sometime later, I discovered that he'd been serious about keeping an eye on me. Serious enough that Kevin West waited in an unmarked car across from the drive and pulled in behind me as I left.

Even assuming Trey's superiors had been convinced of my innocence, I doubted they'd be pleased to find out I'd spent the night at his house. I hoped young Kevin knew how to be discreet.

To be honest, though, I didn't worry very much about it. I had a lot on my mind, none of it pleasant. And what outsiders thought of my involvement with Trey wasn't going to amount to a tinker's damn compared to the rest of this mess.

I sent a silent apology to Choo and drove directly to the police station. Trey's office was empty, and I found Rudy at his own desk.

Looking up, Rudy said, "He's at a meeting with—"

I waved off the rest of it. "Rudy, I need to see those statements again. Somewhere quiet, if possible. And I think I'll need a phone."

He didn't ask any questions.

"The boss won't be back for an hour or more. You can use his office and phone. I'll get the file."

Ten minutes later, alone in Trey's office with the door closed, I took a deep breath and opened the file. I sorted through the statements, found the one I wanted, and read it very carefully.

The key would only work if . . . yes. Just as I'd remembered. One question that hadn't been asked, something that had only just occurred to me. I shuffled through the papers until I found the name and number I needed, then placed a call.

People don't like being disturbed on Sunday. So I lied and said I was a cop, just double-checking a statement. The response to that was grudging, but I got the answer I wanted. I crossed my fingers and asked a second question, which provided me with another name and number.

The second call took nearly fifteen minutes, and I had to use every ounce of charm, tact, and authority I could muster. When I finally hung up the phone, I saw my hand shaking.

One alibi that wouldn't hold up.

Rudy had brought the complete file for me, and I spread the photographs out so that I could see them all. After staring at them for several minutes, I rearranged them into groups. I couldn't look at them for long. I didn't have to.

The pieces were falling into place. I still had questions, but the answers I'd found made sense. More than that, they felt right.

They felt so right it made me sick.

I closed the file and left it neatly on Trey's desk, and then I got out of there. I saw Rudy look up and frown as I went quickly past him, but I didn't stop or explain why I was bolting.

Problem is, there are some things you just can't run away from.

HE FOUND ME in the cemetery. I hadn't been there long. I was standing at the grave occupied by Jeffrey Townsend, staring down at his headstone.

"Montana?"

I didn't look up. "He was a monster, you know," I

said, hearing a weariness in my voice I'd never heard before. "He deserved a lot worse than he got."

"What have you found out?"

I turned then, staring up at Trey. His gaze was sharp, his face intent. Every inch the cop. Last night's lover might never have existed. I knew then, right then, that there was a barrier between us neither of us would ever be able to cross. I didn't know if it was something that would keep us apart, or just separate.

"Trey . . . leave this case in the open file. Let it drop. Bringing Townsend's killer to trial will destroy people, people who've already been hurt enough."

He was frowning. "Murder is wrong," he said tersely. "There's no justification for the taking of another life, Montana. Surely you believe that?"

"I thought I did. But not now, not this time. In the . . . killer's place, I would have done the same."

"No," he protested sharply.

"Yes." I took a deep breath and wondered what was hurting so much in my chest. "He was a monster, can't you understand that? He lived his entire life hurting people, and because he had the name and the money, he got away with it. He wasn't just a ruthless businessman and a cruel husband and a lousy father—he was an animal."

"That isn't up to you or me to judge," Trey said impatiently.

"Then who?" I felt miserable and helpless. "We're all one of those 'twelve citizens just and true,' aren't we? We don't have to sit in a jury box; we judge people every day of our lives. And I know, without a shadow of a doubt, that by killing Townsend someone destroyed a rabid animal because there was no other way to deal with him."

"The courts—"

"Bullshit." My voice was getting harsh, shaking. "The courts couldn't have touched Townsend, and that's a reality. He never killed anyone. He did worse than that. He put the kind of scars on people that don't show on skin. If any of his victims could have been persuaded to testify against him—and none of them would have, because they were terrified of him and his power—what do you think would have happened? Do you really believe he would have been punished? He'd never have spent a day in jail. Bribery. Blackmail. A very expensive lawyer with a lot of courtroom tricks."

"Who killed him, Montana?" Trey asked flatly.

"You see everything in black and white, don't you?" I asked wonderingly. "Right or wrong; good or bad."

"I'm a cop."

I looked away from those hard, luminous eyes. "Yes. But I'm not, am I? I'm just the Judas you picked. Was that tumble of ours supposed to be my thirty pieces of silver?"

"Goddamn you," he said in a voice so low it almost wasn't there.

I was numb by then, and didn't much care what I said. I even managed a smile. Of sorts. "Next time, I'll just ask for money to be left on the dresser. It's a lot more honest."

"Stop."

I vaguely recognized he was so tightly wound he was in danger of snapping, but still I said, "It doesn't matter. You made sure I was in this thing so deeply there'd be only one way out."

He turned and walked away.

My hands were fists in the pockets of my windbreaker, and I couldn't help turning my head to watch him leave. The numbness had worn off, and my chest was hurting again.

I wished he had called me a bitch, or anything else, as long as he raged at me. I wasn't sure, but I thought I'd wanted to bleed a little as well as draw blood. But that control of his had kept him from striking back at me for what I'd said.

Or at least, I hoped that was it. I hoped that Trey didn't believe my accusations had been on target. God, I hoped that wasn't it. Because the last thing I wanted to believe was that I really had been paid thirty pieces of silver.

That kind of truth would destroy a woman.

The odd thing was, I understood Trey's beliefs. He was a good cop, and good cops *do* tend to see things in black and white. They have to. I could even admire and respect that; if you believe in something, you stand up for it. Period. Unfortunately, a lot of my beliefs fall into the gray area between black and white.

Yes, there's no justification for murder. That's the rule, and one I happen to agree with. I also happen to believe that there's an exception for every rule.

Jeffrey Townsend had been murdered, but his killer had been punished already. By bringing that killer to trial, a number of innocent people were going to be all but destroyed. And for what? Jeffrey's killer would never spend a day in jail anyway, because even the stupidest lawyer would instantly plead temporary insanity and/or self-defense. And win.

But the trial . . . that was what would destroy people. The publicity. All the years-old secrets and shames brought out of their various locked closets and rooms and paraded before the gawking eyes of the curious.

And the sad thing was, I thought that most of the officials involved might have taken care of the matter a hell of a lot more quietly if they'd only known what a Pandora's box they were busily prying open. But all the official "friends" of Jeffrey Townsend had fanned the fires of outrage, demanding the murderer's head on a platter. It was too late, now, to quietly arrange a more merciful justice for the killer, who had been far more a victim than Jeffrey had.

I went home to my loft and fed my vastly annoyed cat, then spent over an hour hugging Choo and staring into space. He was unusually docile about being clasped to my chest, something which he generally prefers to be by his choice rather than mine. He purred loudly and rubbed his chin against mine, his declawed forepaws busily making bread on my middle.

God created cats for moments like these.

I knew I had to do it. Though I had (I hoped) unfairly accused Trey of leaving me only one way out of this mess, the truth was that there *was* only one way out. It had gone too far now.

I thought the police could probably get a confession once they knew who to focus on. I didn't feel like much of a detective, but I knew very well that some of the information I had was unknown to the police. The plain truth was that I'd gotten lucky. Some of the stuff I'd gotten more or less by chance wasn't likely to come up in future police investigations, and without those disparate facts, they weren't going to be able to put it all together.

And maybe it would have been less painful for me to just give them a name and what little evidence I'd found. Maybe. But I couldn't do that.

After a while, I released Choo and picked up the phone. I got through quickly, but it was Rudy Flint who answered Trey's line.

"Ms. Montana." His voice was very polite.

I felt puzzled. "Hello, Rudy. I need to talk to Trey."

"He isn't here."

That bear rumble of a voice was still polite—unnaturally so, I thought. Rudy was mad at me, and I didn't know why. I didn't really care. After nerving myself up to speak to Trey with our last encounter in mind, I was feeling a bit touchy myself. "Well, where is he?"

"I don't know."

Checking my watch automatically, I decided that Trey should still be on duty; and he was the kind of man who would always *be* on duty when he was supposed to. Irritably, I said, "You must know. You're his sword arm."

There was an odd sound from the other end of the connection, but Rudy's voice remained flat and polite. "Kevin reported that he left you at the cemetery. He hasn't returned to the office; he isn't answering his radio or his beeper, and when I called, there was no answer at his house."

I caught myself chewing on a thumbnail. "Rudy . . .

where would he go?'' I tried to swallow the lump in my throat. "If he was angry or . . . or upset?''

After a moment, and in a much more natural and definitely worried voice, Rudy said, "I don't know, Lane. He was expected for another meeting an hour ago; he didn't show. And he never misses appointments.''

I could hear the question even though Rudy didn't ask. *What the hell did you do to him?*

"Lane?''

"I'm still here. I'll . . . try to find him.''

I didn't know if I could do it. I had never tried to find a person the way I did objects: by visualizing them and asking myself where they were. With people, I always stuck to good old-fashioned legwork. But that wouldn't help me find Trey now, so I had to try using those peculiar instincts of mine.

I sat in the Blazer for a moment, eyes closed, trying to blank my mind. Where? Where would Trey have gone? And I felt it almost instantly, that queer internal lurch, so strong that I actually jerked. I started the engine and pulled out of the lot, driving with automatic, unconscious awareness, but functionally blind.

Kevin was still following me, I assumed; I didn't bother to check.

Trey. I couldn't have known, of course, not logically. *You don't know him well, after all. Just well enough to have slept with him. Just well enough to have hurt him.*

How long do you know a man before you can follow him to his secret places? Years, I guess. A lifetime. If ever. But I didn't have to wait that long to find the secret places outside Trey's head. Those inside his mind . . . those I might never be able to find.

I didn't know where I was going, except that I would find Trey there.

I stopped the Blazer before I was even aware of it, realizing only when I felt the weight of the keys in my hand and heard the silence when the engine was turned off. I blinked and shook away the lingering feeling of detachment, then looked around.

My peculiar instinct had brought me unerringly to the right place; I was parked beside Trey's Mercedes. I got out of the car and looked at the place we'd both come to. It was a small observatory, virtually deserted this time of the day. There was a kind of concrete veranda built around the big dome, and I could see him from here, standing at the low wall and staring out over the city. He was alone.

I went up the wide steps and around the dome, slowing as he came into sight again. He was slumped, forearms resting on the low concrete wall. His tie was loosened. His face was still. I stopped a couple of feet away and joined him in gazing out at the view.

"You find lost things," he said.

I didn't know what to say to him. Would it have been easier for us if we'd been younger? Maybe. In some ways, at least. If we had been eighteen, the emotions would have been closer to the surface, more easily gotten at and released. There would have been a stormy confrontation with lots of yelling, followed, no doubt, by a bout of passionate making-up.

But that way was too easy for us. We had both learned that answers couldn't be simple because the questions weren't. And what was between us couldn't be thrashed out by yelling and scratching; when we cut each other, it would be to the bone.

Had been.

I didn't know what to say to him. "Rudy's worried about you. You missed an appointment. He said it as if . . . as if the sun forgot to rise this morning." No response. I tried again. "I called your office because I wanted to talk to you about the case. I think—"

He held up a hand, and I broke off. After a moment, he said, "We made love because we both wanted to, Montana."

My throat was hurting. "Yes."

He didn't look at me. "I was right; there couldn't have been a worse time for us. Do you really believe—?"

"No. I don't know. But I feel like a Judas. I feel used." And sick. And tired.

"And it's my fault."

I tried to keep my voice steady. "Somebody else got me involved. Planned to make me look suspicious. But you knew I didn't kill Townsend. You knew you could use me to find out who did."

"I didn't know you when it started," he said in a low voice. "I didn't know you'd hurt like this. I didn't know it would matter so much to you."

"No. But it doesn't change anything, does it, Trey?" I wished I could cry, but my eyes were so dry that the lids scratched against them. "I knew you were using me from the beginning, but it seemed almost like a game. Find the killer. Be a detective."

"Montana—"

"Only it was never a game. I stood at a window and looked into those people's lives like a voyeur. And I probed and I probed until I saw all the things they wanted to hide. All their secrets and shames. All their pain. That's what *you* made me do."

"I'm a cop," he said tautly, swinging around to face me.

"But I'm not." I felt miserable again, and cold, and lonely. "I just wanted to help people find their lost things, the things they cared about. That's all I ever wanted to do, Trey."

He stared at me, his mouth, under the neat mustache, a hard line. Then his face closed down. "I'm sorry," he said.

"So am I." It was over, and the pain of that, for now at least, mercifully dulled my senses.

It's hard to have an ending so soon after a beginning.

Trey shoved his hands into the pockets of his coat and straightened his shoulders stiffly. "You wanted to talk to me about the case?" His voice was remote, formal.

I don't know how I did it, but I kept my voice calm and

steady. "The evidence I have is just bits and pieces. Circumstantial, mostly. But it all fits. And I believe we can get a confession."

"Give me what you've got," he said. "I'll take care of it."

"I've gone this far," I said. "I have to see it through."

"No. You don't."

It wasn't the cop talking. He wasn't worried about procedures, he was worried about me.

I took a deep breath. "I have to. And you owe me this."

He didn't like it, but he must have realized I wasn't going to give him a choice. "All right. What have you got in mind?"

I managed a rueful smile. "Something very old and corny. But in this case, I think it's the best thing to do."

IT WAS a scene right out of one of those old mysteries. All the suspects gathered together in one room, Trey and Rudy and Sarah Jensen (who was present at my suggestion) seated unobtrusively in a corner. Jason, a bit bewildered but alert, was near them.

And yours truly, center stage.

We were in the room where Jeffrey Townsend had spent his final hours exactly one week ago. The couch he had died on was gone; Amy had had it removed the day I'd brought authorization from the police that the room could be unsealed. We had slightly rearranged the remaining furniture so that there was a loose circle, everyone under the eyes of everyone else.

They weren't an especially happy group. Amy sat beside Randal Fane on one couch, a correct foot of space between them. Jeff sat on the other couch, clearly uneasy. Maybe it was because he was beside Luther Dumont, who was slumped and apparently sleepy. Samantha was sitting in a chair with her back to the cold fireplace; she was smiling coyly at Jason, who was in another chair on her right. Completing the circle were Trey, Sarah, Rudy, and me. I was leaning against the bar.

Eyeing me, Randal Fane said coldly to Trey, "I intend to lodge a formal protest with your department, Lieutenant."

"You're free to do so, Mr. Fane," Trey responded.

Quietly, Amy said, "I agreed to this, Randal." Her hands were tightly clasped in her lap, and she was staring down at them.

"I don't see why," Jeff said sullenly. He glanced aside at Luther Dumont and added in the same tone, "And why's *he* here?"

"Because he's part of it," I answered, looking at each of them briefly. "You're all part of it."

Samantha giggled and tore her bright eyes from Jason to look at me. "All the suspects. Just like *The Thin Man*. Where's Asta?"

I ignored that. I wished I was anywhere except where I was. I heard my voice come out flat and toneless. "I explained to Mrs. Townsend that all of this will probably have to come out in court if the district attorney decides to prosecute. Maybe he won't."

"Why wouldn't he?" Fane asked quickly.

Luther Dumont chose to answer. "It isn't an election year," he murmured.

As much as I hated agreeing with him, I couldn't help but reflect that he was probably right. I said, "Maybe he'll agree with me that Jeffrey Townsend's killer acted in self-defense, even though the crime was premeditated."

Jeff looked at me through narrowed eyes. "Are we supposed to believe that you have our best interests at heart staging this little drama?" He was about what I'd expected: a young man with a lot of anger in him. He resembled his mother more than his father in looks.

I didn't try to answer his question. How could I? I was about to tear most of the people in this room to emotional shreds.

I said, "You, at least, couldn't possibly have killed your father."

"Thank you," he said ironically.

"You were too far away, in the presence of too many witnesses," I went on, ignoring the interruption. "Your alibi covered that entire night; there was no way you could have come back here. And Samantha was sixty miles away at a party, with a couple hundred witnesses who swear she was never out of their sight for more than a few minutes from before eight until after midnight."

Deliberately, I let my gaze fasten on Amy Townsend's bowed head.

"Mother was in New York!" Jeff said fiercely.

Maybe it would all have to come out—all of it. But it wasn't all going to come from me. I waited until Amy met my eyes, then said, "Yes. She was. She certainly went to New York. But there was always the possibility of an accomplice." I saw her haunted eyes widen fractionally. She was close to breaking, and we both knew it.

"Who?" Jeff scoffed.

"Randal Fane," I answered, still looking at Amy. She didn't look at the lawyer, but I knew then that she had wondered herself. Amy had caught a plane back to New York at ten last Monday night. The police had kept the time of death quiet, so she couldn't know that her husband had been killed while Randal Fane had been with her.

She had wondered. And hadn't asked him. It was why she had permitted this confrontation. Because she had to know.

"He had no reason to kill Jeffrey," she said softly.

"I was working at my home that night," Fane said at almost the same moment.

Responding to Amy's statement, I said, "He had several good reasons, Mrs. Townsend. He knew how your husband treated you. He knew you were too terrified of Jeffrey's rages and threats to even consider asking for a divorce. And he loved you."

I heard a gasp, and a glance showed me that it was Jeff

who was surprised. Samantha was looking at her mother and the lawyer with a faint frown, but it wasn't an expression of surprise.

Stolidly, Randal Fane repeated, "I was working in my study at home." As long as Amy's alibi apparently held up, he wasn't about to admit that she had been in Atlanta with him; when lovers alibi each other, and both have something to gain by murder . . .

Looking at him, I said, "Alone. No witnesses. No alibi."

The lawyer gave me a disgusted stare. "Miss Montana, don't you think that I would have given myself an alibi—and a good one—if I had planned to commit a murder?"

"As a matter of fact, I do think that. I also think that you could have given Townsend the muscle relaxers, or stabbed him—but I doubt you would have done both. And there are several other elements that don't add up if you were the killer. Small ones, mostly."

"Which are?"

I drew a breath. "The police determined he was given the muscle relaxers in chocolate; I couldn't see you bringing a box along on a visit. In this room—the murder scene—there were several oddities. A missing rug and drapery tie, a carefully vacuumed carpet. I'd be surprised if you even knew where the house vacuum cleaner was kept."

"I don't," he said dryly.

Shrugging slightly, I said, "So I kept looking. One very important thing was the victim himself. The more I found out about him, the more I realized that he . . . wasn't a nice man. I realized that he must have made a number of enemies. I started looking for them."

"And found them?" Luther Dumont asked lazily. Beneath the sleepy lids, his yellowish green eyes were sharp.

"Yes." I looked at him. "Your part in this looked suspicious, especially once you called me, Mr. Dumont."

"Luther," he murmured.

I could feel Trey's eyes on me. I ignored them. I also

ignored Dumont's silky intimation that he and I were on closer terms than existed between us. But the hint irritated me, and my voice sharpened.

"Lieutenant Fortier told you that I claimed Townsend had wanted to hire me for some reason. You didn't waste any time getting in touch with me. You were Townsend's silent partner in a number of questionable business ventures, which could have meant that you had a reason for being worried about his reasons for wanting to hire an outside investigator."

"Curiosity," Dumont said, still lazy and watchful. "I explained my reasons."

"But not all of them." I kept my eyes on his face. "Townsend had been blackmailing you for years." I watched his sleepy lids rise abruptly, saw something sharp and ugly gleam in the yellow-green depths. "You were afraid he'd meant to hire me to find out a few more of your . . . secrets. That was the last thing you needed. You've been getting treatment for a long time now; I noticed in your appointment book that you visit a therapist regularly. But if certain things in your past came to light, it could only hurt your legitimate business reputation."

Into the sudden taut silence, Jeff's angry young voice sounded unnaturally loud. "He fucks kids!"

Dumont didn't look at him or react in any way to the crude accusation. He continued to gaze steadily at me, his eyes veiled now. His face unmoved.

"Is that what your father told you, Jeff?" I asked, still looking at Dumont.

"Yes. Dad told me. When I asked him why he was in business with scum like Dumont, he told me. He said he had to keep him in line, make sure he didn't keep hurting little girls."

Quietly, I asked, "How did he know about that, Jeff?" There was a long silence, and when I looked at Townsend's son I saw an abrupt and uneasy confusion.

"I don't know," he said sullenly. "I didn't ask."

I looked back at Dumont. "A few days ago, a man who

had installed a very special safe in this house approached the police. He'd heard about the murder and thought that the safe, which only he and Townsend knew about, might hold some evidence, so he revealed its location. There was a photograph in the safe. And a set of negatives.''

Trey spoke for the first time in a while, his voice quiet. ''The photo and negatives will be handed over to you unless they're needed as evidence, Mr. Dumont.''

Dumont nodded slightly, but he was still looking at me. ''They won't be,'' he said. ''I didn't kill Townsend. God knows I wanted to, but I didn't.''

''No, you had an alibi for that entire night. But you weren't supposed to, Mr. Dumont.''

He stared at me, frowning. ''What?''

''You told me so yourself, but I don't think you realized just what you were saying. According to what you told me, and what your fellow players told the police, Tuesday night is the regular weekly poker game. You met on Monday night that week because one of the others was getting ready to leave on his vacation.''

Dumont nodded slowly. ''True. What are you getting at?''

''Most people have a number of fixed habits. What do you usually do on Monday nights?''

''I stay at home. Watch football on television.''

''Alone. No witnesses. And so . . . no alibi. Townsend knew about how you spent your Monday nights. True?''

''Yes.''

''So did his killer, Mr. Dumont. You were bound to be involved in the investigation; your partnership with Townsend was quiet, but not secret, not once the police began checking documents. Which they would naturally do. The killer knew about the blackmail, but couldn't lay hands on the proof since Townsend had hidden it. Still, you were likely to be a suspect, with a possible motive and without an alibi. Until you switched your poker night.''

There was a long silence, and then Dumont said somewhat wryly, "I'll have to buy Pat a drink when he gets back from his vacation."

I half nodded. "His vacation was a stroke of good fortune for you," I agreed.

Impatiently, Jeff said, "Okay, Miss Montana, you've now eliminated all the suspects except you and your brother. My money's on you."

"Mine almost was," I said. "At first, it seemed important to find out why Townsend had wanted to hire me. But there was a strong possibility almost from the beginning that he, in fact, hadn't intended to. The message could have been faked somehow, maybe a recording. That seemed even more likely if you consider the wording of the message. He said, 'Come to my house at eleven.' I didn't stop to think about it then, because I knew when the call had come in, and since he didn't say 'eleven *tomorrow*,' I assumed he meant eleven that night. But it was amazingly short notice for a business appointment—hardly his style. Later, I started wondering about that.

"The message was erased from my answering machine, so I had to wonder if it was because I might have heard something odd if I'd been allowed to listen more closely, or if the killer had simply wanted to cast doubts on my motives for being here that night. Whatever the reason, the message was erased from my machine sometime after eleven and before midnight. During the hour after my appointment when, presumably, I would have already been here at the house. The killer assumed I'd be here; nobody says no to Jeffrey Townsend."

"What's your point?" Dumont asked intently.

"Well, I considered two possibilities. Either Townsend was killed *because* he wanted to hire me and that panicked someone, or else I was very neatly framed for his murder. I wasn't sure which way to go, until I found out that the police had discovered a photograph of Townsend in bed with a woman. The woman's face isn't visible, but she looks like me."

I glanced at Amy, feeling apologetic that I had to bring

all this up, even though there was, God knew, worse to come. She was watching me with a faint frown, and I saw that she and Fane were holding hands. I hoped he was as strong as I thought he was. He was going to have to be strong.

Dumont spoke. "Needless to say, it wasn't you?"

"It wasn't me. And I can prove it easily."

"How?" Samantha asked curiously.

"I have a scar on my back; the killer couldn't have known about that. It would have been very obvious in the photo."

"But it pointed at you," Dumont said. "So you realized you were being framed?"

I nodded. "I realized, after I thought about it. Townsend wasn't careless; he wouldn't have left a picture like that in his desk drawer. So I decided that the killer had. And that, added to the erased message and the appointment entered in Townsend's datebook, convinced me that someone had gone to a great deal of time and trouble to focus suspicion on me."

"Why you?" Dumont murmured.

TWELVE

"EXACTLY. Why me? It was hardly likely that a killer had picked my name out of the phone book. Every time I ran into an alibi as solid as a brick wall or—as in Mr. Fane's case—found a suspect who just didn't fit, I kept coming back to that question. Why me? Why was I involved in this? I never met Townsend, had never done any work for him. But there had to be a connection."

"Lanie . . ." Jason's voice was troubled.

I looked at him and felt my lips twist in something like a smile. "Nothing else made sense, Jase. We've been looking right at it all along and just didn't see. The connection was through you."

My brother stared at me for a moment and then turned disbelieving eyes to Samantha.

She laughed. "I was at a party sixty miles away!"

"Are you out of your mind?" Jeff yelped at the same time.

I kept my eyes on Sam. "When I realized that you were the only connection, I took a closer look at that alibi. At first, I only wondered if you might have slipped away from the party. But it would have to have been a long absence, and too many people had sworn you never left."

"That's because I never did," Sam said.

As if she hadn't spoken, I went on. "Still, there were other things that made me believe it could have been you. I looked at the statements from the people at that party,

217

and it occurred to me that nobody had mentioned what kind of party it had been. So I asked. And I found out that it had been a costume party—complete with masks.''

"So what?" Jeff demanded sharply.

"I've been to masquerades. It's amazing how costumes and masks can make you see what you expect to see. For instance, I remember when a friend of mine had decided to go to a masquerade dressed as Queen Elizabeth the First. She talked about it for weeks. But she waited too late to rent the costume—something I didn't know. At the party, I saw Queen Elizabeth and thought that was my friend. I didn't realize my mistake until the unmasking at midnight.''

Jeff looked pale. "So?" he asked, less sharply.

I felt very tired. "So I asked a few more questions and did some checking." I looked at Sam, who was watching me with no expression. "A friend of yours at the party left the next day to return to college, so she was never questioned by the police. It wasn't easy, but I managed to get the story out of her. It seems you wanted to slip out to meet a . . . young man. But everyone knew how strict your father was; he always insisted you be chaperoned. Your friend was sympathetic. She agreed to wear your costume while you were gone. You left the house around seven, just after the party started, and returned between eleven-thirty and twelve. You changed into your costume—and were there for the unmasking.''

Samantha shrugged. "I met a guy. Big deal.''

"His name?" Trey asked quietly.

"None of your business," she snapped without looking at him.

Jeff said tautly, "She didn't have a reason to kill Dad.''

I didn't want to do this. I wished somebody would stop me. But no one said a word. Amy sat, rigid, her features so expressionless that my own face ached. "I didn't think so either, Jeff. Until I started tying a few things together. Mr. Dumont, Townsend was using a photo and negatives to blackmail you. Am I right in thinking that they were taken inside a very private and exclusive, uh . . . club . . . here in Atlanta?''

He nodded. "Yes. I went there only once." His mouth twisted. "Blind drunk. No excuse, of course, not for what I did. But I've been paying for more than ten years. And I've been in therapy.''

I wondered if that poor child he'd abused had been in therapy since that night as well.

"It's out of business now," he went on. "It was raided a few months ago and closed down.''

In a jerky voice, Jeff said, "What kind of club? And what does it have to do with Sam?''

I looked at him. "A while ago, I asked you how your father had known about Mr. Dumont. I wondered about that. I had a hunch that the picture had been taken at that place; because of a case I worked on some time ago, I knew what went on there: that men went there and paid to have sex with children, mostly young girls. The men protected their secret; obviously their careers would have been ruined if word of their activities had been made public. They visited by appointment only and generally wore disguises—even when they were alone in the bedrooms with the girls.

"There were cameras and video equipment in only one of the rooms, obviously so that the customers who wanted to could tape their activities. The police found the equipment when they raided the place, but no tapes or film. Those men were extremely paranoid; the club existed only because it protected their anonymity, and they made sure they couldn't be taped or photographed without their knowledge. And yet, Mr. Dumont had been photographed there, without a disguise and apparently unaware of a camera. So I began to wonder if it was possible the pictures of Mr. Dumont had been taken quite deliberately, by a club member, in order to blackmail him. Mr. Dumont, why did you go there?''

Dumont was frowning. "Like I said, I was drunk. Met

a man at a party who said he knew a place where anything was possible, for a price.''

"Did you ever see that man again?"

"No."

"And you never knew his name?"

"No."

I nodded. "That's what I thought. Townsend no doubt hired him to lure you to the club. Maybe he'd guessed you had certain . . . leanings. Maybe he just waited until you were too drunk to know or care what you did. In any case, Townsend undoubtedly had those pictures taken. He might have taken them himself. But how did he happen to know of a place where anything was possible for a price? The obvious answer is that he was involved in the club himself.''

Dumont shook his head. "That's what I thought, after he started squeezing me. I asked a couple of men I could trust to stake that place out for months. Townsend never showed."

"He stopped going as soon as he began blackmailing you," I said. "He didn't have to go back there again."

"You mean he only wanted a lever against me?"

"No. I mean he didn't have to go back there. He had no . . . personal need for the club any longer." I looked at Sam and took a deep breath. "When did you make up your mind to kill him, Samantha? How old were you the first time he took you into his bed?"

"Oh, my God," Amy Townsend whispered.

"Eight," Samantha said dully.

Jeff made a choking sound, then leaped up and ran from the room. I didn't blame him. I wanted to be sick too.

Randal Fane had an arm around Amy. He was as white as she was, but his voice was steady when he spoke to her daughter. "Don't say another word, Samantha. Do you understand me, child? Not another word."

Her bright eyes met his, and a queer little smile curved her lips. "Afraid I might incriminate myself? Don't worry. No jury in the world would convict me once I confess—

and plead justifiable homicide.'' She glanced at Trey. "Better read me my rights, Lieutenant.''

But it was Rudy who, after a glance at Trey, produced a small card and quietly read the Miranda warning.

Samantha didn't look at her mother. Not once during the next hour did she so much as glance at Amy. She just talked with no expression in her voice. Fane didn't try to stop her. No one could have. It was like a dam bursting.

Rudy produced a small tape recorder. Sam liked that.

SHE HAD planned carefully, she explained proudly. She had planned for months, and then had waited for just the right time. When the party had been announced, she had encouraged her mother to choose that week for her trip to visit an old friend. Jeff was in college and in another state; no problem there. Randal Fane had casually mentioned a business dinner scheduled for that night (which had never existed since he had planned to meet Amy, but Sam hadn't known that), so he'd have an alibi.

Yes, of course she'd known about her mother's affair; she thought it was a good thing. Mr. Fane would make her mother happy. Amy broke down at that point and began sobbing almost silently.

Monday night was Dumont's football night, so he could be a possible suspect—something she wanted. It would be best, she'd decided, to draw attention away from the family by supplying suspects outside it. Dumont was possible.

So was I.

She knew (through Jason's casual conversation while painting the mural in Townsend's office building) that I was something of a loner, hated parties, and tended to drive around the Perimeter to relax in the evenings; there was a good chance I'd lack an alibi for that night. And if, by chance, I'd been at the loft when she called, she had planned to play the recorded message from her father and hang up; he would have sounded abrupt, and I *might* have called to verify the appointment, but nobody says no to Jeffrey Townsend. She was sure I'd come to the house, which would have put me at the scene of the murder, and she had a few things in mind to make me look suspicious.

Why me? Because, Sam said, according to Jason, I found things. She decided to see if I could find a murderer. Of course, she'd meant to confess all along, because no jury in the world would convict her anyway. But she wanted to find out if I was as good as some of her favorite detectives were.

That was why me.

Yes, she'd been in my loft—once. While he was painting the mural at her father's building, which was closer to my loft than to Jason's, he'd had to temporarily store his paints and brushes at my place because he was running late for an appointment. Samantha had offered to help him, and since he was going back by the Townsend building on his way to the appointment and could easily drop her off, Jase had accepted.

Knowing my brother, I figured he'd done it more to please her than because he needed her help. In any case, she'd helped him to carry the stuff into my loft. I hadn't been home, and when Jason had briefly excused himself, she'd had a chance to look around. When she saw my answering machine and realized it was the same one her father used at home, she began to get the idea of using me in her plans.

Jason groaned softly when he heard that. *She followed me around,* he'd said cheerfully, and none of us had thought twice about it.

There had been no need for her to return to my loft. Knowing how the machine worked but cautious enough to test it, she'd called weeks later, planning to hang up if I answered. The machine answered instead, and she left an unidentifiable message. A second call to erase the message by using the push buttons on her phone worked just fine, and a third call verified it.

After that, it was easy.

She had the chocolates all prepared. Her father loved chocolates, and she'd made a habit of occasionally buying some for him. The pills? Oh, she'd taken them from her mother's prescription bottle in her bedroom. Just a few at a time, over the course of a few months. Until she had enough.

She'd timed the drive from the house where the party was being held to this house. Under an hour easy, with not much chance of getting stopped, especially on a week-night.

Was her father expecting her? Well, of course. He didn't know about the party; she'd just told him she was coming home early, and he liked that. They'd have a couple of nights alone in the house before her mother returned from her trip. He liked playing games, so she'd promised him one. She'd surprise him, arrive without warning. She parked her car a couple of blocks away, in a parking lot where it wouldn't be noticed, and then walked to the gate.

She hadn't needed the family code to get onto the grounds, because her father had turned the system off. She'd left her coat in the foyer and come into the room— this room—where her father was waiting. Dressed just the way he liked. How? Well, like a little girl. A frilly white dress and kneesocks, with her hair in braids.

She gave the chocolates to her father—but he wanted to play first. That was what he called it. Playing. It was the first time in ages they'd had the house to themselves (he usually took her to the lake house), and he wanted to play with her on the bearskin rug.

He made her keep her dress on at first. He liked for her to sit on him while he lay on his back on the rug. Her skirt hid what they were doing, and he liked that. He liked for her to squeal and call him Daddy while she rode him. After, he usually liked to relax and eat chocolates while she sat at his feet and talked to him. Until he was ready again.

Sam had counted on that. But, so careful in her planning to that point, she had forgotten one small detail. Her father had ordered her, years before, to regularly use a depilatory—especially between her legs. He didn't like to see hair; he didn't want her to be a woman.

She had forgotten, and her father became enraged. He stripped off her clothes, calling her horrible names, and turned her over his lap, beating her bottom where the marks wouldn't show. Then he got one of the drapery ties and bound her wrists together behind her back. He made her kneel on the rug and ordered her to stay there.

Then he went and took a shower. He returned dressed and stretched out on the couch. He started eating the chocolates, ignoring her.

For the first time, Sam had felt panic. She had begged and pleaded to be set free, terrified that he would die leaving her tied up and helpless.

Which is what happened.

She stumbled to the kitchen and managed to use a knife to cut the cord around her wrists. Her hands were swollen, and her wrists were bruised and chafed. She'd cut one finger with the knife, and had to find a Band-Aid for the cut. Time was running out; it was already after nine, and she had so much to do!

Furious with her father for nearly ruining her careful plans, she returned to the living room and plunged the knife into his still chest.

Then she got busy. She got dressed and cleaned up the chocolate wrappers. She put the box and the ruined drapery cord on the rug and rolled it up. It was stained, and the police would notice something like that; she couldn't leave it there. She used her handkerchief to wipe every surface she'd touched, including the knife handle. She vacuumed carefully and added the bag to her bundle, then wiped the machine to remove fingerprints.

Then she called my loft from her father's study and played the recorded message. Spliced? Oh, no, nothing that complicated. For a school project, she'd (quite openly) recorded her father working at his desk one day months before; it so happened he had left that message on someone else's answering machine.

Simple indeed.

She replaced her father's datebook with the one she'd prepared a couple of days before, adding the necessary appointments, including mine. Then she added the original datebook to her bundle, to be disposed of as far from the house as possible. She left the house with the front door standing open a foot or so and carried the heavy, awkward bundle down the drive and out through the gate. She kept close to the wall so no one would notice her, and she managed to reach her car unseen.

She drove most of the distance to the house where she'd been staying, then found a pay phone. It was well after eleven when she called my loft and signaled the machine to erase all messages; whether or not I'd gotten her message, she didn't want it left on the machine. (If I hadn't gotten it and therefore hadn't turned up on the Townsend doorstep that night, Sam had counted on the datebook and the photo to direct suspicion at me and worried only that I might have had an alibi.) Nearby was an industrial trash dumpster; she disposed of the rug in it.

Then she returned to the house and slipped in, met her friend upstairs, and swiftly changed into her costume. When the masks came off at midnight, Samantha was there.

WHEN SHE FINISHED her confession, Samantha smiled brightly at me and congratulated me for figuring the whole thing out. Because she'd planned so carefully and, really, I'd been smart to put it all together.

I sort of went blank at that point. I was vaguely aware of Rudy and Sarah moving toward Samantha, and of Amy sobbing and Fane murmuring to her. Dumont had a brief word with Trey and then left quietly. Jeff hadn't returned to the room.

And I wanted out.

I felt Trey's gaze, but it was Jason who came to me.

"Come on," he said gruffly. "I'll take you home."

Trey didn't try to stop me or say anything to me. I hadn't expected him to. Or had I?

I was vaguely aware that Jason made one stop on the way to my loft, but I didn't notice or care why. When we got to the loft, he came up with me and fixed coffee while I collapsed on the couch. The first sip of coffee told me why he'd stopped; it was laced with whiskey. I never have liquor at my place since I hardly ever drink.

"Am I in shock?" I wondered aloud.

"You're in pieces," Jason said flatly, sitting beside me on the couch and watching me the way you'd watch a crystal vase on a shaky shelf.

"I'll be all right," I said.

"I know. Eventually. Drink the coffee, Lanie."

I drank. "Where's Choo?"

"On the kitchen counter. I fed him."

"Oh. Thanks." I was still numb, but not quite so cold. "Do you think they'll prosecute her, Jase?"

"I don't know. There's been so much media attention that the D.A. won't be able do nothing. Once he hears her confession, either he'll agree it was justifiable homicide or he'll decide to charge her with murder."

"First degree," I said. "She planned to do it for a long time. But she was right, you know. A jury wouldn't convict her, not if they believed how he abused her."

"It's a hard thing to believe," Jase said.

I heard a little laugh escape me. "Oh, I'm sure Sam thought of that. She'll have proof. That picture of Townsend with the dark-haired woman—that was her, wearing a wig. I'll bet she has other pictures, hidden away somewhere. Probably even videotapes."

Jason frowned. "Could Townsend have been that careless?"

"It's just speculation on my part, but I doubt very much if he ever knew. She probably got the idea after he told her about what he'd done to Dumont; and I'm sure he told her. He liked to brag. That was a mistake. Sam was smart enough to see the possible advantages of having proof of what her father had done to her. She'd taken a video-production class in school. When the police search the lake house thoroughly, I'll bet they find that Sam had rigged one of the bedrooms. It's not that hard to do, maybe through a closet wall or vent or something. Jeffrey was so obsessed with her, he wouldn't have noticed.''

I sighed. ''She cut the brake line on my car while I was at the apartment complex; it would have been easy for her, since her school records showed she'd also taken a course in auto mechanics, and her grades were good. I have the feeling she's often followed me—and the police tail—just waiting for a chance. I doubt that she meant to seriously injure me. I'm just speculating again, but . . . In most detective novels, the sleuth has at least one close brush with death. She just wanted the story to be complete.''

After a moment, Jason said, ''How did you know, Lanie? I never would have seriously suspected her.''

I shrugged, feeling impossibly tired. ''Once I realized that Sam was the only connection I had with any of them, and once her alibi fell through, I started looking for a motive—or, rather, confirmation of a suspicion I had. There were a lot of little things I'd noticed all along, things that didn't mean anything until they were all tied together.''

''For instance?''

''Well, her clothes and hair, for a start. Right after Townsend's death, she cut her hair and bought shopping bags full of new clothes. When I looked in her closet, all the old stuff was very . . . immature. Childish. And she obviously hadn't the faintest idea how to apply makeup with a light hand. That seemed odd for an eighteen-year-old. At the time, I just thought that some fathers didn't want their daughters to grow up, and that's as far as it went.

''She seemed to have no feelings at all about Townsend's murder, except to remark that it was probably a hit man since her father was a son of a bitch. She told me he liked to blackmail people, but the examples she gave me just indicated that Townsend had been a domestic tyrant and made his family toe the line. Her telling me that was deliberate, even though she understood blackmail very well; she didn't want to sound too smart about it, but she wanted me to start looking for a victim and believed I'd fix on Dumont. And I noticed from the bookshelf in her bedroom that Samantha had read every classic mystery you'd care to name, as well as most of the more recent ones.

"But it was a realization about Jeffrey that made me start pulling everything together."

"Which was?"

"The pictures. The one of him in bed was pretty fair evidence that he liked his sex on the kinky side; the one of Dumont was pretty fair evidence that Jeffrey knew about the goddamned club and was possibly a member. If he was, it was because he got his kicks abusing young girls."

"And from there," Jason said slowly, "it was logical to wonder if he was abusing his daughter."

"Yeah." I felt miserable. "Eight, Jase. She was eight years old. He turned his own child into a sexual toy, a baby whore. She may never heal from what he's done to her."

"What about you?" Jason asked after a moment. "Are you going to heal?"

I knew what he meant. "Trey and I . . . we're too different."

"Different isn't always bad."

"No. And maybe if we'd met in another way, the difference wouldn't matter. But it does, Jase. It does matter. He saw things in black and white, and I got caught in a gray place between them."

"Was that his fault?"

"Yes—no. I don't know anymore. All I know is that there's been too much pain. Not just between us, but all around us. I'm tired, Jase. I'm too tired to think about it, or even to care very much right now.''

''Don't run from it, Lanie.''

''Who's running?'' I said.

EPILOGUE

I WAS. I ran as fast and as far as I could the first chance I got.

There was never a trial. As Jase had said, the D.A. couldn't do nothing; he charged Samantha Townsend with first-degree murder. Her defense attorney, rather than pleading justifiable homicide or self-defense, simply made a pretrial motion stating that his client had not been responsible for her actions due to her father's abuse. Samantha's statement to that effect (far more lengthy and detailed than her confession) was backed up by three six-hour videotapes in which Jeffrey Townsend used his daughter sexually in every conceivable way, bound her with a variety of ropes and other bondage paraphernalia, beat her, and tormented her both physically and emotionally. (Sam said that her father had made the tapes in order to keep her in line. I don't know. Maybe he had. But Sam had known where they were "hidden" at the lake house.)

A number of doctors judged Sam unfit to stand trial and stated their opinion (unanimous) that ten years of abuse had left Sam's mind severely damaged.

They didn't say she was insane, and maybe she wasn't. Maybe Samantha Townsend just took all she could—and then stopped.

To this day, I don't think of Sam as a murderess. I think of her as someone who found a tragic way out of an intolerable situation. I've told her that; they let me visit her sometimes in the private hospital where she lives. They tell me she's getting better, and I guess she'll be healed. One day. After she was committed, she sort of reverted to childhood; the doctors say it was because she missed it the first time.

I showed her how to put on makeup when she asked me to, and I bring her books sometimes. She likes murder mysteries. The doctors say that's fine; it provides an outlet for hostilities. I don't know—it didn't the first time.

Anyway.

Randal Fane wasn't arrested for jury tampering, because the photo wasn't strong enough proof and the man he might have paid off couldn't be located. Amy Townsend married Fane very quietly a few months after, and they moved into the suburbs near Atlanta. Jeffrey Townsend III went back to school; I hear he's in therapy, and I think that's good. Luther Dumont is still the half-shady, half-respectable businessman he always was.

And me? Like I said, I ran. As soon as it became obvious that my testimony wouldn't be needed, I stuffed Choo into his carrier, turned off my damned answering machine, and flagged down the first plane headed west.

I spent six weeks at my uncle's ranch in Wyoming, looking at a lot of clean white snow. I might have stayed until the spring thaw, except that Jason called and told me to get my ass back home before he killed *all* my houseplants.

So I came home.

For a few days, I holed up in there, cleaning like a maniac and driving Choo nuts by emptying his litter pan after every visit. I don't know, maybe my cat got fed up and called my brother. Anyway, Jason came and kidnapped me, dragging me to several parties people had invited him to. He told every person he could corner what I did for a living, and I found myself working again.

One of my cases (which turned out to involve a simple runaway who wanted to come home, thank God) took me to the police department. I took vast pains to avoid getting anywhere near Trey—and then almost knocked him down the steps as I was hurrying from the building.

It was the perfect opportunity to tell him I was getting over that Townsend business. To say hello casually and smile and prove I was adult enough to be friendly to an ex-lover. A perfect opportunity. Did I take advantage of it?

Hell, no.

I was very dignified. I scuttled around him sideways like a crab and fled. I think I even blushed.

I was still mentally cussing myself about that when I got back to my loft later that night. I replayed my messages while I was stripping down, listening without really paying attention. But then a voice caught me, just the way another one had at the beginning of the Townsend mess. I'd never heard his voice on tape, so maybe that was why it sounded so different.

Maybe that was why it sounded like chocolate.

"Montana. I've lost something I care about, and I was hoping you could help me find it again. You've got my number. I'll be waiting. Montana . . . Damn it. I'll be waiting."

The machine reset itself while I stood there in my bra and panties, staring at it. Well. I was supposed to be good at finding lost things, wasn't I?

Wasn't I?

After a while, I went over to the phone and lifted the receiver. I took a deep breath and closed my eyes for a moment.

Then I called Trey.

KAY HOOPER is single, in her (very) early thirties, and lives alone—unless she counts her menagerie of pets, and a collection of unicorn drawings and figurines. Kay isn't really quite sure how she wound up as a writer. A love of reading and of words—along with quite a few lucky breaks—just seemed to snowball into a career. Although Kay professes to be faintly bewildered by it all, she'd never choose anything else. She says, ''Someone once said that 'Anyone who writes a book willfully appears in public with his pants down.' I think I feel a slight draft . . .''

IF IT'S MURDER, CAN DETECTIVE J.P. BEAUMONT BE FAR BEHIND?...

FOLLOW IN HIS FOOTSTEPS WITH FAST-PACED MYSTERIES BY J.A. JANCE